Fire & Thunder

Fire & Thunder

by

Sam Sitler

Table of Contents

For my mom, Denise Sitler, and my Grandpa Sonny, who both gave me the racing bug when I was little

Chapter One
The Final Four

And the rocket's red glare

The bombs bursting in air

Gave proof through the night

That our flag was still there

O say, does that star-spangled banner yet wave

O'er the land of the free

And the home of the brave?

The crowd cheered as the ten-gallon-hat-wearing bearded pop country star finished his heavily stylized acapella rendition of *The Star-Spangled Banner.* Three F-22s from Luke Air Force Base nearly drowned him out as he neared the end of his song. The crowd settled into their seats as forty drivers settled into their cars.

Chad Helton swung his right leg over the door of his Ford Mustang Darkhorse. Well, it wasn't exactly a door, but it was where the door would've been had it been an actual road car. Swinging his left leg over into the window opening, he slid into the driver's seat. With some assistance from his crew chief, he buckled the six-point harness that would keep him glued to his seat for the next three to five hours.

"This is it," the crew chief told him. "Just get out there and get at it."

"That's it then?" Chad chuckled. "Come on, Larry, you can do better than that."

Chad was in the final race of his rookie year, and it was one for the books. The baby of five children born to an Oregon grass seed farmer, Chad wanted to distinguish himself from his siblings by choosing a completely different career path. After cutting his teeth racing go-karts as a young child, he got into racing local dirt tracks in the Pacific Northwest by the time he was a teenager. His big break came at sixteen when he was spotted by an ARCA team owner. From there, he rose up the ranks, winning race after race. This culminated in an ARCA West championship. Then it was on to the NASCAR Truck Series when he was eighteen, winning Rookie of the Year and the championship. By this time, he had secured an agent named Ace Valdez. He was eager and ready to move on. His second year in NASCAR was spent with a new team in the Grand National Division. They were a small struggling team, but Chad really brought them together. After an impressive regular season with six wins, he entered the playoffs and ran well. A small mishap on the last lap at Phoenix cost him the championship, but he vowed he would be back. The team owner had made the decision to bring his operation to the Cup Series, NASCAR's top flight, and Chad came with. This was his third and final year with a yellow stripe on his rear bumper. Effortlessly, Chad kept the number 28 Ford Mustang up front. His career highlight came after winning Daytona twice, Talladega once, and Darlington twice all in the same year. With nine regular season wins, he was leaps and bounds ahead of anybody in playoff points, able to relax a little if that was in his wheelhouse. Relaxation when there was racing to be done was not in his wheelhouse.

The regular season of the Cup series consists of twenty-six races. Each race is divided into three stages, save for the Coca-Cola 600 at Charlotte, which is four stages due to its length. Playoff points are awarded at the end of each stage with race wins automatically entering drivers into the playoffs. At the end of twenty-six races, the top sixteen in points battle it out over four rounds throughout the last ten races, each round lasting three races, with the bottom three competitors eliminated. The season concludes in a final round at Phoenix Raceway, where the top four drivers have one final shot. Even though only four cars are eligible to win the championship, a full field of 36 to 40 will race for bragging rights, experience, and money.

So here Chad was, one of four drivers eligible to win the NASCAR Cup Series championship. The playoffs were tough, but he made it a habit to pull through and at least win the final race of each round. Nicknames varied that season from "Wunderkind", "The Ghost", and "The Invisible Man", but the name that stuck during playoffs was "Mr. Eliminator".

For the final time this year, Chad brushed back the bushy thick brown mop from his icy blue eyes, both of which he had inherited from his Sicilian mother. He scratched at the beard he had grown over the last ten weeks, itching to shave it tonight. He never liked it anyway. It never grew in right and came in patchy, leaving an unsightly bald spot on the right side of his lower jaw; all thanks to the eighth of Kalapuya blood he had inherited from his father. For the next three to five hours, his head would be encased in a helmet, completely closed off to the outside world, making the prospect of an itchy beard even more uninviting than it could already be.

"Drivers, start your engines," came a command from a gray-haired, pudgy man from the infield.

Chad flipped his battery and fuel pump switches on and turned the ignition. The 5.8-liter V8 roared to life amid a chorus of 39 other V8 mills.

Larry Truman was a crew chief with some fifteen years' experience. This was his first year in Cup as well after spending the previous fourteen in the Truck and Grand National Series. The old man shared a chemistry with Chad few driver-crew chief combinations had. He knew how to talk to Chad. He knew what it was like to rush from bottom to top quickly. He knew success and failure. He had worked for this day, and he was on his guard. Fifteen years of trying, and he was going to be a Cup Series championship-winning crew chief.

Larry closed the window net on the stock car, sealing Chad inside. The Mustang Chad drove was anything but. A tube chassis caged the driver in while a 5.8-liter Ford FR9 V8 sent power to a five-speed sequential transmission, powering the rear wheels. Over the chassis, a carbon fiber and sheet metal composite body was blanketed. The front clip and rear decklid matched a road Mustang, but beyond that, it was just like any other Mustang, Camaro, or Camry out on the track that day.

The forty stock cars lined up two-by-two behind a stock Toyota Supra with a strobe light on its roof. Forty V8s rumbled as the Supra led them out onto the track. The time to let loose was near. It was just a matter of a few parade laps as the cars zigzagged around, warming up their tires for much-needed grip.

"Sixteenth," Chad thought to himself. *"I'm better than this."*

It was true. He was consistent all year, but yesterday, he was off during qualifying. For some, sixteenth was a respectable place to start, but not for Chad.

"Okay, I know you're in a bad spot," came Larry's voice over the radio. "Just hit your marks and fall into that inside lane as soon as possible. Remember, you have 312 miles to work your magic."

Chad took a deep breath. Seven rows ahead of him, an official in the flag tower waved the green flag. Row by row, the stock cars gunned it. Chad tried for it, but the driver in front of him spun his tires.

"Come on!" Chad shouted.

"There's an opening coming up behind you," a second voice chattered through his radio. "Take it in three, two, one..."

Chad swooped down to the left, falling in line with the inside lane.

"Thanks, Hawk."

Scott "Hawk" Hawkins had been an aspiring driver several years before. Barely making it to the Cup Series, he struggled to even qualify.

He found a home up above the track in the spotter's perch, owing to his keen eyesight.

Chad kept to the rear bumper of the number 99 Camaro. He knew he couldn't stay there long. Phoenix Raceway is a strange track. Its asymmetrical tri-oval layout proves a challenge to every driver. The turns and backstretch are narrow, allowing for close action that tests a driver's skills. The frontstretch is a tri-oval turn with a wide apron that extends the racing surface several lanes. There, drivers have the choice of staying high in the banking and keeping momentum going into turn 1 or cutting distance and going hard on the brakes. Chad chose the latter.

The Mustang charged ahead, passing five or six cars.

"Opening!" shouted Hawk. "Take it now!"

Chad moved to the right, cutting off the number 54 Camry.

"Idiot!" the driver yelled at his crew chief. "'Mr. Eliminator', I'll eliminate his butt."

"He's racing for a championship," came the driver's crew chief's voice. "Just keep pushing."

Chad was oblivious to the scene behind him. He kept the leaders in his sights. Scooting up close to the outside wall, he shot down the backstretch. Before he made it to turn three, yellow lights on the catch fence began blinking. The leaders in front of him slowed down.

"Tower's called a caution," Hawk's voice came from the radio.

"What's going on?" asked Chad.

"Fifty-one was running slow again," Hawk answered. "Thirty laps in, and that kid's already out."

"How does he still have a ride?" marveled Chad.

"Nepotism," was Hawk's response.

The remaining thirty-nine cars lined up behind the Supra as they passed the wreck of what was the 51 Ford. Chad's spine tingled as he observed the yellow stripe on the former rear bumper of the Mustang. How could this be the same rookie class?

"Hey, the leaders are pitting," said Larry. "Come in. We can make up some of that position. Just fuel. I think our tires are good until the end of the stage."

"Where am I, Hawk?" Chad said.

"You've made it up to seventh," Hawk replied.

"You guys ready?" asked Chad.

"Did you have to ask?" chuckled Larry.

Chad followed the leaders onto pit road as the back markers stayed out. One by one, the cars broke off from the pack as they slid into their pit stalls. In the 28 Tom Morris Ford Dealers Mustang, the radio was abuzz with chatter as Larry got his men into place.

"Three, two, one."

A single crew member jumped the wall, carrying an eleven-gallon fuel can. He plugged it into the fuel tank. Within five seconds, he had emptied its contents and retreated back over the wall.

"Go, go, go, go, go!" Larry shouted.

Chad tore out of his pit stall like a bat out of Hell. To his amazement, the other competitors were barely behind. Some had taken tires. Ahead of him, the number 20 Toyota was just making its exit. It would be close. He moved to the right to clear the yellow and black Camry as he crossed the pit road line.

"You beat him!" Hawk cheered into the radio. "Looks like you'll start ninth, but those guys will have to pit before the stage ends."

Chad caught up to the pack zig-zagging behind the pace car. He held his breath as he waited for the flag to drop. One by one, the other cars joined the pack, lining up behind him. After two more laps, the green flag was dropped. Chad gunned it, driving his nose mere inches from the car ahead of him.

The laps began to wind down for the first stage, and the leaders began to pit. Chad was busy battling the 91 Chevrolet for position, and they were catapulted into the lead. Chad ducked low as the two raced side by side coming to Lap 75. He wanted this stage win. Chad bombed back up into the low banking of Turn 1 right up on the door of the 91. They dueled around the turn and through the backstretch. Again, Chad cut it low against the apron in 3 and 4, staying there through the dog leg. He downshifted, giving himself a small burst of acceleration to carry his Ford across the line first. The green and white checkered flag waved. The first stage belonged to Chad Helton.

"Okay, let's bring it in when pit road opens," Larry instructed Chad. "That was a good run. Just remember to save it for the rest of the race.

The Supra darted out of its stall and onto the track, its strobe light a beacon to the thirty-nine remaining cars. They lined up behind it, parading around the track. As pit road opened, nearly everyone, with the exception of a few gamblers, ducked down into the pits. Chad slid his car into his pit stall, and a carefully choreographed dance of tire carriers, tire changers, and a fuel man began. As soon as the Mustang entered the pit stall, five men jumped over the wall. Mike Rogers and Quizz Jones were tire carriers. Another couple carried air impacts with one of them also carrying a jack. They were Josh Lopez and Kyle Franklin. The fifth who stayed on the driver's side and fueled the car was Dan "Noodle" Lee. He was the character of the pit crew. What started out with everyone calling him "Dan" turned into the childish "Dan Dan" until someone made the connection with "dan dan noodles", and everyone just started calling him "Noodle". Like clockwork, the four crew members jacked the car up, removed the wheels, and attached the new ones within seconds. Their job on that side done, they rushed to the driver's side where the tire carriers already had their load in possession. The car was jacked up again, the old wheels removed and the new ones placed. With a couple good hits with the air impacts, the single-lug wheels were secured to the car, and they let it down. The whole operation took less than thirteen seconds. As soon as the wheels hit pavement, Chad gunned it out of there.

The race off of pit road was just as intense as the race on the track. Thirty-five cars jockeyed for position at 45 mph. The pit exit bottlenecked at the end, so it was very tight. Unfortunately for Chad, the number 22 Ford barely edged him out.

"You're back in sixth for the restart", Hawk informed Chad.

"You got this," Larry reassured him. "Just take it easy this stage. They know what you can do. Save the car for the third stage, and let us work everything out for now."

Chad needed not say a thing. He gripped the wheel as he watched the lights on the pace car three rows ahead go out. The little Supra ducked back into the pits, and the number 1 Chevy led the field to the green.

Larry was right. Chad was no slacker, but he held back and saved precious tires and fuel throughout the stage. It was lucky for him too. The stage went caution free. The strategy was a wise gamble.

Naturally, holding back would cost positions, but the savings made up for the position. Not even halfway through the stage, the leaders began to pit, allowing Chad to make up the position he lost. Chad passed much of the field as they sat in the pits. Their quick stops were no match for his triple-digit speeds. By the time much of the field had cycled through green flag pit stops, Chad was in the lead again by Lap 60, lapping much of the field.

"I think we have a good cushion for pitting," said Larry. "Bring it in now. Two cans of fuel and four tires all around."

Chad brought his Mustang in, and some of the others who hadn't pitted followed him in. Again, his crew performed their dance around the car. 12.9 seconds was sufficient to service the car and get Chad back out sitting in the top ten. Chad now had the advantage on fresher tires. Fifty-four laps later, the green and white checker waved over Chad as he crossed the line in fifth. Not a bad effort for not giving it the beans.

"Bring it in for fuel," Larry instructed. "Go for right side tires."

The whole field came down pit road as they prepared for the final leg of the race. Clint slid into his stall as his crew jumped over, barely missing his front tire carrier. The crew jacked the right side of the car up as the wheels were once again switched out. His fuel man rapidly emptied the contents of his can. The crew cleared the way, and Chad gunned it out of his stall, only to be blocked by the number 33 Chevrolet, another rookie, this one making a limited start before declaring for next year. The Camaro had entered his stall at a bad angle, blocking Chad's way out.

"Get him out of the way!" Chad shouted.

Too late, the car was lifted, and the crew was working on it. Precious seconds were wasted as they took their time changing the tires and refueling.

"You gonna change his oil too?" Chad taunted.

The Camaro was let down, and its driver took off, but not before Chad was able to gun it and cut him off.

"Okay, you're a few spots back from where we wanted you," said Larry. 'Don't worry about it. You have 122 laps to work through the field."

Chad lined up in 23rd.

"Take it easy, Chad. You have plenty of time. Don't let him blow it for you," Larry reassured his driver.

Chad's world slowed down as his own heartbeat became audible to him over the roar of thirty-nine engines. His reverie was ended as the green flag dropped. The cars took off like jets. Chad elected to hold back as he followed the bottom line around the track.

"Caution!" Hawk said sharply into the radio.

This wasn't just an unskilled rookie spinning his car. Across the frontstretch, several cars jockeyed for position, going nearly six-wide through the dog leg. The bottleneck at Turn 1 turned out not to be the deal breaker as they fought their way to maintain position. The turn proved too much, and a pileup ensued. Ten drivers' nights were ended as their mangled wrecks either limped or were towed back behind the wall.

"Looks like we're under a red flag. Might wanna shut it off," said Larry.

Chad shut his engine down as his Mustang sat crookedly on the dog leg of the frontstretch. The temperature inside a stock car is already nearly unbearable. An air hose is attached to the driver's helmet to supply some fresh air and slightly cool the driver down, but with no air being generated by the car moving, it was useless. Chad began to choke on the hot, stale desert air as he waited for the cleaning crews to finish their work. Finally, after what seemed like an eternity, the lights on the catch fence changed from red to yellow, and the Supra emerged from the pit road. The remaining twenty-nine cars fired up their engines and lined up in position behind the pace car.

"Pit road is opening next time by," said Larry. "Why don't you stay out? You have a hundred to go. They're bound to get desperate and wreck this close to the end."

Chad watched as several cars ducked into the pit lane as he stayed out, gaining several spots and reeling in the Supra.

"Perfect," Hawk commented, "we're in fifth."

Chad swung his car left and right, heating up his tires adding some much-needed grip. His eyes narrowed on his twelve, longing to see the green flag drop and make his way to the front. He didn't know what the points situation looked like. He had no idea whether or not he was ahead of the other three championship hopefuls or behind. All he knew was he was going to win thar race, that way, it wouldn't matter.

The green flag dropped, and Chad gunned it once again. Crossing the start/finish line, he swung down into the dogleg, making his way to the front row and cutting off the leaders. First was his. Lap after lap, Chad grew his lead, but soon he had another problem. His lead began to shrink as the competitors behind him with fresher tires pressed their advantage. Within seven laps, the second-place car was on his rear bumper, and he was one of the Championship 4.

"Come on!" Chad verbalized. "Someone, mess up!"

Chad's wish was granted as the right rear tire of the number 23 Toyota blew, sending him careening into the wall. The yellow flew, and the number 20 Toyota that had been tailing him backed off as the Supra once more took to the track.

"Bring it in for a quick splash of fuel and left-side tires," Larry instructed. "We're gonna gamble this one to the end. Give it all you got as soon as you get out of here."

Chad brought his car in. As he slid into his stall, the crew jumped over, wasting no time. They rushed like their lives depended on it. The car was let down, and Chad darted out of his stall.

"Kyle, did you make sure that rear wheel was tight?" Larry asked the rear tire changer.

"I'm pretty sure I got it," Kyle responded.

"Okay, it looked pretty quick," Larry responded. "Keep your fingers crossed and pray we got it."

Chad re-entered the track behind a pack of gamblers. He knew he could make it to the end and win this thing. Again, everything went silent. This was it. It would be flat out from here to the final lap. This was his championship to win. History would be made tonight, and nobody would get in the way of that. If they wanted it, too bad. All other competitors would have to get out of the way or be mown down by his Mustang.

The green flag dropped, and the symphony of V8s resumed. Chad wasted no time making his way back to the front, utilizing the dogleg to make his passes. One by one, the laps ticked down until Chad finally made a pass for first. It wasn't easy. The number 20 Toyota knew how to make his car three lanes wide. He wanted that Cup trophy, but

Chad wanted it more. He found his opening and forced the Toyota to check up in Turn 1. Using Turn 2 to slingshot, he hugged the outside wall of the backstretch, using every bit of aerodynamic advantage he could find. The vacuum created by his car and the wall cut down the wind resistance, boosting him forward.

In quick succession, the laps wound down, but the Camry never left Chad's rear bumper. The advantage would soon be lost with two to go as Chad noticed the rear of the car rattling.

"Guys, the car's vibrating like crazy," he snapped into his radio.

"Come on, Kyle!" Larry shouted, then he turned back to his radio mic. "Do you think you can make it last?"

All or nothing," said Chad as he gritted his teeth.

Chad fought the car around the track, silently praying it would hold together. The Camry, on fresher tires, made his move around the outside, making the final lap a drag race. The crowd stood on their feet as the two drivers engaged in an all-out battle around the tri-oval track. Through Turns 1 and 2, the cars remained neck and neck. They gained speed through the backstretch, the Camry taking the advantage with fresher tires, but Chad bombed it down into Turn 3, regaining his position.

Out of Turn four, Chad cut it low again, but the tension was just too much. The weak old tires on the right of the car gave, and he blew the right rear. The rear of the Ford kicked out, slowing just enough to give the Camry the advantage to cross the line first.

The rear of the Mustang slammed into the wall as the car crossed the line. The force of the impact bumped the already-loose left rear wheel off, sending it bounding toward the infield; a path cleared for the loose projectile. Dead in the water, Chad shut his eyes, hoping his Mustang would be seen and avoided. With the coast clear, he let down his safety net. As quick as the remainder of the field returned to the pits, the driver of number 20 Toyota Camry performed his victory burnouts while a red Toyota Tundra emerged from the infield and hooked itself to Chad's Mustang.

As Chad stepped out of his mangled Ford, he took stock of what had just happened. To his relief, an ambulance arrived to take him to the infield care center. He needed this. He was in no state of mind to talk to the press until he had had some time to cool off.

After fifteen minutes, he was declared free of concussion or other injuries and released from the care center. Outside, the press had gathered like a swarm of mosquitoes. Chad was still speechless.

"Why can't they just interview the winner?" he thought.

"Can you tell us what happened?" asked one reporter.

"Tire blew," came Chad's curt reply.

"Can you tell us what happened leading up to it?" asked another reporter.

"Look, you have a guy in Victory Lane who was there for the whole thing," said Chad. "He has a much more interesting story and can probably tell it better than me. Good night, folks."

Chad fought his way through the mob to the hauler and took refuge inside until they figured out he wasn't going to talk. The herd of reporters pressed around the MorrisSport hauler, ignoring the poor sap in Victory Lane who had just won his first championship. The interest in Mr. Eliminator was just too much, no matter what he did.

Chapter Two
Offseason

One would think that the offseason is a time to relax and get your mind off of work. That is far from the truth for a stock car driver. At the conclusion the season, the press takes every opportunity to get to the nitty gritty about the lives and plans of the drivers, owners, and crew members. The silly season officially starts as teams and drivers start playing musical chairs, signing contracts and making changes to the teams.

After a few interviews with a couple of the major national sports networks in mid-November, Chad made his way back to Oregon to spend Thanksgiving and Christmas with his family before making his way back to North Carolina to prepare for Daytona.

Before actually going home, Chad's first stop would be an extended stay with his Aunt Charlene and Uncle Rob over the Thanksgiving holiday at their home in Seaside. It had been a long journey across the country. He hadn't shaven in over ten weeks. It was peer pressure brought on from other drivers to grow a playoff beard. He constantly scratched at the patchy growth on his face. He was glad to get it off. He wetted a brush with hot water and stropped his blade. He nicked himself on the first stroke. Oh well, it takes ten weeks to make or break a habit, and he was way out of practice.

Chad's twenty-first birthday fell three days before Thanksgiving. The baby of five, he always felt a bit left out of everything his siblings did, leading to his racing career. With two boys and two girls, Chad was his parents' tie-breaker. Oldest brother, Will, had followed in their father's footsteps: a grass seed farmer. Jana, the next in line, had gone off to Bible college in Arkansas for her M.R.S. degree years before and had married some pastor out of Arizona. Chris, the middle child, worked the farm with their father. Vickie, the closest to Chad in age, was the closest thing they had to a black sheep. Her husband, Todd, was a hard worker, pulling long hours at the Freightliner shop down the highway; but Vickie, she was a social media influencer – a mediocre social media influencer. At least she tried. So, that left Chad.

Working a farm wasn't for him, and he knew he didn't have the face for social media. When he was five, the family took a trip to Sonoma. A family friend purchased them tickets to the NASCAR Cup Series race at the local track. Chad was hooked. After a year of begging and pleading his parents for a go kart, they finally relented and bought one for his seventh birthday.

At the Thanksgiving table, the family discussed plans for the upcoming year and what they were thankful for; the normal Thanksgiving conversation. As much as they supported what he did, Chad knew his family was less than interested in what he did. Even though he probably brought in more money than all of his siblings combined, he still felt he could never measure up to Will or Chris. They had real jobs. They contributed to society. They didn't, as Will put it at an unfortunate moment of indiscretion, "get paid to drive around in circles for five hours". Chad said very little about his plans. They were simple: he was going to win the Championship.

After Thanksgiving, Chad could finally go home. He left early Friday morning, even beating the lion's share of Black Friday shoppers, and made it to the Willamette Valley by sunrise. After another hour, he cruised down a two-lane blacktop in the middle of the countryside outside of Salem. There, hidden behind some roadside hedges, was a narrow gravel driveway. This was the portal to his home.

Chad's massive paychecks from his contract and race wins paid for the ten acres outside of Salem where he had just finished building a modest home in the center. He drove his Ford GT down the long paved driveway, leaving it in the massive garage attached to the house. Three bedrooms with two-and-a-half baths wasn't bad for a single man of only twenty-one. The garage was a different story. Besides storage for ten cars, the garage included a shop where Chad could service his collection. He parked his GT next to an R34 Nissan GT-R and walked inside. Everything was bought outright, and the only costs to him were utilities and the insane property tax imposed by the State of Oregon.

Chad laid his keys on the counter and went into the living room where he crashed on the couch. He turned the TV on to one of the sports channels. There was his interview from a couple weeks before.

"That's strange," he thought. *"Why would they be showing that so late?"*

He sat up on the couch, his interest piqued. Very soon, a terrible truth became clear. He reached for his phone and dialed the team owner.

Tom Morris ran MorrisSport Racing. What began as a humble dirt team out of the many in North Carolina had turned into an ever-growing NASCAR empire. After years as a struggling team barely keeping their nose above water, they had hit their stride in the last two years. Even with their recent success, sponsorship was always a struggle. The team had factory support from Ford, mainly from the local Ford dealer Tom owned (the logo of which donned the sponsor areas on the hood, decklid, and quarter panels), but that only went so far; and primary sponsors pay the bills. On occasion, a small company would put together enough money to slap their name on the hood of the number 28 Ford.

"Why am I hearing about this on TV?" Chad asked his boss. "Who said we're shutting down?"

"I'm just as stunned as you," Tom explained.

"I mean, what do we do?" Chad continued. "How is it that we finished second in the Cup as a rookie team and not have a sponsor."

"You know no one wants to sponsor a team," Tom told Chad. "How does Mars leave Kyle Busch or Lowe's leave Jimmie Johnson? Look, I know you're contracted through the end of next season, but if we can't get a sponsor, we'll have to close up shop."

"Okay," Chad said, calming his breathing, "so do we brainstorm when I get back in January?"

"Maybe something like that. Honestly, I think the best strategy is to win Daytona. Rick March already called me and asked about our charter. I'm sorry, Chad. If you want to look for another ride, I understand."

"Yeah, me too," said Chad as he hung up the call.

Chad laid back on his couch. He flipped on his streaming service to get his mind off of work. This was the off-season. He needed a break. Nothing came up that would help. *Days of Thunder, Cars, Talladega Nights, The Love Bug* – it was all racing all the time.

"For once, I might want to watch Anne of Green Gables or some chick flick garbage like that," he thought to himself.

Chad shut the TV off and went to bed. Maybe he could sleep away his thoughts. That was a failure. When he wasn't tossing and turning, he was dreaming about work, waking up several times in a cold sweat, lying in position as if he were seated in his car.

The next three weeks before Christmas were brutal as Chad did his best to avoid the press. The answer to any question was "no comment" or "Ask Tom". He truly had no idea what was happening.

When he visited his family for Christmas, his mother commented on his haggard look. He had barely slept in the last few weeks, and he knew he wouldn't rest until he had a chance to get back to North Carolina and start trying to put the season together. He sat restlessly on his mom's couch as his family opened their gifts from him, mostly racing memorabilia.

Growing up, Chad was always close to his cousin Emily. Being born around the same time, they were raised together like brother and sister. If there was a baby picture of Chad, Emily was in it. They remained inseparable until they reached middle school, then with the changes that came along with that, also came a change in interests, she with becoming the undisputed beauty of the school and Chad with racing go-karts and eventually stock cars. Though their interests changed, they still remained somewhat close. By their sophomore year, the *Sweet Home Alabama* and West Virginia jokes could be quieted when Emily met the love of her life. By their senior year, Emily was engaged to her high school sweetheart, Mike Stewart, and Chad was preparing to go full time in NASCAR. By eighteen, they hardly saw each other as Emily had married and moved to Austin, Texas to begin her new life with her husband. Christmas was a time to bond again as she would return with her family from Texas. As opposite as they were, their relationship was magnetic, even to the point of Emily's husband wondering if they were, in fact, kissing cousins as had been their unfortunate, albeit untrue, reputation growing up.

Chad had crawled under the tree as if he were working on a car. At least, that's how he always pictured it. Reaching in like it was an endless cavern, he pulled out the final Christmas present. With childlike excitement, he handed the parcel to Emily. His old playmate gleefully ripped open the packaging.

"Chad Helton t-shirts!" she exclaimed with feigned excitement. Racing wasn't her thing, but she always proudly supported her cousin, often wearing a Chad Helton or MorrisSport t-shirt to work. As little interest she had in motorsports, she rarely missed a race. Sunday afternoons at her house were usually filled with the roar of forty V8 engines, much to the chagrin of her husband.

"There's one for Mike and Kevin," said Chad.

Mike was Emily's husband. He and Chad had an awkward relationship. He had replaced Chad years earlier as the man in Emily's life, and the two never really hit it off. They didn't hate each other, but they didn't exactly like each other either. They were cordial though and still got along well, with Mike even sporting a Chad Helton shirt from time to time. A former high school football star, by twenty-one, Mike already owned a successful construction company. A muscular offensive lineman, he still knew how to save all that power and energy and hurt you with his wit. When brains inevitably failed, brawn was an easy alternative, and Chad knew to stay off his bad side.

Kevin was Mike and Emily's two-year-old son. Much to Mike's dismay, he wanted to grow up and be just like his cousin Chad. Perhaps that had something to do with the rather lukewarm relationship he had with his cousin-in-law. It was that bond between the two that led to Kevin calling him "Uncle Chad". Emily often found occasion to dress her son in racing outfits, even going so far as to take his one-year photos with him in a tiny MorrisSport firesuit Chad was able to supply from his shop. Mike worried their son wouldn't take his interests, but Emily reassured him that he could do both. On a deeper level, Mike had an irrational fear that Chad would replace him as the father figure in Kevin's life, even as much as he tried to shake that notion off. It didn't help that Chad had already given the boy a NASCAR slot car set already this year.

"They're the special edition playoff shirts," Chad explained.

"They're wonderful!" said Emily as she unfolded them, examining the design of the black t-shirt.

Emblazoned on the front was a sketch of Chad's number 28 Mustang over the words "Chad Helton: NASCAR Cup Series Playoffs". On the back was written in red "MorrisSport".

"Kevin, come here," Emily beckoned her son.

The little toddler wobbled his way over to Emily, his tiny head doubled in size by the toddler-sized helmet Chad had given him, where she picked him up and removed the dinosaur t-shirt and the helmet he was wearing. She replaced it with the tiny t-shirt Chad had bought along with the helmet and let him down. Kevin ran around the room as fast as his little legs could carry him, humming and screaming to himself in imitation of a stock car.

"I'm just like Uncle Chad!" he half-mumbled, half-shouted with delight.

"So, Chad," Mike turned to his cousin-in-law, trying to find a way to bond and to also get his mind off of his young son's desire to follow in his cousin's footsteps instead of his, "got any plans for this year? I could always use some help framing houses."

"Mike," Chad began, trying to figure out whether or not to come back with his own thinly-veiled insult or be serious, "my plan is to continue racing, win Daytona in February, and carry my team into the future."

"And what happens if they close?"

"I can always find another team," Chad answered. "In fact, Tom called me and suggested I start looking around as soon as possible."

"Sounds like he's not even confident," said Mike.

"Well, that big leak didn't help either," replied Chad.

"Well, if this racing thing doesn't work out," Mike's voice actually indicated a more serious tone, "look me up, and I can get you working."

"Thanks," said Chad, "but I think I can find a team. Not to toot my own horn, but I think I have enough marketability to make an even bigger team."

Chad's confidence was grossly misplaced. Silly Season was in full swing by this time. Ace Valdez made calls around as December turned into January. Nothing was happening. Teams that had vacancies were already filling up with rookies coming in from the Grand National Series. To top it off, nobody seemed to want to sponsor a NASCAR team, not even a breakout team like MorrisSport. Chad couldn't even find sponsorship for himself to carry to another team.

Chad returned to North Carolina uncertain of his future. The mood around the MorrisSport garage was melancholy. They all knew the risk. Come February, it was do or die.

As the crew members arrived, Chad and Tom gathered them into the open floor of the garage. There was finally a development that could bode well for the team. Chad's heart raced as the two of them would deliver an opening pep talk. No one took the situation as lightly as Mike had the previous month. A trembling Tom took the stand first, barely able to speak as had come so easily to him over the past couple years. All there, including Chad, would be surprised by the news Tom would give.

"My friends," he began, his voice quivering under the stress, "This last year was the biggest success and achievement of my life, as I'm sure it was all of yours. My financial advisor told me that my dealer can only afford sponsorship for Daytona and the Clash for now. This news came as a shock to me in November as it did all of us.

"As scared as we all are, there is hope. How many of you would like to see SportStream on the side of that car?"

The crowd of workers whispered to each other in excited confusion. SportStream was an up-and-coming company, the same as MorrisSport; this one in the television streaming business. Any and all sports broadcasts were available through this service through broadcast deals with major networks, driving up viewership around the globe and even making MorrisSport a household name in the most far-flung of regions.

"They are offering full season sponsorship if we win at Daytona."

The crew burst into applause at the prospect of their livelihood being saved. Tom gestured for the crowd to pipe down before he continued.

"Here's the catch, here's the catch: They'll throw their logo on the deck lid and quarter panels at L.A. and Daytona and provide exclusive in-car cameras and telemetry to subscribers. We win Daytona, and you'll never have to worry about your jobs again. Take it away, Chad."

Chad stepped up to the center to face his crew, ecstatic at the news Tom had obviously been keeping secret since he had arrived in Charlotte. These men sacrificed just as much as he did over the past year. Their sweat, blood, and tears went into every piece of those race cars. It was Chad who had truly led MorrisSport to victory over the past two years, and it was Chad who would give the final motivating speech.

"Right now," he began, there are thirty-five other teams out there guaranteed a spot at Daytona. There are thirty-five other race teams sitting pretty without a care in the world. Thirty-five cars that will start all thirty-six races next year. We are the odd man out. I know many of you have already started looking around for more work. I can't fault you. Tom will never fault you. It's a wise decision. I understand it's unwise to gamble, but mark my words: we will win Daytona, because those thirty-five teams don't have the greatest crew to ever come along in the NASCAR Cup Series. Those other guys don't put even half the heart you do into their work as you do!"

The crowd let out a deafening cheer and applause as Chad spoke those words.

"Is it possible to lose? Yeah. We may fail. It won't be an easy start either. We'll be down a regular crew member and our car chief for the first three races due to that tire issue at Phoenix. But we will fight to the end to win that race. Folks, Daytona is just the beginning. We have a month and a half to get these cars dialed in. This year's NASCAR Cup Series trophy is ours to win. Give me 110%, and I promise to give you guys 111%."

The crew let out and even bigger cheer and applause as Chad stepped down. There was no doubt that while Tom Morris owned MorrisSport, Chad was king.

"Now let's get to work!" Chad shouted as the crowd dispersed to their work stations.

Chad stepped out of the shop and into a small room. Situated inside was a simulator. A custom racing seat sat upon a tube frame, three large curved LCD television monitors sat mounted to the front of it, mimicking the windshield of his car. A steering wheel, gearshift, and gauge cluster completed the simulator. Chad sat down and began running laps in his virtual car with Larry in his own office crunching numbers and adjusting it from his own computer. Chad had to get those lap times down.

It wasn't enough this year to start Daytona and last. The assignment was to win and win big. The goal was to start from the front and stay out front until after Lap 200. He would not rest until then, and everybody knew it.

Chapter Three
California Feelin'

The California sun gleamed against the rainbow of automotive wraps. Forty stock cars staged outside the L.A. Memorial Coliseum for the first race of the season. A non-points race, the Clash was open to all teams. It was a chance for bragging rights and some extra much-needed cash. For a few weeks following the Rose Bowl, the football stadium would be converted into a quarter-mile short track.

MorrisSport was on fire that weekend. Things were looking up as Chad flew around the tiny oval within 13.741 seconds, a track record. This captured him the top seed in the first qualifying heat race. Twenty-five laps would decide if he was in the feature.

Tom Morris Ford was still able to provide some sponsorship. Their logo adorned the hood, but from the doors back, it was SportStream. The retro paint scheme chosen consisted of the white background of the previous year's Tom Morris wrap that was abruptly cut diagonally front and bottom to rear and top by a 45° teal line that divided it from the black rear half of the car – SportStream's corporate colors.

Crowds packed into the stadium this first day of the weekend, benevolently open to all free of charge. To the cameras, it was a good look. Racing was alive and well, and it was all happening right here in Los Angeles.

A Mustang with a strobe light led the ten cars onto the track. The ten stock cars swerved back and forth warming up their tires as the hearts of ten drivers practically beat out of their chests in anticipation for the green flag. Soon enough, the Mustang dipped into the makeshift infield, and the ten cars laid on their accelerators. Twenty-five laps would decide who would make it into the feature. Chad could hear fans shouting his name as he weaved back and forth during the opening parade laps. He was thrilled that his fans who may not have that much money would actually be able to see him race in person.

Chad held the gas pedal down as long as he could, trying to brake late in an attempt to enter and exit the corners as fast as possible. He kept it low, gaining a car length on second place and allowing him to slide up in front of the path of the field, blocking any challengers.

Television viewers from around the world would be treated to an exclusive show as SportStream not only showed the local broadcast of the race, but also split the screen with exclusive angles from Chad's car as well as live telemetry. Subscribers would see every rise and fall in RPM, every gallon of fuel burnt, every depression and lift of the accelerator and brake pedal. For SportStream's subscribers, they would know everything Chad and Larry knew. This was the price to make the season, and the MorrisSport guys knew it. Chad, Larry, and Hawk had worked up a code, knowing people would be watching the telemetry and listening to the scanners. They still had their secrets to keep.

"Don't go too hard this round," said Larry through the radio. "We don't want to screw the car up before the main event."

Chad obeyed as he quickly caught up to the last-place car. He held back as long as he could until he could find a way around. This continued until the penultimate lap when the 24 Chevrolet rode up on his rear bumper as he was trying to lap a car. The 24 tapped his rear as he sent it into Turn 3. This broke Chad's rear traction and sent the MorrisSport Mustang into a spin.

Seconds seemed like hours to Larry as it seemed NASCAR was taking forever to make a decision. "Throw the caution," he whispered through gritted teeth. His prayers were answered before the 24 could get around Chad. Their heat was ended with the caution. Chad was safe.

Chad brought the car into the garage area outside the stadium. Larry and the crew met him there. Larry knew Chad would be hot under the collar after being spun.

"It's short track racing," he told Chad, trying to calm him. "Besides, you can rest easy. You're in the main. Drink some water and have a banana.

Chad, always camera-shy, snuck off to the hauler to relax on the couch. A NASCAR hauler isn't just any regular trailer. Rather, it is split into two levels. The upper level is only about four-and-a-half feet tall, just enough to fit two cars, the primary and back-up, into it. The lower level is the team's command center and storage. Aside from a small lounge with a sofa and television, anything the cars will need, up to a spare engine and transmission, are kept here. More often than not, the drivers bring their own campers to stay in, but not Chad. He was the great uniter. Where the team went, he went. This meant staying in the same hotels and resting in the team hauler.

The opening laps of the heats were a snoozefest. Each driver would be overly cautious at the beginning, not wanting to wreck their car before the main show. However, by the time the twentieth lap came around, caution turned to desperation. As had happened in Chad's qualifier, drivers itching to make it into the feature at the last second made bold moves. Bumpers were banged. A few cars spun into oncoming traffic. This was pure short track racing.

Between heats, Chad would run to the refrigerator to grab a Monster. Between 64 ounces of the diuretic and three or four bananas, he was wired. After the final heat, Chad snuck to the camper his team provided him. Though he generally liked to hang in the hauler, he decided he needed the privacy now. As much as his sponsor was also the press, he still wished to avoid the mosquitos. The effect of the caffeine in his system was short-lived, and he passed out on the couch.

Anxious to start racing the next day, Chad downed two more Monsters before presenting himself to the public. In a desperate attempt to avoid wetting himself, he made a mad dash for the restroom, missing the broadcast of the first "Last Chance" qualifier, a true last chance for some lucky few to make it in who didn't finish in the top three.

By the time he made it back, the second "Last Chance" had gone green. These heats were fifty laps apiece. Chad began his stretch routine. Today, he'd be stuck in that car for 150 laps. Sure, it would only be about forty-five minutes tops, but the car still got hot and cramped. After some stretches and a couple more bananas, he was ready.

Chad climbed back into his car without a word. As he secured his steering wheel onto the column, Larry closed his safety net. This was it; 150 laps to $2 million.

"What're you gonna do with that $2 million?" asked Larry, trying to hype up his driver.

"A second house out in Charlotte?" chuckled Chad.

It was go time. The officials waved the cars back out onto the track. Chad pulled in behind the Mustang leading the procession of twenty-seven stock cars. The track fell silent to Chad as the pace car ducked back into the infield.

"Show time! Go! Go! Go! Go! Go!" shouted Hawk into the radio.

Chad wasted no time speeding into turn one. He bounded forward ahead of the second-place car to his right going into the corner, exiting turn two a car length ahead of the competition and allowing him to throw a block up against the backstretch wall. As quickly as he exited turn two, he met with turn three. The same process repeated itself.

For anyone who thinks NASCAR is just people driving in circles and making left turns, they would be right, except for the fact that these drivers must contend with up to thirty-nine other cars at speeds of up to 200 MPH, often mere inches from each other. Each track presents its own unique challenges. At Los Angeles, the track is the smallest on the circuit, and it can fill up quickly. Within one or two laps, Chad was staring down the rear bumper of the number 11 Toyota.

"Out of my way, old man," Chad mumbled to himself.

With lapped traffic, Chad would be held up, allowing the leaders behind him to catch up. It would become a game of who could make it through this obstacle course in one piece and come out in front. Chad made it past the first two or three back markers until he met the yellow-striped bumper of a rookie. The inexperienced driver was a fresh talent brought up from the Grand National Series. Going into turn three, the rookie threw a block on Chad. This was tolerated in the lower series, but here in Cup, you get out of the leader's way.

"Someone black flag this clown!" Chad hissed at Larry.

"If you think you can keep the car in one piece," began Larry, "move his silver spoon butt out of the way."

"Rubbin's racin'?" asked Chad.

"Rubbin's racin'," replied Larry.

Chad brought the nose of his Mustang to the rear of the rookie's Camry as they powered down the frontstretch. The leaders were gaining on him, so he would have to act fast. Going into turn one, he didn't let up until the last second. The momentum of the push threw the rookie's Camry off balance, forcing him into the outside lane on turns one and two and allowing Chad to safely continue his strategy of outdriving into the turns and taking the short way around. Chad waved from the inside lane to the rookie as he sailed past. The rookie showed his displeasure by flipping Chad the bird. He didn't care. He was here for one reason and one reason only. It didn't matter to Chad or anyone at MorrisSport what the world at large thought of them. This was a fight for survival, and anything they could find at their disposal was fair game.

"Woo! That'll show 'em!" laughed Hawk.

The laps wound down quickly, this being the shortest track they would visit that year. Chad's brakes glowed red hot as he entered the corners. With every lap, their hold on the wheels weakened as they wore out. 150 laps would take less than forty minutes if they went caution free. Chad prayed it wouldn't happen. His prayers were answered as he passed the second-place car. He had lapped the entire field within seventy-five laps. There were seventy-five remaining. NASCAR has a policy regarding lapped vehicles during cautions called the "Lucky Dog". In this, the first car a lap down will be able to regain that lap under caution and restart on the lead lap. This means that even if the tower threw a caution, Chad would only be competing against one car. That moment never came.

What was set to be an eventful race turned uneventful as Chad dominated the track. The rookie even learned to respect him as Chad lapped him a second time, sticking to the outside lane as the Wunderkind passed him.

Chad crossed the line in record time, leading a caution-free Clash in under thirty-seven minutes. Any other day, Chad would've been bored to tears winning in such commanding fashion, never really facing any adversity; but today was different. MorrisSport was a team in desperation, and this looked to be an omen of things to come. If Chad and the team could carry this momentum into Daytona in a couple weeks, the SportStream sponsorship would be secured, and MorrisSport would be saved. He reasoned within himself that this could be easy. Now with the support of a major sponsor, they could afford all of the good parts and maybe even some better training equipment. The simulator was good, but it could be better; that was Chad's main complaint.

Chad rested easy that night, the giant trophy gleaming in the moonlight shining into the living room of the team hotel suite. No more did he dream about work as he dozed off to sleep. It was the best night of sleep he had had since November, and he had no plans of waking up early the next morning.

Chapter Four
Duel

Across the continent from Los Angeles, the NASCAR season really got its start at Daytona. The Clash was just a little warm-up before the real thing. Daytona would be the first of thirty-six points-paying races on the schedule. Often billed as the Super Bowl of Stock Car Racing, the Daytona 500 draws the biggest crowds and television ratings all year.

While most races throughout the year include a qualifying session before the race, NASCAR has chosen to make the Winter Daytona race a bit more special by adding twin 125-mile qualifying races, known as the Duels or the Twin 125s preceded by a title sponsor, after the first qualifying sessions. These races are seeded according to how each car qualified, save for the front row which is set during individual qualifying laps. If a car qualifies on the inside lane, an odd-numbered position, he will start in the first race, and likewise the second race with cars in even positions from the outside lane. This way, if more than forty cars showed up, there would be multiple opportunities for a team to make the race, other than just scraping up enough money to show up to Daytona with a NASCAR-spec car and be sent packing after only two or three minutes on the track. Thirty-six teams hold charters purchased from NASCAR, guaranteeing them a starting position in all the races throughout the year. This leaves four spots open for the taking during the Duels.

Chad had qualified fifth. It wasn't the best spot, but he could manage it. He had 625 miles to make it work, starting with the first Duel. His fifth-place qualifying run put him third in the first 125-mile race. Chad relaxed in his pit box, enjoying a chopped banana and a sugar-free energy drink. The day of the Duels included some preliminary events like Spec Miatas and some ARCA practice. After a while, he got bored.

"Hey, I'm gonna get up and walk around," he told Larry.

"Just be careful of those cameras," Larry replied. "If anyone asks, everything's fine."

Was it though? Sure, Chad had won the Clash, and he was starting inside the second row for the first Duel; but the deal was to actually win the big show. Second place wouldn't do. If he lost even by a mere one thousandth of a second, his ride was gone. Chad heeded very little of Larry's warning as he walked down the pit lane. With his head down, buried in his thoughts, he didn't see the woman approaching him directly in his path. She didn't see him either. They collided with enough force to knock the wind out of the both of them, sending the poor woman to the ground.

"Holy crap!" Chad exclaimed, almost shouting for the whole world to hear. "I'm so sorry. Here, let me help you up."

Chad reached out his hand and lifted her off the ground.

"Oh, it's perfectly alright," she said, a noticeable and thick British accent.

Off the ground and standing face to face, Chad was able to get a good look at her. First were her bright green eyes, almost like a pair of green LED headlights that stared into your very soul. Zooming out, he noticed her turned-up nose and conservatively glossed bee-stung lips that just slightly opened in the center as if she was whistling while they rested shut. Her raven hair tumbled down a little past her shoulders, ending in what were probably once some reddish gold highlights with possibly some brown interwoven in it; he couldn't exactly place it. Her skin tone? Well, he wasn't sure. It wasn't pasty, but it wasn't dark; "healthy" was what he could best describe it in his mind. She was even dressed conservatively, maybe a little overdressed. Most of the women here at the track wore a spaghetti strap tank top and short shorts. Even in February, the Florida humidity can be miserable. And this woman looked like she had just exited Narnia back into World War II-era England. She wore a brown sweater, a white button-down blouse exposed underneath, with a darker brown skirt. She had to be melting in this heat, but he couldn't detect a drop of sweat on her face. She definitely was not here to just sit and enjoy the race. Her presentation was totally that of business and professionalism. She wasn't dressed to impress, but she certainly made an impression on Chad.

"England?" Chad asked, trying to make conversation with the woman.

"Blackpool," she replied.

"I've never heard of that country," replied Chad, somewhat confused. "Is it near England?"

"It's my town," the woman giggled. "Yes, I'm from England."

"Oh," chuckled Chad nervously. "I've never left North America. The only geography I really paid attention to was where our tracks were."

"No worries, driver," the woman replied.

"Uh, Chad Helton," he stuttered out, extending his right hand.

"Gemma McKenzie," the woman replied, firmly grasping Chad's hand. "Pleased to meet you."

"Likewise," said Chad.

"Well," Gemma began, "I had better be going. I'm here on business, not holiday. I'm sure you'd understand."

"Likewise," replied Chad.

"Cheers," Gemma said as she departed, twirling back around and walking back with a small skip in her step.

Chad watched as she disappeared into the crowd. He felt something. It was something he had never felt before. It was attraction. At least he thought it was. All throughout high school, Chad had never dated and never had anyone on his mind. His career was his sole focus. That's not to say no girls tried. There were many who wanted him, but his mind was on other things. Contrary to popular belief, he wasn't gay. He certainly liked women, as evidenced by the few times he caught his gaze following an attractive woman. He even took a girl to prom, but much to the date's disappointment and dismay, he stumbled through the entire night and communicated very little afterwards; but this was totally different. He actively wanted to pursue this girl; not in a creepy way, but to actually have a conversation with her and maybe even somehow get to know her. Their whole future flashed before his eyes: the proposal, the wedding, the first child, the heartbreak, the forgiveness, the growing old, and eventually, Gemma sitting by his bedside as he drew his last. So, this was what disappointment felt like. And to top it all off, he knew practically nothing about her other than the fact that she was beautiful and British; not exactly two things that he thought were mutually exclusive.

"Will the starters for the first Duel make their way to the grid?" a disembodied voice spoke through the loudspeaker.

Well, that wasn't much of a walk. Chad returned to his box and chugged a bottle of water.

"You're gonna pee yourself," said Larry.

"Not with this humidity," chuckled Chad as he mounted the driver's window.

Chad swung his left leg up and lowered himself into the car.

"*Okay, focus*", he thought to himself. "*Cute girl does not exist anymore. Don't look for her.*"

Chad peered out his rearview mirror as he buckled his harness at the new rear tire changer. Poor kid would probably only get one shot, and barely out of college. Apparently, he wasn't good enough for the NFL.

"You're all set," said Larry as he closed the window net. "Just get out front and stay there."

"Isn't that the game?" replied Chad.

"Right," said Larry. "And don't forget, there's probably millions of people right now paying $20 a month for SportStream Premium just to see you race right now, so keep it clean."

"Hey, it's not me I'm worried about," said Chad. "It's those yellow stripes that scare me."

Chad finished putting on his helmet as the cars began leaving their pit boxes to take their spots behind the pace car, this time a Camaro. The MorrisSport Mustang sported a new wrap. The Tom Morris Ford logo was still present on the hood, but SportStream took over midway through the car. The wrap chosen for Daytona consisted of the same white background of the old Tom Morris Ford paint scheme Chad had run the previous year, but it then faded to SportStream teal and then to black. With any luck, the whole car would be completely SportStream teal and black in Atlanta.

As with every race Chad had started, the world slowed down on the final approach to the green flag as the Camaro pace car ducked down into pit road. The flag dropped, and Chad laid on the accelerator as hard as he could.

Daytona is a 2 ½ mile superspeedway. Once the cars are on the track, there is no braking or lifting off the accelerator. It's pure open throttles the whole time. This provides close action as well as some of the fastest speeds in NASCAR. In the late 1960s and early 1970s, Ford and Chrysler duked it out on these tracks with the Ford Torino Talladega and Mercury Cyclone Spoiler II versus the Dodge Charger 500, Dodge Charger Daytona, and Plymouth Roadrunner Superbird. These cars were aerodynamically enhanced versions of the normal street cars with rare examples of street legal cars sold to meet NASCAR's homologation rules. By 1971, new rules put in place by NASCAR all but ended the Aero Wars, but tracks like Daytona and Talladega still provided high speed action, including regular speeds of over 220 MPH until the late 80s when the high speeds eventually turned so dangerous that they endangered spectators. With the end of unbridled speed came restrictor plates at these two tracks, as well as pack racing where cars would bunch up within inches of each other while still at full throttle. This new type of racing caused massive pileups that were affectionately known as "The Big One". Adding to that little bit of excitement was an extra challenge. Superspeedways have an out-of-bounds that other tracks don't have. While drivers can cut down as low as they can without wrecking, the big superspeedways have a double yellow line below the inside lane. Drivers are not allowed to advance their position below this line, though enforcement and the definition of "advancing position" seem to be blurry.

Chad loved and hated superspeedway racing, and with a recent reconfiguration at Atlanta, a 1 ½ mile quad-oval, NASCAR added two more such races, owing to some new banking that mimicked the high banks of the two big tri-ovals. Chad loved the prestige a win at any of these tracks would bring, but they were a challenge. With the prestige of winning at Daytona and Talladega also comes some doubts. While it takes some skill to be consistent at the superspeedways, it is still very possible to be taken out of the race through no fault of the driver. The pack racing is dangerous, but also puts more emphasis on the draft. A driver can have the fastest car on the track, but if he doesn't have the help of another car pushing him, he'll fade to the back. These two aspects have led to many fluke wins, and many believe that the key to winning Daytona or Talladega is to just keep your car in one piece and be in the right place at the right time.

By the time the field had reached the backstretch, Chad had snuck in between the two pole-sitters. Now running second, he sought to separate the leader from the pack, hoping to tag team throughout this first run before pitting.

Caution-free races can be great, except for one thing: green flag pit stops. Much time is lost when being limited to 65 MPH on pit road and stopping for tires and fuel while everyone else is doing upwards of 200. Pitting under caution was ideal. If everything went right, the pit stop would be completed before the field rounded the track, allowing the driver to catch up and only have to fight through traffic until those foolish enough to gamble had to bring their cars in under green. Chad's crew held out for a caution, and their wish was granted.

Friends, the situation wasn't good, at least for those involved. The backmarkers had bunched up flying down the backstretch. A lone car driven by a rookie making only his third start fell out of line. The driver, used to taking risks in the lower divisions, swerved back up into traffic, only to cut off another car, sending that one into another and causing a massive pileup. The rookie's car was rear-ended by another backmarker who was even further back, sending the car up onto its nose, its rear end visible sticking straight up in the smoke and debris.

"Yellow, yellow, yellow," said Hawk from his perch above the track.

It would be an unfortunate moment for a couple drivers who didn't have charters. They would be going back to Charlotte. As for Chad, he fell in behind the Camaro pace car.

"How about scuffs and one can of fuel?" said Larry, more giving an order than asking a question.

"How long do we have left?" asked Chad.

"Thirty-five to go when they decide to wave the green," answered Larry. "Pit window's forty laps. I think you'll have more than enough to finish if they don't screw around out there."

As soon as pit road was open, Chad guided his Mustang off the track. He felt honored to be given the first pit stop of the season. He hoped there would be many more. Chad slid into his pit stall, and the crew set to work. Everything was done in under thirteen seconds.

"Keep your fingers crossed those lugs are tight," said Chad.

Chad took his position back in the pack. He was sandwiched in the middle. This scared him a bit. This was where all the bad things happened. Get between the wrong people, and your day is done. The green flag waved, and Chad gunned it again.

"*Not today, Satan*," he thought to himself as he pushed his line ahead.

Chad hugged the double yellow line as he rounded the corners, careful not to let one millimeter of a tire to even touch the yellow paint. Chad knew if the race stayed green, the leaders would have to pit.

"How we doin' out there?" asked Larry.

"I told you I don't like crowds," joked Chad. "Got a path for me yet, Hawk?"

"23 is losing momentum on the backstretch," answered Hawk. "If you could just sneak your way in there in three, two, one."

Chad's Mustang moved into the open spot like the final piece of the puzzle snapping in place. This line proved to be the ticket. It kept him away from much of the danger.

One by one, the laps counted down. Roughly about every fifty seconds, Chad crossed the start/finish line. With twenty-five to go, the leaders began to pit. That was it. Just take it easy. Slow and steady would get him out front. Chad sailed by the former leaders as they pulled off the track every lap or two. Now he was in third. This could be interesting.

As the final laps began to count down, Chad had hooked up with another Mustang. In the outside lane were two Toyota teammates. It looked like it would be a tandem drag race as they flew underneath the white flag. Chad wanted that trophy. He needed that trophy.

Chad pushed the other Mustang hard down the backstretch, but the Toyotas remained neck and neck with the two Fords. Here it was. They slingshot off of turn four. It was now or never. Chad knew his car had momentum. There was room between the two leaders. The hinder Toyota competitor thought so too. Chad beat him to the spot as they approached the start/finish line. The lead Toyota saw Chad and tried to duck down to block, a stupid move. The Yota got loose and began to slide, tagging the other Ford with his nose before swinging back around and smashing the wall, collecting his teammate who had nowhere to go. With the other Ford careening out of control toward the infield, Chad was able to keep his car steady and cross the line, carnage ensuing behind him.

Chad was one of the few drivers still who waited to celebrate until he reached Victory Lane, and what a celebration it was. Larry jumped Chad and hugged him.

"You son of a gun!" Larry shouted. "I knew you could do it!"

This year was shaping up to be the shot in the arm MorrisSport needed. How could they lose the Daytona 500? They got their answer as the officials announced the grid for the next Duel.

"And starting inside row three is Blackpool's own Nigel McKenzie in the number 88 SportStream Ford Mustang Darkhorse."

"SportStream?" Chad blurted out confused. "He's not with us, is he?"

"No, I don't think so," replied Larry.

The announcer went on, "Nigel is here for Project 88 with SportStream, making a selective start here in NASCAR over from Formula One, where he is the current World Champion."

"I think I'm gonna call Tom," said Larry.

"McKenzie, McKenzie," Chad repeated as if he were searching for the word. "Where have I heard that name today?"

He decided to take a run up to the press box and watch the race from there. As the race was underway, he kept his eye on the other SportStream car, this one all teal blue with no overt sponsorship from Ford. His method seemed odd. Actually, it seemed downright stupid to Chad at first. By the time they had exited turn two for the first time, the fool had already fallen out of the draft.

"What's this moron doing?" thought Chad. *"How much is SportStream paying this clown?"*

The race was still green by lap thirty. Nigel was still in the back. Those poor subscribers. They were paying to see this guy put on a show, not freak out because he had to make a left turn.

Nigel kept it easy and pitted on lap thirty-one. Their pit strategy appeared very similar to what Chad did. Of course, they had SportStream sponsorship and could probably see everything Chad and Larry had cooked up. Nigel wasted no time exiting the pits. At least he was quick about something here.

As the field began to spread out due to green flag pit stops, Nigel appeared as if he were left out to dry. What Chad didn't know was that Nigel was just holding back.

With five to go, the field had all but bunched back up again with a few cars lapped by the leaders. Nigel's Mustang was the last car on the lead lap. It was go time. He hooked onto the rear bumper of a Camaro and pushed the lucky winner through the pack.

"That son of a gun!" Chad whispered to himself.

If the driver in the Camaro thought he was receiving a gift, he was dead wrong. Over four laps, the pair pushed their way through traffic. As the white flag waved over them, Nigel began to make his move. Coming off of turn two, Nigel kept his Mustang low. The Camaro had the advantage as far as momentum, but Nigel was choosing the short way around. They were neck and neck going into three, still neck and neck out of four. It would be close, but Nigel had the inside lane advantage.

"Three one thousandths of a second!" the commentator shouted.

Chad sat back in shock. He had a challenger, an interloper no less. What was his race to win was now his race to lose. Two cars with one sponsor meant someone was playing them off of each other. He gulped with despair.

The victory lane celebration was just as big as Chad's. He watched the broadcast from the flatscreens mounted in the press box.

"Nigel McKenzie," began the pit reporter as he made his way into victory lane, "Formula One World Champion and now a winner in the NASCAR Cup Series. What do you have to say about that."

"Well, first of all," Nigel began, "I'd like to thank my sponsors. This SportStream Ford Mustang Darkhorse was tremendous out there. Also, my owner, Colin Singleton, for giving me this opportunity. And finally, I need to thank me agent, Gemma McKenzie, who's also me sister."

And there she was: Chad's girl. The gears started turning. He was crushing on Nigel McKenzie's sister. That's where he heard the name.

"*Well, Gemma,*" he thought to himself, "*I'm afraid I'll have to break your pretty heart come Sunday.*"

Chapter Five
500 Miles

The weather was pretty much the same over the weekend: hot and muggy. Chad paced around his pit box as reporters and news personalities milled around, getting the scoop on every driver and crew member's opinions ahead of the race. He was nervous. He never liked talking to the press much. He wanted to leave the pit box. He wanted to sneak out and find the other SportStream team. A good word with Nigel McKenzie could get him close to his sister. Was his thinking wrong? Maybe. How long before the national anthem? A half hour. He could do it.

"Hey, Noodle," he gestured to his fuel man, "lend me your helmet."

"What for?"

"To pass through Mordor unseen," replied Chad.

Noodle handed Chad his helmet, and Chad put it on.

"Come on, Noodle," said Chad as he attempted breathing through his mouth, "why does this thing smell like pad thai?"

"Man gets hungry doing all this athletic work," chuckled Noodle.

Chad spun around and left the pit box, pushing through the crowds and searching for Nigel.

As it had turned out, Nigel was racing directly for SportStream. Company owner and CEO, Colin Singleton, had decided to field his own entry in the Daytona 500 ahead of the Formula One season. He chose his primary driver from that series to fill the seat. Nobody from MorrisSport could believe their ears hearing this news. It seemed as if Singleton wasn't interested in MorrisSport. If he was, wouldn't he have bowed out of running an extra car until after Daytona? Wouldn't it make sense to do everything in his power to help the team he's looking to sponsor win, not some one-and-done non-charter team? Larry concluded that this was probably some rich guy with tons of cash to blow and throw at anything on a whim.

Chad caught his breath as he emerged from the crowd into the SportStream pit box. He had never met Nigel McKenzie, even in the drivers' meetings throughout the week. He had been just one of several faces that would come and go. There he was in the flesh. The man was a bean pole, around 6'3" Chad guessed. He indeed looked very British. His hair reached almost down to his shoulders, really a big mess of a brown mop on his head. His teeth were prominent, but not in that stereotypical way Americans like to tease Brits for; they at least looked clean and all there, as well as being somewhat straight for the most part.

"Good afternoon," Chad greeted his teammate, extending his hand. "Chad Helton, MorrisSport."

Nigel sheepishly accepted Chad's handshake.

"Nigel McKenzie, SportStream."

"That was some racing you did last week!" said Chad, trying to drum up some conversation.

"I'm hoping I can replicate it," replied Nigel.

"Have you done something like this?"

"Like what? It's a lot of firsts."

"500 miles. Endurance. Sitting in a car for up to five hours."

"I've done Le Mans once or twice. We're usually pulling three-to-six-hour stints in those cars."

Chad was taken by this guy. He would clearly be a challenge, but a worthy challenge. He thought Nigel could see the same thing in him as well. The conversation was interrupted by a sound that made Chad's heart flutter.

"Nige, I just got off the phone with a representative from Auburn. They've offered 30 million quid over one year."

The voice belonged to Gemma. Chad spun around. His blood pressure rose. For some reason, he felt exposed, almost naked. The girl was still wearing that plain brown anachronistic business attire.

"Tell them I'm not interested," replied Nigel. "I already have my home for this year."

Gemma regarded her brother with some skepticism. Turning down £30 million seemed foolish. Oh well, his loss. Gemma wheeled around and noticed Chad.

"Chad Helton," she stated his name with that exclamation that sounds somewhat like a scold, but a happy scold.

"Gemma, isn't it?" said Chad, just excited to be able to even see her face to face again, to share some space with her.

"Correct," she replied.

"I'm glad to see you again," began Chad. "I had no idea Nigel was…"

"My brother," Gemma cut him off. "It's true, I guess. I'm also his agent."

She twirled one of her corkscrew curls with her index finger. Chad found this attractive. Was she into him, or was he just reading into things?

"Well, it was nice meeting you again, Gemma," began Chad, "but I'd better go. They're about to do the prerace ceremony. See you guys after the race."

Chad waved the Brits good-bye. He caught what looked like a wistful wave from Gemma, like one of those "come back soon" waves you see women giving their men in those old war movies and westerns.

"See you in victory lane, Nigel," Chad shouted. Maybe he could shake this guy a little.

Chad returned to his pit box just in time for the invocation given by a local pastor.

"Oh, Lord Heavenly Father," he began. He was really going to milk this one. "We thank Thee for this opportunity to gather here today to partake in this great tradition of auto racing."

Really laying it on thick with the King James English, Chad thought to himself as he bowed his head, sneaking a peak with one eye from time to time to see if he could spot Gemma somewhere.

"We thank Thee for the cars, for the drivers, and the teams. We thank Thee for the manufacturers of Ford, Chevy, and Toyota. We thank Thee for Thy care over these drivers as they climb into their cars to risk their lives over five hundred miles. I thank Thee for my church, my congregation, and my smokin' hot wife."

Chad could feel the tension. Did he just hear what he thought he heard? Did those words come out of this man's lips after such fancy prose? Chad peaked around even more to see if anyone reacted. Of course, old Noodle was there at the end of their formation stifling a laugh.

"In Thy name we pray, amen."

Without missing a beat, another country artist began her rendition of "The Star-Spangled Banner." Now with their hands over their hearts, Chad could really look around. To his surprise, even the Brits showed some modicum of respect to his nation's flag as the NPC musician sang a song about Americans standing against the British.

Chad reveled in the irony. He also wondered how many ways such a beautiful song could be butchered and turned into pure torture. He was sure agents at Gitmo played this on a loop. Waterboarding had nothing on it. Finally, the torture was over. The F35s flew over, shaking the very ground Chad stood on. It was a sight that never got old.

The same routine as in Phoenix began to play out here in Daytona. Chad slid into his seat through the window and began to buckle himself in as Larry closed the window net. He always kept his helmet and HANS device in the space next to his seat. He switched out his SportStream cap for both and began to fasten the two. The helmet matched the car's paint scheme, fading from white to teal front to back with a 28 on each side. A Ford logo was stuck on the space above his visor, a SportStream emblem covering the rear of the helmet.

Chad held on to hear the command to fire up his engine. For a race like Daytona, they couldn't just get any old person to be the grand marshal. This year, they picked some celebrity from some big action movie coming out that Chad didn't care about. However unimportant this joker was to Chad, at least he showed some enthusiasm for the job.

"Gentlemeeeen," he held out the second syllable of "gentlemen", "start your engines!" This time, he paused for a bit between each word.

Chad flipped his battery and fuel pump switches on and turned the ignition once again. The engine roared to life. The deafening noise drowned out Chad's worries as he was right where he belonged. Forty cars staged two-by-two along the pit road, lining up behind the Camaro pace car. As soon as the Chev advanced, the racers made their move.

The conversation was lively up in the press booth. Three middle-aged men in suits and ties stood in front of a camera amidst a background of the track.

"In our starting lineup today," one began, "we've got Tyler Morgan inside pole in his number 26 Dream Mobile Toyota Camry for Wolfe

Motorsports. Next to him on outside pole is Kyle Rooker in the number 78 Central Welding Supply Chevy for McGuiness Racing."

"And on the second row," another commentator picked up the conversation, "we have a very unique combination. Inside is last year's Rookie of the Year and championship runner-up, Chad Helton. You'll see the MorrisSport Ford Mustang Darkhorse is sporting a new paint scheme this year with Tom Morris Ford and SportStream splitting sponsorship. News in the garage is that SportStream is offering full sponsorship throughout the year if he can win. Let's certainly hope so after the bad news the team received this past November."

"I'm just gonna butt in here and mention the newcomer outside row two," added the third commentator. "Nigel McKenzie from Blackpool, England is piloting the number 88 SportStream Ford, a one-off sponsor-owned operation. SportStream, as you know, owns a successful Formula One team. They've yet to make an announcement if this foray into NASCAR is an omen of things to come, but it's exciting nonetheless. Nigel surprised us in qualifying and the Duels. They've told us that he had never sat behind the wheel of a NASCAR Cup Series car until qualifying last week."

The aura of anticipation was thick and visible. The roar of the crowd nearly drowned out the roar of the stock cars even as the commentators introduced the remaining thirty-six drivers on the grid. Chad zig zagged his car to warm up his tires. He looked to his right and noticed Nigel in the outside lane. How was that for optics – two cars that shared a sponsor starting side-by-side? Chad saluted his British teammate as they crossed through the tri-oval start/finish line.

"Going green next time by," Hawk chattered into the radio.

"Okay, son," began Larry. "It's all you out there today. You got three stages and two hundred laps to make a miracle happen."

Chad's heart beat in anticipation as the pace car ducked down into pit road. This was it. There was more at stake here today than there was at Phoenix. There, it was just a championship. Today, it was his job. Today, a championship did really seem like such a little thing. All that was out of Chad's mind as the number 26 Toyota launched through the restart zone and across the start/finish line under the green flag. The Daytona 500 was officially underway.

If Chad had any objective at any other Daytona race, it was to survive. Sure, he'd be doing that today, but the stakes were too high to just merely survive. As critical as a win was today, he knew he had to be patient. The race isn't won on the first lap. The first two stages were sixty-five laps, capped off with a final seventy-lap stage. Even with playoff points up for grabs, they would be of very little help to Chad if he didn't finish that final stage first.

Nigel had no such reservations. With nothing to lose, he pushed forward, accelerating his line past the inside lane. Nigel was here to win.

"Hold back, Chad," said Larry. "Conserve your fuel. Just find a line and stay in that draft."

"What about dirty air?" asked Noodle off radio.

"When the time comes.," replied Larry.

The most dangerous thing for Chad at this point would be being stuck in traffic. If any cars to his side were to wreck, it could easily spell disaster for the MorrisSport Ford. Chad kept quiet as he sat comfortably in fourth. The leaders lined up single file down the backstretch.

"Well, it looks like the everyone is playing follow the leader as Nigel McKenzie moves to the lead," said a color commentator perched up in the press box.

"Shall we give them a show?" Nigel asked his crew chief.

"I say give it all you got," replied the crew chief. He was a veteran of just as many years' experience as Larry. As talented as Nigel was, he knew he couldn't do anything without a good crew.

The situation continued for several laps. By around lap thirty-eight, it hadn't improved. The drivers were afraid of the dreaded Big

One, and for good reason. It would be foolish to take such big risks so early on. That would have to be saved for the final stage.

"How's the fuel situation in there?" asked Larry.

"About an eighth," replied Chad.

"Crappy mileage," muttered Larry. "Okay, we'll need to bring you in. We'll follow Plan Phoenix today."

"Plan Phoenix" was code for "Repeat what we did in Phoenix". Larry wasn't taking any chances to reveal his pit strategy. He needed the edge. With the first stage going caution-free, everyone would have to pit under green anyway.

"Should I gamble it?" asked Chad. "I could stay out and lead a few laps. I need some clean air."

"Just get that air when you come into the apron," replied Larry. "Don't put yourself in a dangerous situation. We've still got a whole lot of racing left to do today."

Chad obeyed his crew chief and broke off from the pack, the first car to do so. Some other drivers and crew chiefs saw Chad's strategy and came to the same conclusion. Green flag pit stops had begun.

"Be ready in three, two, one," came Larry's commands as Chad slid his Mustang into the pit box. Like Phoenix, it would be one can of fuel, but also right-side tires as the high speeds of Daytona eat at tires like acid. Within six seconds, the service was completed, and Chad bolted out of his pit box even as the other drivers who had mirrored his decision were sliding into their boxes.

Chad hated green flag stops. In addition to the time lost to the leaders, there was the problem of rejoining the track with cars already nearing 200 miles per hour.

"Looks like everyone else is pitting," said Hawk as he watched everything from his perch. "How's about we take the lead on this thing?"

"Hey, cut it out," yelled Larry. "We don't need to go giving the kid any bad ideas."

Larry knew that Chad wanted nothing more than to win the race. To win the race, you have to be in front. To be in front, you have to be fast. Chad was fast. He knew it. Larry and their car chief, Smokey Childers were masters at setting up the car. Smokey was known for fudging things up a bit. Many people said he was responsible for 50% of the rulebook changes on the Next Gen car, but this week, he was under strict instructions to keep it as clean as possible. They couldn't risk having the car disqualified in the position they were in. Smokey didn't need to cheat anyway, and Larry made double sure that their set-up was free of any of Smokey's "innovations". Larry believed they had created the ideal perfect car, and he was proud of it.

"Leaders coming up behind you," said Hawk. "Wait a second. Okay, go for it."

Chad gave it all he had. The beast roared out onto the backstretch, catching just the tail end of the draft, drawing him closer to the leaders as they entered turn three. Chad's excitement grew as those leaders began to peel off and enter the pits. He was leading now. The MorrisSport Mustang had speed.

"Let's let these subscribers get their money's worth," chuckled Chad.

"He is gonna lose this race," muttered Larry under his breath.

Maybe not yet, because Chad maintained his lead throughout the remainder of the stage. He held a private miniature celebration to himself in the car as he crossed the line under the green-and-white checkered flag.

"Two cans of fuel and tires all around when you bring it in," said Larry as the field lined up for the caution between the stages.

Chad brought it in, watching his RPMs carefully so he wouldn't speed. NASCAR stock cars are not equipped with speedometers, and speed is tracked by timing lights along pit road. Chad knew his car, and he knew exactly what engine speed he needed to stay legal but fast. The car slid into the pit as his crew jumped the wall. Their routine was flawless. That was until a spark from the left rear lug nut making hard contact with the impact gun ignited fuel that was spilling out of the gas can and the fuel tank. Not only was the rear quarter panel of the car ablaze, but so was Noodle. Pandemonium broke out as Mike and Quizz grabbed fire extinguishers and doused the flames. The car was safe, except for some peeling of the wrap where the fire had eaten through the gasoline. As happy as everyone was about the car, they were more thrilled that Noodle was unharmed.

"Get out of here!" screamed Larry. "Go! We've lost time, and we're losing more!"

Chad bolted out, losing some position as the potential disaster cost them valuable seconds.

"I guess we oughtta start calling you Fried Noodle," laughed Chad as he rejoined the field.

The commentators got a kick out of the fire just as much as Chad did. The scene of Noodle dancing around with flames roaring off of his firesuit was replayed over and over. It was sure to make the rounds on social media as well.

Chad impatiently waited in twelfth as the rest of the field lined up behind.

"Green flag next time by," said Hawk.

Chad zig-zagged, heating up his tires in preparation for the next stage. Same deal as the first stage.

"Where's McKenzie?" asked Chad.

"Don't worry about him," said Larry. "Just hit your marks and be out front at the end."

"I'd just like to know," said Chad.

"If you must," Larry relented, "first."

"Crap," Chad muttered onto his live mic.

"Well, it does help if you're not busy putting out your crew members," chuckled Larry.

The conversation was cut short as the green flag waved. The stakes were raised now, and Chad was stuck in the front half of the middle of the pack. Chad tried desperately to find a safe spot, but to no avail.

Disaster struck on the twenty-third lap of the stage as one of the Chevrolets dipped too far down in turn three, losing control and swerving back up into traffic. The ensuing pileup sent another car careening toward the inside lane before being launched into the air by another car. The airborne Toyota missed Chad by millimeters as he drove right underneath. The car crashed back down onto the ground and slid for several feet until finally coming to rest in the infield grass off of turn four.

"Is that a code brown?" asked Larry.

"Negatory," replied Chad. "Shorts are clean."

The commentators watched the scene in awe as car after car disappeared into the cloud of smoke. Some flew out intact at speed, some exited spinning and damaged, and some were lost in the cloud.

"Who knew the Big One would come so soon this year?" one of the commentators said.

The carnage extended the entire width of turns three and four. There was no choice for the officials but to red flag the race. Chad brought his Mustang to a stop on the entrance to turn one and shut it down. If the Arizona heat was bad during the red flag at Phoenix, the Florida humidity made it even worse.

"I'm going to need a liter of water and a banana when I pit," said Chad, clearly going cotton-mouthed.

After what seemed like hours, the lights turned yellow, and the pits opened. Chad fired up the engine and brought his car in. He didn't want to be out there anymore, and Larry knew it. He knew his driver well.

"You'll feel better after that banana," said Larry. "Also, we filled that tumbler with a sports drink. You're low on electrolytes."

Chad was thankful for the care as the crew finished servicing the car and sent him on his way.

"How are we looking?" asked Chad as he sped up to find the pace car.

"You'll restart third directly behind Nigel," said Larry.

Chad brought the car to within a millimeter of Nigel's rear bumper.

"Smile for the cameras," Chad whispered to himself.

All over the world, SportStream subscribers got a screen full of Mustang grill, virtually blacking out their view until Chad backed off.

"Okay, Chad, stop showing off," groaned Hawk who could see everything Chad did.

The green flag dropped, but as soon as it dropped, the yellow came out again.

"What for this time?" roared Chad as he slowed back down.

"Some B.S. debris caution it looks like," replied Hawk.

Sure enough, there was a plastic bag that had made its way onto the track.

"Did NASCAR really think that was that important?" Chad complained to Larry.

The bag was, in all reality, of very little concern. At the worst, it would get stuck to someone's grill, but that could be mitigated by drafting up behind another car to disrupt the airflow and send it over the car.

"Green next time by," said Hawk.

The Camaro pace car left the track back for the pits, and Nigel punched the accelerator as he crossed the line for the restart zone. Row by row, the other cars followed suit.

"If we're thinking about putting on a show," Larry began, "I bet you'd make the subs really happy right now if you pushed Nigel for a bit."

"You mean actually race?" asked Chad.

"Well, more or less. Just make sure you can save the car for the third stage. Get you two separated from the pack. You might keep the both of you safe just in case someone does something stupid."

Chad did just that. He linked up his nose with Nigel's tail, and the two of them took off. The pair on the outside line tried, but couldn't synchronize. Nigel must have known what Chad was doing, because he kept him in his rearview mirror, lining up perfectly with his fellow Ford driver.

"Green checker next time by," said Hawk.

"Should I go for it?" asked Chad.

"If you want," said Larry. "Do it if you think you can do it safely. Those are old tires."

Chad chose the safer option. Instead of going for a second stage victory and possibly sweeping the race, he pushed Nigel across the start/finish line. Today was all SportStream.

"Bring her in," said Larry. "This is it."

A lap after the Camaro emerged from the pits, every single of the remaining cars ducked into the pits. The stage two Big One had ended the hopes of thirteen drivers. Four or five others managed to make it back out with some damage, but they were ailing too.

MorrisSport's perfectly choreographed ballet had no match. A couple more like this, and the Daytona 500 would be a sure win for Chad. The SportStream crew nearly kept up, but it was all Chad as he edged Nigel out onto the race out of pit road. Chad lined up directly behind the Camaro.

This was it. This would be the last stage. Seventy laps would decide the fate of MorrisSport. Chad had gambled his NASCAR career on this moment. Following his example, every single crew member and staffer at MorrisSport followed him in doing the same. Outside of the one or two pit stops remaining, all hopes rested on Chad's shoulders. What could be a story of a failing team going out with a whimper could turn into the greatest triumph story in the sport's history. The moment would play on recaps for years and years. But Chad had to get there first. 175 miles to save MorrisSport. Was he up to it? He forgot all that as the Camaro ducked into the pits. The green flag waved, and Chad mashed the throttle as soon as he crossed into the restart zone.

"Okay," Larry began as Chad flew down the latter half of the frontstretch, "now's the moment we've been waiting for. Don't hold back. Give 'er all you got."

Larry didn't have to tell Chad twice. Chad knew exactly where to carry his momentum into turn one and keep it coming out of turn two, allowing the car to slingshot to within millimeters of the backstretch wall. The G-forces glued Chad to his seat over the 31° banking through the turns. The backstretch widened and flattened to 3° as Chad flew down it before rising again to 31° in three and four. All the while, Chad paid no mind to whatever events unfolded behind him. Coming out of four, he would get another reprieve as the frontstretch tri-oval flattened to 18°, just enough to carry some momentum and speed in front of the grandstand.

With five extra laps on the stage, the pit strategy would change a little. The whole team collectively prayed for a caution, but it didn't come.

"Bring it in," said Larry with fifty to go. "They're bound to mess up the closer we get to the end.

Chad heeded his crew chief and brought his car in under green. Nigel did the same.

"That snake is following everything we do," Chad told his crew chief.

"Well, he's been a threat all day," Larry explained, "and if he's following us, he may be the only thing we have to worry about. We've got a fast car. We'll be fine. We're going Pearl Harbor."

"Pearl Harbor" was Larry's code to Chad for four tires and one can of fuel. Larry had come up with the morbid name for his strategy based on four and one, which led to forty-one. He associated forty-one with 1941. The significance of that year was the attack on Pearl Harbor. While it was somewhat cringeworthy, it worked.

MorrisSport moved quickly. Chad's goal was to stay out ahead of Nigel McKenzie.

"Where's the limey?" Chad asked, making sure he wasn't on a live mic.

"One step behind," Larry yelled back.

Once the driver's side of the car was dropped, Chad peeled out of the pit stall. He rejoined the field about a lap down. The position wasn't bad though. He was the lucky dog – the first car a lap down. If there was a caution for any reason, he'd end up back on the lead lap. Chad silently prayed for a caution and just one more caution. That would likely eliminate Nigel's chance of catching up and posing a serious threat.

That caution came with thirty-five to go. A rookie, who up to that point had been running well, messed up and exited turn two too fast. He was unable to react in time and smashed the passenger side of his Chevy into the backstretch wall.

"Thank you, Connor Westmoreland," Chad chuckled into his radio as he circled the field to regain his lap.

"Pit road is open next time by," said Larry. "Bring her in for a British Wood Special."

"British Wood Special" was Larry-ese for "Two right side tires and one can of fuel". It was British, because British automobiles are right-hand-drive. The Wood was for the Wood Brothers' number twenty-one; the numbers two and one.

Chad brought the car in, and the crew did their thing. It was perfect. Due to their abridged pit stop, Chad had gained even more position. Nigel was out of the picture, unless he remained the first car a lap down if a caution came out.

Green flag, and another restart. Chad weaved his way through the field, edging one car out in one and three then pulling a slingshot in two and four. Things couldn't be better as the front row came into view. After another lap, Chad was back in the lead.

"Trouble!" shouted Hawk as carnage broke out behind Chad with five to go.

"Bring it in," said Larry. "We're going to make you fast."

Chad brought the car down pit road one last time. He had a little extra time for reflection as he rejoined the pack seconds later. The wreck cleanup had extended the race into overtime. Chad was already low on fuel when the yellow flew. The splash of fuel Fried Noodle had put in the car kept it a little lighter. Fresh tires would allow him to overtake easily. Chad lined up seventh as he passed the carnage. Luckily, it had been more or less relegated to the large run-off along the inside of the backstretch. It was still gnarly. Some of the cars had bunched up jockeying for position. Someone failed to check his mirror before he moved to block, and he was dumped. The pack racing and sudden deceleration caused a chain reaction. Now only seventeen cars remained. And who should be right behind Chad in ninth but Nigel McKenzie?

"Going green one more time," said Hawk. "Two to go."

"Go, go, go!" shouted Larry.

Chad didn't wait. As soon as he crossed the start/finish line, he made his move. He knew that as much of a threat Nigel was that he would also push him to the front. They did just that, and by the end of the lap, Chad crossed under the white flag.

This was it! MorrisSport was saved! Chad sailed down the backstretch at almost 200 MPH with Nigel's Mustang practically welded to the rear bumper of Chad's Mustang. Nigel kept in line perfectly with Chad. Coming out of four, all bets were off. Nigel made his move. He performed a slingshot and took the high lane, using his momentum to overtake Chad.

"Not today," said Chad as he lightly broadsided Nigel.

"What the blazes is he on about?" Nigel shouted to his crew chief.

"This ain't Formula One," the veteran quickly explained. "Rubbin's racin'. Give it back."

Nigel did just that. The next five seconds seemed like five minutes. Nigel was right on Chad. They were side-by-side. The crowd roared as they ran parallel to each other. They crossed the line together.

To say it was an historic moment would be an understatement. To the naked eye, they crossed the line at the same time. Even NASCAR's timing lights couldn't tell who won; but this year, they had a new tool. In addition to sponsoring two cars and streaming the race, SportStream had provided a super-slow-motion camera placed at the bottom of the wall at the start/finish line. It would record footage at 10,000 frames per second, an incredible frame rate. The result was a NASCAR record: a winning time differential of one five thousandth of a second for Nigel McKenzie in the number 88 SportStream Ford Mustang Darkhorse. MorrisSport was now defunct.

Chapter Six
Moonlight Sonata

Chad remembered very little of the end of the race. He held out hope that perhaps Nigel's car would be disqualified during post-race inspection. In fact, it would be his car. NASCAR quickly tore down the top three cars plus a random finisher directly after the victory celebration and found that some foam in the nose of Chad's car behind the wrap was slightly misshapen. Did it really matter in the long run? Not in the slightest, but NASCAR issues strict rules for the teams to abide by, and that means even some of the most meaningless infractions can ruin the day. Chad's second-place was demoted to a fortieth-place finish.

Nigel McKenzie was loaded. Formula One is known for its lavish lifestyles, and Nigel was no different. In the weeks leading up to Daytona, he had sent his yacht to Florida in preparation for a grand party he wanted to throw for his fellow drivers, win or lose. Anybody who was anybody was in attendance. Grudgingly, Chad went as the designated driver for his team. He didn't drink, but he thought one last hurrah before they returned to North Carolina to clean out the shop would be in order.

The atmosphere inside the yacht was loud and obnoxious. Forty drivers, plus their team members, team owners, NASCAR officials, television personalities, and random celebrities packed onto the 150-foot yacht. Even for its size, the yacht seemed like a dinghy bobbing up and down just off the Florida Coast. The distinct smells of tobacco smoke and alcohol wafted through the air as partyers lit victory cigars and the booze flowed into priceless glass flutes. Chad left the claustrophobia for some fresh salt air. The stifling heat and humidity of the day had faded into a chill in the low 60s. After acclimating to the previous climate, it felt anything but pleasant, almost as if he would soon be able to see his own breath. Gone were his firesuit and SportStream cap. He had settled for something a little more casual: some blue jeans and Johnston & Murphy sneakers with a Ford Racing polo and his old high school letterman jacket from the one year he did track and field. He stood out on the deck, resting his left arm on the rail while dawdling over a Styrofoam cup of steaming black coffee. He still hadn't had time to process the disaster. He wasn't even sure if he could forgive Smokey for screwing up the car. It was just a piece of foam, but had he won, he still wouldn't have won. As much as he failed his team, if he were honest with himself, he felt somewhat that his team had failed him.

"Catching some air?" came a familiar voice from behind him.

Chad spun around to see Gemma dressed stunningly. No more was she the living anachronism. Now she was dressed in a shimmering red strapless dress and standing a little taller on matching heels. The red seemed to bring out even more of the green in her eyes as if he were looking at Christmas personified. Her tumbling raven hair which had been styled with precise minimalism to look professional was now done up with a few remaining corkscrews dangling around the side. She had gone from the world of C.S. Lewis to a night on the red carpet.

"Well, that's a bit of a change," Chad commented. "I like the look."

"Well, I'm off the clock," Gemma waved the comment on. "Anyway, I get to play designated driver tonight to my brother once this yacht makes port. You?"

"Same," replied Chad. "It's the price you pay when you're the outsider on a team of good ol' boys."

"So not even a glass of Nigel's finest?" asked Gemma.

"I'm what your people would call a teetotaler," replied Chad.

"What led you to that decision?"

"My Baptist church back home," laughed Chad.

Chad glanced at the girl. He was tempted alright. It would be so easy too, but he averted his eyes before he could do something stupid.

"Got cold," he said, trying to change the subject from drink choices.

"Could you believe it's only 16°?" replied Gemma.

"Well, I don't think it's that cold."

"Sorry, I forgot to change my phone from Metric," explained Gemma.

"Allow me," said Chad as he removed his letterman and placed it on Gemma's shoulders.

"Thank you," she said.

"Well, I think you need it more than me. So, tell me, what actually brought you here? I mean, how does someone like you become a sports agent?"

"What exactly do you mean?" asked a puzzled Gemma.

"I mean my agent, Ace Valdez, is one of those sleazy types. It seems like they all are from everyone I've talked to."

"And I'm not?"

"I haven't gotten that impression."

"I don't have to be," Gemma said proudly.

"So how did you get here then?"

"Why are you so interested?"

"I'm just making conversation. How long do you expect this thing to go on tonight?"

"Well," she began, "you'll need to be wired on caffeine, because Nigel has a tendency to party until sunrise. The deckchairs on the stern make for rather comfortable sleeping if you don't mind back pain in the morning."

"Brilliant," mumbled Chad.

"Are you wanting to hear my story or not?" said Gemma, stomping her foot to feign a childish impatience.

"Of course," answered Chad. "Fire away."

"Well," she began for real, "both Nigel and I were born in Blackpool, Nigel six years before me. Mum and Dad liked to travel a lot. Of course, Nigel was already racing karts when I was born, and that fed their habit. I always had tutors when I started school, never leaning with other children. It was fine that way, I suppose. I always had the best education. When I was twelve, Nigel was racing Formula Three in Austria. Mum and Dad decided to go skiing while they were there with him. They were on a ski lift when," she started to tear up here. "I'm sorry."

"Don't worry about it," said Chad, trying to comfort her.

"No," she replied, "it happened years ago, but it still gets to me sometimes. There was an avalanche that took out the ski lift. They were the only passengers at the time. They only found the bodies after three days. I was sent to live back in Blackpool with my nan until I graduated four years later. I forgot to add that I was years ahead in my schooling since my tutors taught me year-round. I went to Somerville and got my degree in business communications. Representing Nigel is my first real outing since I graduated in May."

"Four years?" asked Chad.

"Four years," Gemma confirmed.

"That would mean," Chad looked up as if he were searching for something to say, "you're what? Twenty-one?"

"Not until July," Gemma replied. "Which is one more reason I haven't had any of Nigel's fantastic brandy. I tried to get him to sail to international waters, but he thinks it'll scare some of these guys. He still thinks some of them aren't very bright."

"Well, to tell you the truth, I think he might be right with some of them," laughed Chad.

"I think you've changed his perspective on Americans," Gemma explained. "You genuinely scared him. You know what he told me before he went out there? He said that he felt like the only person he needed to watch out for was you."

"Funny," said Chad. "I thought the same thing about him."

"He was surprised he was able to make that last lap pass."

"Well, you know," began Chad, "he wouldn't have even needed to pass me. My car got disqualified."

"That's tough," said Gemma. "Perhaps you'll have better luck next week?"

"I don't think so," replied Chad.

"Why not?"

"Because I lost my ride."

"How could you lose your ride after a race like that. I thought you were some 'wunderkind'. I've read about you. You finished runner up in the Cup Series Championship and won Rookie of the Year last season. On top of that, you had a record-breaking fourteen wins on the season. How do you lose your ride like that?"

"Sponsorship," Chad answered. "If people don't want to pay the bills, the lights don't stay on. SportStream only promised to fund the team the remainder of this season if we won Daytona."

"It's a wonder then why nobody would sponsor you," Gemma replied, still trying to process such a thing.

"Nobody wants to sponsor a NASCAR team anymore," explained Chad. "Some pretty successful teams have shut down because their sponsors decided to take their funds somewhere else."

"So these big companies can't find anywhere in their budget to sponsor a car?"

"Not enough viewers," Chad continued. "Back about twenty or twenty-five years ago, we were second to the NFL in ratings. Nowadays, we can barely bring in two million television viewers outside of Daytona. The optics just aren't there."

"So where will you go now?" asked Gemma.

"I'm not sure," replied Chad. "My feckless leach of an agent couldn't find anybody willing to take me."

"You see," interrupted Gemma, "this makes absolutely no sense to me. Forgive my ignorance, but are you not supposed to be the greatest NASCAR driver ever or something like that?"

"Something like that. Unfortunately, there aren't any vacancies."

"Nobody?"

"Well, the best I can do," Chad continued his explanation, "is to go to Atlanta next week and hope someone falls sick."

"And if that doesn't work out? I mean, you can't possibly go on like this forever."

"Maybe it's time I find a different line of work. It's just that I've been working toward this since I was a little kid. Like Nigel, I was racing karts since I was a little kid. Twenty-one years old, and I feel like my life's been derailed."

"Don't worry," Gemma tried comforting her new friend, "lots of people don't start their lives until much later."

"I don't know," Chad continued complaining. "I look at my cousin Emily. She and her husband are my age, and they already own a house and a business, and they have a kid. I'm there with the house, but that's not what I want to live for."

"What were your plans?"

"I don't know. Winning a NASCAR championship was my dream. Now that it's out of my reach, I feel like there are other things of greater value. I just wish there was a way I could support a family and do what I love."

"Aren't there any other driving disciplines that would allow that? I'm sure you'd be in high demand."

"Not any that would pay the bills," answered Chad. "Listen to that. I'm complaining to you. I'm sorry if I sound like I'm whining."

"No, no," said Gemma, trying to comfort him. "I get it. It all seems so simple, yet it's complicated."

"So what about you?" asked Chad.

"Me?" asked Gemma, confused at the sudden turn in the conversation.

"Well, I think we've established that I'm pretty much screwed for the time being," Chad explained. "What's next for you?"

Gemma took a deep breath at this.

"Well," she began, "we race in Bahrain at the end of this month. As soon as we get back to Daytona, we fly back to headquarters in Austin. For that time, I'm fielding phone calls with sponsors and advert people. Would you believe that even up until the first race, there are still other teams trying to get Nigel?"

"Seems like you'll be pretty occupied," sighed Chad.

"You could say that," Gemma replied.

The two designated drivers remained outside while the party raged on through the night. They discussed hopes and dreams, interests and passions. By around 3, they found their way to the stern where they both crashed on the deckchairs. Four hours later, Nigel decided he had had enough and requested his yacht make for port. An hour later, the host of inebriated party guests stumbled off onto the pier.

"No, this side," said Gemma as she guided her hammered brother from the driver's side to the passenger seat of his Aston Martin.

"We're number one!" he shouted, though it was hardly intelligible through the alcoholic slur.

After she was finished buckling Nigel in, Gemma turned around to see Chad waiting for her.

"Oh, it's you," she said, not knowing what to actually say. She felt awkward, what with stuffing her brother into the car like a toddler and this man she just met standing there staring at her.

"I just thought I'd come and say good-bye before we shove off to our hotel," Chad explained.

"Oh, well I apologize for you having to witness my brother's behavior."

"Not at all," continued Chad. "You should see the group of wombats I get to drive."

"Then I'll just stick with one alcoholic today," laughed Gemma.

"Well," Chad continued with some longing in his voice, "I guess if this is the last time I see you, thank you for last night. You actually made designated driver duty fun."

"I enjoyed it too," said Gemma, "and I doubt this is the last you'll hear from me." And with that, she lowered herself into the Aston.

Chapter Seven
Second Chances

Gemma was not lying about those deckchairs. As soon as he had made sure his crew members were safely in their hotel rooms, Chad found his room and crashed.

Gemma's face, yea her very presence occupied Chad's mind as he drifted off to sleep. If his first meeting provided just a vision of their life together, his sleep provided the whole thing played out as if he were living it. The human mind is very powerful, able to imagine the unimaginable. He dreamed of everything about her. It seemed he experienced seventy years within an hour or so. It was the unwritten story of their life. His heart raced even as he slept. He was happy. Forget the racing career. Gemma was his life now.

Then, he woke up. Disappointment began to set in as he looked around his hotel room. It was dark. In that confusion everyone has upon first waking up, he didn't know where he was. Only a few seconds later, that smell that all non-smoking hotel rooms have told him exactly where he was. Chad looked at the bedside alarm clock. It read "1:27". He had been asleep since 9:15 in the morning. Four hours? No, sixteen hours. It was 1:30 in the morning. Even after all that sleep, he still wasn't refreshed. As he began to move around, he felt grubby. He looked down and noticed he hadn't undressed from the previous night's party. His shoes were still neatly tied. Chad got out of bed and stripped down. A shower was in order. Even if he had no one to impress, he knew the shower would be relaxing.

After finishing the hot water massage with a quick rinse of ice-cold water, he emerged from the shower and found the bathrobe provided by the hotel. What to do, what to do? It was now 2:15. He found the television remote and settled on the sofa in his suite. When he was bored, Chad liked to flip through the channels. There was never anything good on television these days. Even with thousands of channels plus the thousands of available programs on the streaming services, nothing piqued his interest. The boredom sent him right back to sleep, this time leaning over on the couch.

The morning Florida sun broke through the balcony door when Chad's phone woke him from his slumber. Groggily, he reached for the device and stared at it for a second. The readout told him that it was Ace.

"*Great*", he thought to himself. "*Just the idiot I want to talk to at stupid o'clock in the morning.*"

With no excuses to be found, he accepted the call.

"Go for Chad," he spoke into the phone, his tired voice somewhere between Richard Sterban and Adam Sandler.

"Hey!" came the voice on the other end of the line. It all sounded all too enthusiastic and forced, as if Ace were a performer for his clients. "My main man!"

"*Can't he just cut to the chase?*" continued Chad's inner monologue.

"I got something big for ya," Ace continued.

"Come on," replied Chad. "Stop fooling around. I literally sat around for two months waiting for something. How much am I paying you again?"

Ace could hear Chad pulling the phone away. He knew his job was on the line. Sure, he had other clients, but if he couldn't work something out for his biggest client, those others would be gone soon as well.

"Wait, wait, wait!" he said, his plea ending in a crescendo ensuring Chad would hear him. "Are you still in Florida?"

"Yeah," Chad replied. "We fly out at five. Why?"

"Fancy a road trip to Miami?"

"That's almost four hours," Chad complained.

"Someone wants to take a look at you," Ace explained.

"Who wants to take a look at me?"

"Some guy named Lars Ströh."

"Do we even know anything about this guy?"

"Not much," Ace replied, "but he thinks you'll be a fit for his team."

"I've never heard of anyone named Lars Ströh," said Chad. "Is he ARCA?"

"He didn't say," replied Ace.

"Then why would you send this to me?"

"To be honest," Ace explained, "it's a last-ditch effort to save my butt. Look, if you go down to Miami, and it's a dud, fire me. But at least give it a chance. Better yet, if you go down there, and it's a complete scam, I'll reimburse you on top of letting you fire me."

"Where exactly in Miami am I meeting this Lars Ströh?"

Ace breathed a sigh of relief. Maybe he was getting somewhere.

"Do you know where Hard Rock Stadium is?"

"I've heard of it," replied Chad. "And that's the place?"

"That's it."

"One more question, Ace," Chad began. "How did you get this offer?"

"I don't know," replied Ace. "Some chick called me an hour ago and relayed everything. I'm just as mystified as you."

"Okay. Hey, Ace, if this turns out, you'll be the man of the hour."

"Well, you know me," laughed Ace. There was that old overly-confident sleazeball back.

Chad hung up and started packing his bag. As he rushed out his hotel door, he caught Larry in the hallway.

"Hey, I'm going to Miami," he told him.

"Miami!" exclaimed Larry in confusion. "When are you going to be in North Carolina? We have a shop to gut out."

"I don't know," replied Chad. "I'll charter a flight to Charlotte tonight. I may have a job lined up."

"Well, think of us while you're down there, alright?"

"I won't forget you guys," said Chad. "I'll catch you in Charlotte tomorrow."

Chad rushed out of the lobby and handed a ticket to the valet manager. Within three minutes, a nineteen-year-old who made less than half a percent what Chad would make sped into the driveway with his Mustang Darkhorse. Chad tossed the kid a $100 bill and peeled out of there without a word. It would be just under four hours to Miami if he didn't hit traffic. That would put him there around 1 PM.

After bending a few traffic rules, Chad beat his GPS to Miami. As he approached the stadium, he noticed a familiar sight. Parked in the lot across from the stadium was a tractor trailer dressed in the SportStream livery. As he neared it, he could tell it was a hauler. This wasn't the NASCAR hauler MorrisSport had leased, nor the one used by the SportStream NASCAR crew. This one looked more refined. A NASCAR hauler would be garish, often sporting an image of the car or the driver. This hauler was plain, the wrap starting out bright teal up front and fading to black down the length of it. The only decoration was the official SportStream logo.

"This must be it", he thought to himself. *"Why would SportStream screw MorrisSport over and then ask me to come here? Were they trying to poach me?"*

Chad pulled up to the hauler. The place was abuzz with men who were obviously pit crew members.

"I'm looking for a Lars Ströh," said Chad as he approached the crew members.

"Yes, you are looking for me," came the reply from a man with a Dutch accent.

Lars Ströh was an imposing figure, as are many of the Dutch. Standing at 6'5", he towered over the entire crew. He stretched forth his right hand, and Chad took it. He had a good, firm handshake. Chad could see getting along with this guy.

"Chad Helton," he replied, introducing himself to the human skyscraper. "So, why exactly did you call me here?"

"To see if you can drive that," replied Lars. He gestured toward the hauler.

Chad's heart raced as two members emerged from the hauler. At first, he could only see the rear wing, but it all came into focus as they pushed a SportStream Formula One racer off the ramp.

"Do you have your gear?" asked Lars.

"Yeah, I left it in my car," replied Chad.

"Well, throw it on," said Lars.

Within minutes, Chad was back in his MorrisSport racing gear. He had never raced open wheel. Up until this point, he had driven heavy stock cars. Everything was totally different. For starters, he had to step into the car and then lower himself into the seat, practically lying down. The steering wheel wasn't even a wheel. It looked to Chad like a fancy game controller with a heads-up display. Everything he needed to know would be on this. He felt the floor with his feet; no clutch pedal. This was still a sequential transmission, but it was a clutchless manual with paddle shifters on his steering wheel. His heart raced as they fired up the engine. The little 1.6-liter turbocharged V6 roared to life. It was much louder than the big 5.8-liter V8 he was used to, but it lacked that pulse-pumping rumble he liked.

"Have you ever driven one of these?" asked Lars.

"Never," replied Chad.

"Gewelding, gewoon geweldig," Lars mumbled to himself in Dutch. "Okay, this may be a learning curve then. You know this track?"

"What track?" asked Chad.

"This is where the Miami Grand Prix is raced," Lars explained. "It's a temporary course, kind of like your L.A. Coliseum. See all these cones? Those mark your boundary. Give it a spin around the track, and when you're comfortable, we'll time you."

Chad glanced at the Dutchman for a second then hit the accelerator. Timidly, he took a Sunday drive around the course, trying to get a feel for the new car.

"Do you think we're wasting our time?" a crewman asked Lars.

"I don't know," Lars replied. "Apparently McKenzie and Mr. Singleton saw something in him."

"Same guy Nigel beat on Sunday?"

"Same guy," Lars continued.

"Yeah, but, like, only by one five thousandth of a second," another crewmember chimed in as Chad drove like a granny down the winding backstretch. "They practically tied."

Chad brought the car around the final turn. He waved to the SportStream crew members as he crossed the line at a blistering thirty-four miles per hour.

"*I think I can do this*," he thought to himself. "*Next time by, we'll give it the beans.*"

"Oh, would you look at that," yet another crew member laughed. "He's actually driving the thing."

Chad was gaining speed through the backstretch. He would show them. At least he hoped he would.

"Lars," Chad began through the radio. "Start that clock this time by."

Chad punched it down the final straight and smoothly entered the final set of turns. He pulled a slingshot out of turn 19 and crossed the line to start his hot lap. This car handled nothing like his Mustang. With half the weight and twice the torque, the throttle response was out of this world. As quickly as he reached top end, he had to brake for the first turn. Chad held on for dear life as he went through the first set of esses. Miraculously, the car stuck to the pavement. Exiting from turn 8, he picked up speed. The track arced through a left turn, allowing for Chad to open the throttle before braking hard into turn 11. He kept to the inside of turn 12 on the apex. This was the slowest point in the course with three 90° turns before the final straight. He held to the outside lane on this long straight before hitting the brakes hard again in turn 17, arcing through 18, and then swopping through 19, and flying across the line for another lap.

"Lars," a crew member addressed the principal, "you better take a look at this."

The giant peered down at the monitor the crew member was holding.

"Impossible," he whispered.

Chad completed two more laps. He couldn't believe how easy it seemed. After the third hot lap, he brought the car in. Adrenaline coursed through his veins as he hopped out of the car.

"I thought you said you've never driven a Formula One car!" exclaimed Lars.

"I never have," said Chad.

"Then how do you explain this?" Lars pointed to some stats on the tablet he was holding. It was the lap times, the fastest clocked at 1:29.699.

"What am I looking at? My times? What's so exciting about that?"

"You set a track record," replied Lars.

Just then, the side door on the hauler opened, and out stepped three figures. Two of them Chad recognized. It was Nigel and Gemma McKenzie. His heart fluttered at the sight of the girl he had spent the evening with just two nights ago. The third figure was unfamiliar to Chad. He was of average height, but he carried himself like he was the biggest man at the track. His neatly-trimmed goatee spoke something of an everyday man. Dressed casually in khaki slacks and a SportStream polo, he didn't exactly scream "multi-billionaire", but that's exactly who he was as Chad would find out.

"Bravo!" he exclaimed as he clapped his hands. "Bravo! How did you ever do that?"

"I don't know, sir," Chad stuttered.

"Oh, where are my manners?" the billionaire exclaimed. "Colin Singleton."

Colin Singleton owned SportStream along with many other business ventures. Raised on the wrong side of the tracks in Johannesburg, he was determined to make something of himself. He applied himself in school and received a scholarship to USC. He turned his business major and market savvy into a successful small computer repair business in Anaheim. With the sale of that business, he chose to invest in several other ventures, compounding income from those investments into further investments. By the time he was twenty-seven, he had made his first billion. His biggest investment so far was SportStream, a streaming service dedicated to sports. Branching off from SportStream were various sports teams all sponsored or owned by the former. The SportStream Formula One team was just one of many of those ventures.

Chad shook his extended hand. His right hand was nearly crushed in the billionaire's death grip.

"Do you think you could replicate that in Bahrain?" asked Mr. Singleton.

"Hold up," Chad began. "You want me to drive that?"

"I'm looking for top talent," Mr. Singleton explained. "Sure, you missed the mark on Sunday, but it was impressive nonetheless. I need a secondary driver, someone to back Nigel up."

"But I barely know the first thing about Formula One," Chad tried to excuse himself.

"Nonsense," said Mr. Singleton, brushing Chad's concern off, "if anything, we need a butt in the seat. It'll just be that the butt is attached to a body that had some amazing talent."

"Am I even qualified to do this?"

"Just barely," Lars butted in. "You need forty points for your Super License. Since they raised the number of points awarded for NASCAR, you just barely have that with your runner-up finishes and your Truck Series Championship. Also, we can administer your tests in the next few days."

Chad pondered the offer for a nanosecond. It was really a no-brainer. A big change, sure, but it was an opportunity.

"If I take your offer, might I make one request?" asked Chad.

"Of course," replied Mr. Singleton, still beaming from Chad's incredible hot lap.

"I have eight crew members that lost their jobs on Sunday. I can't get along without them."

"I could always do with more mechanics working on the car," said Mr. Singleton. "I'll see what I can do. We may have some open spots."

"Then it's a deal," said Chad as he stuck his hand out for another bone crushing.

"Perfect," said Mr. Singleton as he once again crushed Chad's hand. "If you can get all your things ready by Saturday, we'll fly it all out to Austin and have it all there for you."

"Austin?" asked Chad, knowing what this meant.

"Yes, our race headquarters are in Austin, Texas," Mr. Singleton explained. "You'll stay right at home here in America. Well, I must be off. The Bundesliga commissioner wants to negotiate broadcast fees again."

And with that, a silver Bentley appeared and whisked Mr. Singleton away.

"Okay, boys," Lars began, "that's a wrap. Get it loaded up."

Chad watched in awe as the crew began picking up cones, turning the circuit back into a parking lot. He looked over at the two Britishers. He had a new teammate. This would be a new experience for him after being solo for the last few years.

"Congratulations, Helton," said Nigel as he shook Chad's hand. "Now, let's see what you can do on a real track with other cars out there."

He bumped Chad's shoulder as he headed for his Aston.

"What's with him?" Chad asked Gemma.

"I think you scare him," she replied. "Remember what I told you on the boat?"

"Is it that big of a deal?"

"I guess you don't really know how this works, do you?"

"No, enlighten me."

"Nigel is the primary driver. You're the secondary. He's supposed to win. You're supposed to do research and development and maybe finish second."

"Okay, and what's wrong with that? Does he want to do R&D. I'll gladly trade places."

"No, it's not like that at all. He knows you're as good as him, if not better."

"Well, when I drive, I drive to win," said Chad indignantly.

"I know that, and that's why I'm worried."

Their conversation was interrupted by the Aston Martin's horn.

"Come on, Gemma, we're going to be late for our flight," Nigel yelled across the parking lot.

"I'll be there in a minute," she shouted to her impatient brother. "Well, it looks like I have to go."

"Will I see you again?" asked Chad.

"I'll always be around wherever Nigel is," she answered.

"Then I guess I'll see you on Saturday."

"Yes, you will."

Gemma walked to Nigel's car, skipping a couple times like a school girl, something that tickled Chad's fancy a bit. Underneath all the stuffy business and Oxbridge education, there was still that little girl that wanted to enjoy life and actually have fun.

Before the hauler left, Chad changed back into his street clothes and drove to Fort Lauderdale to catch a plane back to Charlotte. Just when his life seemed to be over, a new chapter had just begun.

Chapter Eight
Cameras and Carts

Cameras flashed as Chad sat seated next to his new boss at the SportStream racing facility outside of Austin. To his right sat Larry Truman. The old redneck looked out of place among the high-class European-style characters present. He would've retired a happy man to his farm back in Alabama after MorrisSport shut its doors, but Chad wouldn't have it. Along with Chad and the MorrisSport pit crew, he received a crash course in how Formula One works. When he would have been reading his Louis L'Amour books before bedtime, he found himself studying the FIA rulebook. The old man was proof that you can teach an old dog new tricks as his wife would quiz him every morning during his workout routine.

"We are excited to announce the signing of Chad Helton to the SportStream Formula One team," Mr. Singleton announced. "Along with Nigel McKenzie in our primary car, we hope to be the top team at the end of the season. He has already far exceeded our expectations by setting a track record at the Miami International Autodrome.”

“I and my crew members are excited to embark on this new opportunity,” Chad added in his prepared speech. “We've been busy preparing for Bahrain next week and dialing in the car. We are all looking forward to show the world that we can do more than drive a Mustang in circles.”

The crowd let out a collective chuckle at this. Larry's aged eyes scanned the audience. Something just didn't feel right to him. Maybe he felt like he was being judged. It wouldn't have surprised him if that was the case.

“Along with Chad, we were able to bring his entire crew over from the MorrisSport NASCAR team,” Mr. Singleton continued. “Larry Truman will be crossing over from NASCAR to serve as assistant team principal. He will be directly communicating and calling the shots for our mechanics. I understand he's been studying long and hard, and it shows. I've watched the team dialing the cars in, and it looks like he's been doing this for twenty years.”

Larry sunk back in his chair as the crowd applauded the announcement. He just wanted to be out of there as quickly as possible. Who were these people anyway?

“We look forward to the upcoming season, and we can't wait to see you all again next week in Bahrain,” said Mr. Singleton. “Chad, Larry, other crew members, welcome to SportStream.”

And with that, the delegation stood up as one from the table, exiting stage right. Multiple conversations between the crew members filled the hallway as they all dispersed. Chad noticed Larry moping as they walked through the concourse.

“Hey, old man,” Chad addressed his crew chief, “what's going on? You look like they just announced that Talladega was being torn down.”

“Look at these people,” Larry began. “They're not us.”

"What do you mean?"

"Couldn't you see how they looked at us? They think we're inferior, stupid fat Americans."

"I didn't get that vibe. Don't tell me you're having second thoughts."

"You know how they view Americans in Formula One, right? You know what they say about us?"

"Yes, I know," Chad conceded. "They say we're rubes and ignorant hicks, but we need to prove them wrong. I didn't ask you to join me just out of the kindness of my own heart. Don't get me wrong, I would have, but I asked for you because you have always been able to put me out front at the end of the race. I can't do this without you."

"And prove that F1 isn't just for rich muckamucks?"

"Show them that the hoi polloi can drive a car too."

"Then let's win some races," replied Larry, his spirits raised slightly.

"Look, I don't know about this second team crap," said Chad. "When I get out on that track, I'm racing to win."

"Don't tell Nigel that," Larry added, feigning worry. "Remember, I'm running a crew now for two cars."

"I'm not here to be another butt in a seat. Nigel's finishing second next week."

"I don't doubt it," said Larry.

"In fact, I'm going to win the championship," Chad added. "That's what we've moved halfway across the country for, right?"

"Then let's give 'em a show," said Larry, his familiar grin returning to his face. He gave Chad a slap on his back before he turned and walked away. Chad watched his chief walk through the doors before looking down at his watch.

"Crap! I gotta go!" he shouted his thoughts for everyone to hear.

Chad had promised to help his cousin Emily with the grocery shopping for the week in return for them letting him crash on their couch while he found a house near headquarters. He ran out to his

Mustang and peeled out of the parking lot. It seemed like he was always in a hurry, even off the track.

Ten minutes later, he found himself parked next to Emily's Explorer in the Sam's Club parking lot.

"Sorry I'm late," he said as he jumped out of his Mustang. "Press announcement went long."

"Never mind," said Emily. "Could you grab the grocery bags out of the back?"

Chad ran around to open the tailgate as Emily began the complicated process of unbuckling her squirming two-year-old. The little tyke was restless, having stayed awake his entire naptime.

"He's a bit tired," Emily explained, straining as she reached for the toddler, "but he couldn't wait to see you again. Here, could you hold my purse?"

Emily handed Chad the enormous Coach purse, Mike's gift to her that Christmas. Chad held it like a rag dripping with dog vomit. It wasn't that he was unwilling to do things for Emily. It was more of the fact that he thought people might get the wrong idea. Any idiot with a camera could snap a picture of him holding a purse, sell it to a tabloid, and convince the whole world that he was gay or something. Emily was finally able to wrangle Kevin out of his car seat and into the back of the shopping cart.

"Thanks," said Emily as she reached for her purse, "I know it's heavy."

Kevin continued to wiggle around trying to reach for Chad.

"Stay put," Emily told him sternly.

The little guy huffed as he finally settled in the seat. Chad was glad he could spend time with his cousin. This would be his first opportunity outside of the holidays to do so. The pair talked like old friends as they walked through the doors, even though Chad had been living in their den for the last two weeks.

"Are you getting excited for next weekend?" asked Emily as she started inspecting some honeycrisp apples.

"A bit nervous actually," answered Chad. "I've never left the country except for that one time we went to Toronto for that exhibition. That's hardly another country. Bahrain, though, it's like hardly anyone I know has heard of it. Noodle asked if was somewhere near Omaha. Boy, is he in for a surprise! We're taking bets to see who can get deported first."

"Well, I guess it'll be an exciting experience for all of you," replied Emily.

"It's all so different," Chad continued. "The cars are different. The culture's all different. We're based here, but most of our races are in Europe. We have a shop in England."

"So you'll be gone to England a lot?"

"Yeah, but the schedule isn't as packed as the Cup Series was. We go from March to early December with only twenty-four races. They got rid of the Las Vegas Street Course, and we're going to Sonoma for the penultimate race. We have that and COTA here in Austin that I'm familiar with."

"That'll be nice," Emily replied somewhat absent-mindedly, picking through the bunches of cilantro in the coolers. "So, enough of the racing. Anyone new I haven't met?"

"Tons," replied Chad. "It's a whole new team. I brought as many people as I could from MorrisSport, but our pit crew is four times bigger. I guess that's mitigated by the fact we have to share a pit crew between two cars. The guys on the Cup team had to multitask. They were shocked when they found out they'd only have one tiny thing to do. Both of my tire carriers share a wheel. My tire changers only loosen and tighten the lugs. Poor Noodle and Hawk have whole new jobs entirely, because we don't fuel during the race, and I don't get a spotter. Instead, they get to be my stabilizers. They keep the car steady when it's lifted off the ground to change tires. Other than Larry still being my crew chief, the rest are all a bunch of guys I've never met. It'll take me a while to learn everyone's name."

"Have you gotten to know any of them?" asked Emily as they walked side by side through the meat department.

"Well, Lars Ströh's our team principle," Chad answered as he snuck a package of carne asada into the cart. "That's what we actually call the guy who runs the show. He basically oversees the operations of the team since Mr. Singleton doesn't really have an interest in actually running the team. Then there's Nigel McKenzie, if you've heard of him. He's the other driver."

"Anyone else I should know about?" asked Emily, adding more intensity to her questions.

"How do you mean?" asked Chad right back.

"You know what I mean," Emily scolded her cousin. "You're not getting any younger."

"Still single," replied Chad.

"Nobody in mind?"

"Nobody."

"Are you sure?"

Chad was puzzled as to why Emily kept pressing him. Did she know something he didn't? Or was she just that desperate to get her cousin married.

"Maybe," said Chad through gritted teeth.

"What's her name?" giggled Emily.

"Like I said, she's nobody," Chad groaned.

"I got you cornered. Now what's her name?"

"Gemma," Chad surrendered. 'Gemma McKenzie."

"Any relation to Nigel McKenzie?" asked Emily as she inspected bags of frozen chicken breasts.

"His sister."

"That sounds like it'll be complicated."

"Yeah, did I tell you he doesn't like me?"

"Because you like his sister?"

"Unless she's told him, I think he's completely in the dark on that. No, Gemma says I scare him. Apparently, he thinks I'm going to steal wins from him or something."

"Aren't you paid to win?"

"Yes and no. I'm doing research and development, so Nigel gets all the best stuff. Same car, better support. We apparently get 'team orders'. If they tell me to let Nigel pass, I have to back off."

"I've never known you to not at least try to win," chuckled Emily. "White or wheat?"

"I'll take wheat," said Chad. "That white stuff has too much sugar. Did you know we have to keep under a certain weight? That's why Nigel is such a beanpole."

"Well, it sounds like you've had a big change in the last couple weeks."

"Honestly, if you would've told me that Sunday in Daytona that I'd be moving to Texas to race Formula One, I would've called the police to serve a welfare check on you."

"I never would've guessed it either," said Emily.

"You know," continued Chad, "I never see Mike around lately."

"He's busy," replied Emily. "They're building that new development outside of town, and they're way behind schedule."

"Is that it? I was beginning to think that maybe he didn't like me."

"I don't think it's anything like that. You might've hurt his feelings when you turned down his job offer at Christmas," she joked.

"Maybe I could make him feel better if I just ask him to build my house," laughed Chad.

"Maybe," giggled Emily. "Here, could you push the cart for a minute?"

Kevin was ecstatic as Chad obliged his cousin. Emily began inspecting the milk jugs. With her back turned to Chad as she found the 2% with the latest expiration date, Chad put his finger over his lips.

Little Kevin was smart and clued into what Chad was telling him. The toddler signed zipped lips at his uncle. Chad stealthily reached into another cooler and pulled out a gallon jug of chocolate milk, placing it in the cart before Emily could even find the 2% she wanted.

"There!" exclaimed Emily when she finally found milk that suited her liking. "You'd think fresh milk would be easier to find. Um, where did that chocolate milk come from?"

Kevin regarded his mother, zipping his lips. Emily then turned all of her attention to Chad.

"For Pete's sake, Chad," she sighed. "You're going to teach him bad habits."

"Is that not my job as the 'funcle'?"

"That boy will follow you anywhere," Emily stated. "If it gets him hurt, I'm going to kill you, resurrect you, and then let Mike kill you."

"I'll share the chocolate milk," laughed Chad.

"I'm being serious," Emily replied, failing to hold back the laughter.

"I miss this," said Chad.

"Miss what?"

"Just hanging out with you. It feels like old times; you know, before life got in the way."

"I happen to love life," said Emily.

"I do too," replied Chad. "As excited as I am about this new job, I miss the simpler days. It just seems like it doesn't come easy anymore."

"I don't think it's meant to, Chad. Did you honestly think everything would come to you on a silver platter?"

"Not necessarily," Chad answered. "I just thought I was great at what I did."

"You have a lot of dedication to what you do," Emily continued. "And I think you are the best. That comes from your dedication. You take it seriously. All your life, you've been focused on one goal; and now through no fault of your own, that's been taken from you. You have to learn that you can't control everything, but you can control how you respond to it. I think the change will be good for you."

Chad once again regarded his cousin. Her face glowed like an angel.

"*Why did I have to be related to her?*" he thought.

"Oh," Emily added, "and please let me know everything about Gemma."

"What?" mumbled Chad as Emily's voice brought him out of his daydream.

"When am I going to meet her?" asked Emily.

"Meet who?"

"Are you even listening? Gemma."

"I don't know," answered Chad. "I barely know her."

"Then you need to get to know her," said Emily. "Or else some other man's going to get her."
"You're really trying to ship us, aren't you?"

"Why not?" Emily giggled as she reached for an 18-pack of eggs.

"Can you just let me go at my own pace?"

"Of course," said Emily. "I'd just like to reiterate that you're not getting any younger."

"Hey, not everyone can get married to their sweetheart right out of high school," laughed Chad. "Give us some time. We're still young, and we'll have plenty of time to get to know each other.

Chapter Nine
British Racing Green

Chad paced around the garage stall. The car was good, really good. Having passed all of his tests with flying colors, Chad found himself in Sakhir, Bahrain. Stepping out of the airport, he immediately knew he wasn't in Kansas anymore. While he had seen burqas, hijabs, and niqabs on women whenever he visited big cities, he noticed every woman was wearing them. The bigger shock was the men still wearing the same garb as their ancestors 1,500 years before. He kept his mouth shut and instructed his crew members to do the same.

"We're not ignorant redneck rubes," he told them. "Don't let them believe the stereotype."

Once they arrived at the track, they wasted no time getting the car out on the track, getting a feel for what was to come. Most Formula One tracks are flat with little to no banking in the corners. Due to their light weight, the cars are still able to carry a bunch of momentum through those corners. Chad experienced this first in Miami, and he put it to good use in Bahrain. In the first two practice sessions, Chad trailed right behind Nigel. Agreeing to show the team what they could actually do, Chad and Larry conspired the next day during the third session to push the car a little harder, surpassing Nigel's lap times.

Closely monitoring the primary team's lap times, Larry had Chad hold back a little to give Nigel the benefit of a better starting position. It pained both of them to do that, but it could be mitigated during the race.

Qualifying in Formula One is much different from NASCAR. Though positions are still set by lap times, all twenty cars go out on track instead of individual qualifying laps. Within the first one or two laps, a group of five are eliminated, setting the positions 16-20. This is repeated again, and 11-15 are set. After this, the cars are given a fresh set of tires and sent out again. This sets a shoot-out to set the top-10 in the field.

Both Chad and Nigel made the shoot-out. Now was the time to see how they could race together. Chad lined up directly behind Nigel for the start. The Bahrain International Circuit is a 3.363-mile road course. While it has its share of turns and esses, it also contains many straights, allowing for cars to build up speed before cornering. This also allows for long DRS zones. DRS, or drag reduction system, is a technology used in grand prix racing. This type of active aero moves the wing on the back of the car to reduce the wind resistance on the back of the car, allowing it to go faster and make passes on the straight. It can only be used on certain areas on the track, usually a long straightaway.

Chad stayed glued behind Nigel as they made their way around the track. The two cars tandemed down the first straightaway coming out of turn 3. Into turn 4, they met a set of esses that ended in a near hairpin turn in 8. A short straight ended in turn nine which closed off into turn ten, opening again into a short straightaway along the backstretch. After two more turns, they entered the third sector of the circuit, making a sweeping right turn in 13 to another straight. This ended in a sharp turn 14, which opened into turn 15, the final turn. The frontstretch is the longest straightaway, and the two cars flew by, exceeding 200 miles per hour.

Chad kept on Nigel's back. It could really be SportStream taking up the front row on Sunday. Larry checked the telemetry. Chad was trailing Nigel by mere thousandths of a second. They had one more lap to do it again. It was only around ninety seconds more, and they reappeared on the frontstretch. Their final times: Nigel – 1:29.827 and Chad – 1:29.828. The closest time was a Mercedes qualifying at 1:30.213. It was a SportStream front row.

Chad's crew swarmed the car as he pulled back into the paddock. His Formula One debut was going better than expected. One would think he had already won the race if not the championship.

"How did she feel out there?" asked Larry as he helped Chad remove his helmet and HANS.

"These things stick to the ground like it's nothing," replied Chad excitedly. "Try carrying speed through those corners in a stock car!"

The cheers were interrupted by the cold remarks of one Nigel McKenzie.

"Let's see how you do when the heat is on, Helton," he said, just as if he were one of those stereotypical brooding British villains. Chad could almost imagine his teammate stroking a goatee and donning a dark cape.

"Well, good luck to you then," Chad replied, shaking off any worry Nigel's remark may have caused.

"Good luck, Chad," this voice came from Gemma.

Chad spun around to the girl he had been thinking about nonstop for the past month. He had barely seen her since he had moved to Austin. Work was crazy busy.

"Um, thanks," was all Chad had to say.

"No, I mean it."

"Thank you," replied Chad, still a nervous wreck.

"Well, I'd better go," Gemma said as she turned toward Nigel's direction. "Good-bye."

Chad waved her off as she chased Nigel down, still speechless. He watched as she disappeared into the crowd.

"*Great, now if that didn't unnerve me,*" Chad thought to himself.

"Here, have a banana," said Larry as he snuck up behind Chad. "You need the potassium."

Chad accepted his snack and disappeared into his motorhome. He didn't want to think about anything. He just wanted his mind to stay blank – to just go black and wake up in the car on Sunday.

"*Is he using his sister?*" he thought. "*He can't be that cold. No, that's sick. But she is super-hot. No, not super-hot – beautiful… and super-hot.*"

Chad crawled into bed. There wasn't much to do here. Internet was restricted. It wasn't like he was going to go out and pick up women either like Mike and Quizz.

The only thing NASCAR and Formula One really have in common is the fact that they race. That's it. The MorrisSport guys received the biggest culture shock of their lives coming over. Here in Bahrain, it was a party. Nigel's Daytona 500 afterparty was just a foretaste of what they'd experience here, and Chad wouldn't be there to enjoy it. Instead, he took a nap and read. He had to remain sharp and sober.

The next morning dawned, the hot desert sun heating the track surface hot enough to boil an egg. Noodle even tried it and was successful. Chad gathered with his team in the garage. Here it was: their first go at a Formula One race. The left side of the car was compiled of his old MorrisSport crew, but he had barely any time to get to know the guys servicing the right side. Today would be a test to see if this arrangement actually worked.

Chad climbed into the car, keeping the cute agent from the other side of the paddock in his periphery. He could barely keep his eyes off her. It was that indescribable feeling you get when you like somebody and see them afar off; they're busy and inaccessible at the moment, but something about seeing them at work makes your heart pump faster and harder. That's what Chad was experiencing at the moment.

The team pushed the car out to the open pit box for staging. The paddock was crowded with drivers, crew members, dignitaries, and press representatives of every nationality. Chad wasn't camera shy today. He kept a stone-cold poker face on as the official SportStream camera flew by his crew.

Chad tried to keep his eyes off of Nigel, but it could barely be helped. He and his entourage were stationed in the pit box in front of his. He stole quick glances to his right, hoping to catch a glimpse of Gemma as a local imam said a prayer of invocation. He wasted no time climbing into the cockpit as soon as that prayer was given. He was also ready to get away from the snickering and mocking of the Arab organizers from his team; they would go on throughout the night hacking and speaking gibberish in parody of the imam.

On the command, Chad fired up the turbocharged 1.6-liter Ford V6. A silver Mercedes-AMG GT bearing a strobe light pulled out in front of the field. Nigel took off behind it, and Chad followed. After a couple parade laps, they took their spot on the grid just short of the start/finish line. Here is where Formula One further differs from NASCAR. With stock car racing, the pace car ducks down into pit road, and the racers simply accelerate from a lower speed; otherwise known as a rolling start. In Formula One, drivers perform a static start, rocketing from 0 to 200 like a drag race.

Chad closed his eyes and said a little prayer as the world went silent around him. He took one more look to his right, noticing Nigel calm and collected inside his car. The timing lights slowly lit up. On green, he launched his SportStream-Ford into action.

Turn one was a sharp 45° right-hander. Nigel had the advantage, and Chad fell in right behind him. The turn opened up into a softer left-hander, straightening out after an even softer right-hander. Chad kept behind, chopping down his following distance in the slip stream. Flying into turn four, Nigel cut down in front of Chad, forcing him to brake hard. Chad fought to regain control of his car as Nigel sailed off through the sweeping turn five.

"Judas Priest!" Chad shouted into the radio. "Did you see what he just did?"

"Careful," said Larry. "Don't forget, the race isn't won on the first lap. They're already wreckin' in turn one. Yellow in that sector."

Larry knew Chad wouldn't take a move like that lightly. Exiting out of turn fifteen, he was back on Nigel's tail.

"Fifty-six to go," said Larry as Chad crossed the line. "You have completed one fifty-seventh of the race. Keep diggin'."

Nigel and Chad whipped around turn one once again. After the first lap, DRS was available, and Chad took full advantage of it. Once he was within a second of Nigel on the straights, he activated the DRS. The rear wing flattened, lessening his wind resistance, but it wasn't enough to catch him. The other eighteen competitors weren't even a factor. Chad was out for blood, and Nigel knew it. He knew Chad was good, but he had to prove he was better. He would later say in interviews that Chad only kept up because he was just copying his every move. That was true in part, but Chad also took every door that opened up to him. Nigel was just smart enough to catch it and shut it. Every time Chad had the advantage in the turn, it seemed that Nigel could sniff out his next move and go in for a block. These cars, much more fragile than the stock cars Chad had come up driving, seemed like they would disintegrate at the mere mention of contact.

As the middle of the race approached, drivers started to pit. Some had already retired from the race, whittling the field down to around seventeen cars. As Nigel slowed his car to enter the pits, Chad did the same.

"No, no!" cried Larry. "Just Nigel. You stay out, Chad. Build some time on him. We could build that distance. When I bring you in, you might be able to keep it. I don't think you can get around him any other way."

Chad did as Larry said. He mashed on the accelerator and flew by the pits. That was on lap 28. Chad flew solo for the next couple laps. He knew he couldn't hold on forever. Larry watched the telemetry and grid lineup as the cars cycled through their pit stops. Nigel was beginning to gain on Chad.

"Okay, pit this next time by," Larry called to Chad as he rounded the final turn on lap thirty.

Chad slowed it down and ducked into the pits. If Nigel could regain his position, it would likely be over for Chad, but he wasn't a quitter. Chad slid into his pit box, his crew already waiting in position. He was stopped for less than three seconds. Instead of a carefully choreographed dance between man and machine, a Formula One pit stop is more like the function of an assembly line. Each tire had three crew members. There were two jacks – one at the front and one at the back. The car would be lifted. Four men held impact guns to unbolt the lug nuts. Four men would remove the tires while four others would mount the new tires. This would all be finished off by the same four men with the impacts bolting the lugs down. Chad could never imagine that in a NASCAR race. He rejoined the track just as Nigel crossed the start/finish line. Nigel's greater speed gave him an advantage in turn one as he overtook Chad on the outside.

Aside from Nigel, Chad had no other rival today. The two-car tandem had built an incredible gap between them and the rest of the field. As the laps were winding down, Chad used every advantage given him, but it was no good. Nigel was a master.

"Calm down, Chad," said Larry as they crossed the line for the final lap. "You got fifteen turns to make it happen. When the door opens, take it."

Chad kept on Nigel's six. Every move was a perfect mirror of what Nigel did. On the straights, he kept within millimeters of the rear of Nigel's car. If he weren't so afraid of damaging his car, he would have bump drafted. Exiting turn thirteen, Chad found his opening. He activated the DRS and pulled out to the left from behind Nigel. He had the speed, but would he have the advantage in the corner? Could he beat Nigel in the corner? Halfway down the final straight, Chad found himself neck and neck with Nigel. Turn fourteen would be a sharp right-hander.

"*Outlast him*," Chad thought to himself.

The hard right-hander of turn fourteen loomed in the distance. Nigel McKenzie, ever the master of his craft, prepared for the turn the way a professional would. He let up off the gas, allowing Chad to sail by on the outside. First position belonged to Chad for approximately five seconds as he sent it into the turn.

Chad realized his mistake right away as he attempted the turn. The brakes overheated as he slammed on them. Chad turned the yoke, but the car kept going straight for longer than he desired. When the front wheels finally found grip and responded to his input, the rear wheels kicked out. Chad, in a panic, overcorrected and sent the car spinning to the left. He came to a stop on the frontstretch facing the wrong way as Nigel sailed by for the win. Chad fired the engine back up and spun the car around, narrowly avoiding being plowed by oncoming traffic. He joined the pack and raced home to a not-so-impressive ninth place finish; though, it was good for two points.

After a cool-down, Chad brought the car into his pit box. He was miffed. It felt to him as if he had snatched defeat from the jaws of victory. Nigel had played him expertly. He was determined to not let that happen a second time.

Chad slammed his helmet down on the car as he climbed out. He watched with envy as the top three drivers mounted the podium, spraying each other with champaign.

"That could've been me if I hadn't been so stupid," he thought.

Chad also knew that there would be an afterparty here and back at headquarters. He'd have to attend those. Even in the haze of a post-race chaos, he still paused to weigh his options. It could mean another night of playing designated driver with Gemma while Nigel and everyone else got completely hammered. It could also mean having to be at the mercy of Nigel McKenzie, a rival he was shaping up to be. What else would there be to do but wait until everyone else was ready to fly home?

He chose the former option. If he wanted to avoid Emily playing matchmaker between he and Gemma, he may as well talk to the girl at any chance he had. Chad chugged a tumbler of water as the swarm of reporters stampeded into the paddock.

"Can you tell us what happened on the last lap?" one asked.

"What kind of implications does this have going into Saudi Arabia?" another chimed in.

"How did the car perform?"

"Do you think Nigel McKenzie is playing dirty?"

"Was there anything you would have changed about the race?"

Chad held up a finger as he gulped his water. He wanted it to last forever. He hated reporters. They're always meddling, never giving you any time to compose yourself after a race or think for five seconds. His dehydration gave him an excuse to stick it to them in a way. Oh, how they wanted their answers from Chad so they could go back and write their little stories about the American who almost won Formula One but failed at the last possible second! If Chad couldn't have the satisfaction of finishing on the podium, at least he could ruffle a few of the reporters' feathers.

"Okay, where were we?" gasped Chad as he finally lowered the tumbler from his lips.

The rabble started again, and Chad once again raised the tumbler to his lips. He smiled behind his drink as cries of "custard", "rhubarb", and "watermelon", or something like that all gathered into one noise. And you know what? He actually felt better.

Chapter Ten
Second Place, First Loser

The dry heat had cooled to a breezy 73°. The sun had set over the Gulf of Bahrain, turning the distant sight of Saudi Arabia pink and orange with its final glows. On this particular night, a Formula One star's private yacht circled the island nation.

Chad meandered through the crowds of smartly-dressed men and bikini-clad women. The free-flowing booze and over-application of cologne, itself a nauseating cocktail of scents, mixed together, almost becoming one with the nitrogen and oxygen in the air. He held his breath, only taking necessary gulps of air when he felt his head about to explode. Chad was on a mission.

Then, as if it were a dream, he found his quarry. The crowds parted, and there she was, leaning on the rail over the stern of the yacht. Chad was half relieved but also half disappointed that she wasn't among the bikini-clad women.

"All in good time", he thought to himself, thinking of some of the highlights of their life together he had already envisioned countless times. He forced himself to feel relief that there could be some things left to the imagination, only to be revealed at the perfect time.

This time, the top half of her shimmering dress was still red, but the bottom half was white; the two colors bisected by a zig zag, the colors and design of the Bahraini flag. Chad was still amazed how Gemma could go from British schoolmarm to red carpet model so quickly.

"Designated driver again?" he asked as he walked up behind her, trying to break the ice.

"You know it," she replied.

Chad stared down at his hands, then to Gemma's, then back to his. He thought he could easily break through the ice, but that wasn't happening. He lucked out when Gemma was the first to speak.

"I hate it here," she started. "In fact, I hate a bunch of these countries. If they had it their way, I'd be covered from head to toe in a black sheet."

"Well, I'm glad they can't have their way," replied Chad. The line sounded corny, as if he were an actor just phoning it in. In his mind, he was saying, *"You are a romantic genius, you devil. You are a secret agent now."*

"I'm not so much of a fan of this anyway," Gemma continued, gesturing at the dress. "It's much too busy, and it gets cold."

"Well, it is very beautiful," Chad said before he could think. Inside, his inner being was scolding him, *"No, you muppet, not that. Now you look like a fool. It's so cliché and lame. Why would you just say that. It's so obviously beautiful."*

"It is?" Gemma replied, considering what Chad had said.

"No, really," Chad stuttered. Even he knew he had now locked himself into this. It was all or nothing now, and he knew he did not want to lose this chance to be with his dream girl. "It goes really well with your eyes." "*Eyes, eyes. You went for the eyes. How cliché, you dolt. Everyone mentions the eyes.*"

"Thank you," Gemma said. "You clean up nice too for an American." She giggled at this.

Chad had changed into a tuxedo, but he had exchanged the jacket for a woolen Portland Timbers sweater by this point. Besides the sweater, he was almost dressed to match every other man on the yacht. Remembering his last meeting on a yacht, he removed the sweater and handed it to Gemma who kindly accepted the warm knit.

"Are you enjoying your time here?" said Gemma, picking up the conversation.

"I don't know," replied Chad. "it's so different from anything I've done. Is it like this every week?"

"Like what?"

"No passing," Chad answered. "Where you start is where you finish unless you wreck or something."

"Pretty much," said Gemma.

"All the more reason I need to qualify better," said Chad.

"Or practice more," added Gemma. "You've proven that you're already one of the best out there, and that was only the first race."

"So you're saying Nigel is the best, and the only way to beat him is to practice?" asked Chad.

"Pretty much. I'm sure Nigel has some weakness you could exploit. But what do I know? I'm just his agent."

"Was that sarcasm, or were you serious?" Chad asked nervously.

"I can't reveal all of his secrets," giggled Gemma. "That would be helping the competition."

"Not even a clue?"

"Could you imagine how outraged Nigel would be if he found out?"

"Why does he have to know?"

Chad had found his opening. At least he hoped he had. He moved in closer, almost instinctually.

"It wouldn't be the ethical thing to do," she whispered.

Chad could almost feel it. Her perfume filled his nostrils as he breathed in the heavenly scent. Her green eyes sparkled in the Arabian moonlight. He was so close.

"All's fair in love and war," he whispered.

Even he knew it was cheesy, but he was drawing closer. Chad had never kissed a girl in his life; except for one time in the first grade when he kissed Emily. That was scandalous within itself, though just an elementary-school dare. This was real.

"Is this war then?" Gemma pondered out loud, but even quieter than Chad.

"May as well be," Chad merely breathed.

He was there. They were about to lock lips when out of the blue, a drunken Nigel stumbled out of the main dance hall.

"Hey, Gemma," he slurred, "come in and join the fun."

"No, Nigel," she replied in a tone reminiscent of a teenaged girl reminding her parents that she's all grown up. "I have to drive you back t' 'otel."

Chad couldn't decide whether to be angered by the interruption or further turned on by Gemma's Northern accent. He concluded the way she pronounced "the" by barely saying it at all made his heart skip a beat.

"But one drink won't hurt," he continued.

"They lady said no, Nigel," Chad butted in. He chose both. This would be his chance to impress her.
"Who are you to say, loser? Mister second place secondary driver," blurted Nigel right before he belched loudly in Chad's face.

Chad's face wrinkled and contorted from the cocktail of alcoholic drink vapors carried by the carbon dioxide of Nigel's breath. He could barely stand when it was all over.

"Take it easy, Chad," he thought to himself. *"He's smashed. He's not in his right mind. You are in control."*

"Nigel, I think it's time for you to head back inside," said Gemma as she ushered him through the door.

"Mister second place loser driver," Nigel mumbled.

"Look," Gemma said like a mother talking to her toddler, "there's a girl over there waiting for you. Go see her."

Nigel straightened up and stumbled across to one of the many faceless bikini-clad women he had invited to his afterparty.

"And stay away from my sister," Nigel shouted into the ether, still slurring his speech.

Chad was sure the Brit was talking to him. Either way, he didn't care.

"I'm so sorry about that," said Gemma. "He's not usually like that."

"He really is afraid of me, isn't he."

"You do realize he has never had someone stay on his tail like that the whole race? Of course, he's scared of you. He'll never admit it to your face, but you are the best driver he's ever raced against; and he's raced against all of them: Hamilton, Verstappen, Pérez. On top of that, you're an American. Americans don't race Formula One, let alone almost win."

"So you're saying he respects me?"

"You could say that," said Gemma. "Don't forget, he's drunk. Also, because he's scared of you, he's going to try and discourage you. Don't let him get you down. What's it your crew chief says? 'Hit your marks'? Practice, practice, practice. That's all I can say without giving away the secrets of the trade."

Chad pondered this a second. Did Nigel actually believe he was his equal?

"What do I have to do for Nigel to admit he actually respects me?" asked Chad, almost certain of the answer.

"It's simple, but not exactly easy," replied Gemma. "Beat him. No DNFs, no disqualifications. Flat out racing. You beat him in a full race, he'll calm down."

"At least that's the hope?" asked Chad.

"Hardly anyone's ever beaten him. That is the hope. He'll hate you, but he'll at least not actively try and put you down like this."

"Could he at least act like we're on the same team? I always thought teammates help each other."

"You've never been around Formula One, have you?"

"Not until a couple weeks ago."

"Being the face of the team comes with many perks," explained Gemma.

"I kind of get that," said Chad. "I was the one and only face of MorrisSport."

"So it's kind of like that," Gemma continued. "I guess you could say my brother's a complicated character in a complicated world."

"Do you find me complicated?" asked Chad.

"I'm still trying to figure you out," replied Gemma. "I think I'm getting a pretty good picture of who you are though."

"Who am I?"

"You're a man who likes to drive fast and not hold back. That's what I've got so far.

"I guess that's kind of me in a nutshell. Do you have any plans when we get back to Austin?" asked Chad, changing the subject.

"What are you getting at?" asked Gemma.

"Well, this is now the second time we've spent the evening on the decks of this yacht making sure our drunk friends don't kill themselves."

"Continue," said Gemma, now intrigued that Chad was making some actual moves.

"Do you like Tex-Mex?" asked Chad.

"What's that?"

"It's hard to explain," said Chad. "There's this really good place my cousin's husband showed me in Austin."

"Chad Helton!" Gemma exclaimed. "Are you asking me on a date?"

It was the way she said his name. It had been spoken hundreds, if not thousands, of times over by announcers and television personalities; but to hear it shouted in surprised glee from this amazing girl with her Lancastrian accent, made it new all over again.

"A date?" he repeated, finding the right words to say. "Yeah, I'm asking you on a date. Would you like to go on a date with me when we get back to Austin?"

"You know Nigel will kill you if he finds out," said Gemma.

"Didn't I just get done saying all's fair in love and war?" chuckled Chad.

"Chad, you wouldn't!" exclaimed Gemma, dramatically feigning shock.

"I might shove him in one of the lockers and leave him overnight," joked Chad. "Anyway, what's the worst he can do?"

"You're not the first man who's come after me," said Gemma.

Chad could not figure out for the life of him why this shocked him. He wondered if the whole wartime British girl look was just a weird thing just he himself had.

"You looked surprised," said Gemma, noting the look on his face. "Am I that unattractive?" she jokingly pouted.

"No, not at all," said Chad, trying to find an excuse for his expression.

"It doesn't matter," said Gemma. "I'm only joking. Anyway, I had one man ask me out at Oxford. Nigel got wind of it. I never saw what happened; but needless to say, when I tried talking to him the next day, he turned the other direction. I was angry at Nigel; I wanted to kill him, but I got over it. He's always tried to protect me since our parents died. He really does mean well."

"I can't blame him," said Chad.

He really couldn't. He reasoned within himself that if he had a sister half as beautiful as he found Gemma, he would not only beat the living daylights out of any suitor, he'd make that suitor wish he were dead, if not never having been born. As dangerous as Gemma made Nigel out to be, Chad found her hard to resist. Overprotective brothers be cursed, he would go out with Gemma no matter what. He would marry that woman and then live out the rest of his life with her. Chad was so lost in his thoughts that he didn't even notice the awkward silence.

"I still don't get it," Gemma said, trying to move the conversation along.

"You don't get what?"

"Why you guys do it," Gemma answered.

"Do what exactly?"

"Why do you guys race?"

"That's a strange question for someone who represents a driver," said Chad.

"Believe me," Gemma began to explain, "I've asked Nigel several times." She rolled her eyes at this. "All he has is some beat-around-the-bush abstract explanation that makes no sense to me."

"I guess," Chad started, "it's the adrenaline rush coupled with competition. You know how they say guys naturally need something to conquer?"

"That sounds like something Nigel would say."

"Well, at least we can agree on one thing," Chad laughed. "It's a scientific fact."

"But seriously," Gemma pressed, "what are you trying to prove? Even outside of sports. I've seen you and Nigel both speeding around in your own personal cars like you're chasing demons."

"Chasing demons," Chad repeated.

"Why are you guys in such a hurry?"

You've never gone faster than 70 on land, have you?" asked Chad.

Chapter Eleven
Land Speed Record

Gemma held on for dear life as the Mustang drifted around a curve. She had seen Chad in action enough to know that he knew what he was doing. She had never exceeded 70 miles per hour on land (Nigel was always careful to follow the speed limits when she was present.), and now Chad was pushing the car with her in it in excess of 100. She held down her gorge, unprepared for Chad's high-speed shenanigans after the fajita lunch she had just finished with him. Chad was lucky enough to even get her in the car, surprised enough that she didn't try and barrel roll out once he had entered the freeway. What surprised Gemma more than Chad's apparent recklessness was the fact that he was barely keeping pace with the mid-day Texas traffic. Chad had installed various radar detectors and laser jammers; not that he needed them here. Law enforcement here was just as bad about speed control as everybody else on the road. At one point, a good-ol'-boy (as Chad put it) in a lifted Ram 2500 rode up on their tail and refused to take the passing lane around them. That was when Chad decided to exit the freeway for a second. He found an exit and drifted the Darkhorse Mustang through a Texas turn-around and back the opposite direction. Chad gunned it up the onramp and back onto the freeway.

"Okay," said Gemma, still trying to catch her breath after the latest stunt, "I think you've made your point."

"Not yet," said Chad as he pulled onto the shoulder and slid the pony car to a stop. "Now it's your turn."

"My turn?" Gemma squeaked with shock. "Chad, I don't even have an American license. I've only driven from port to t' 'otel in Nigel's Aston, and that's auto-stick." Her pale olive cheeks flushed bright red with embarrassment.

There was that Northern accent Chad loved so much slipping through the posh Oxbridge façade. He made it a mental note: "Get Gemma flustered whenever and wherever possible". The blush was just the icing on the cake.

"It's easy," said Chad nonchalantly. "You just balance right foot and left foot." He unbuckled and hopped out of the car.

Gemma waited for a moment longer as Chad walked around and then unbuckled. Chad opened the door for her.

"You'll do fine," Chad reassured her.

"If we die," Gemma started, "it's on you. Don't forget what I said about Nigel."

"Yes, I'll be the first man to die twice," chucked Chad as he hopped into the passenger seat.

Gemma adjusted her seat as she tried to figure out the pedals. She knew the concept well enough, but she had never needed it. Her Vauxhall Astra she drove around during her Oxford days was a two-pedal snoozefest. Nigel's Aston Martin Vantage that he owned was a dual-clutch like their own Formula One cars; she would shift through the gears in that, but there was no clutch. Chad's Stang, on the other hand, was pure, old-fashioned, unashamed American Muscle.

"Left pedal is the clutch," Chad began, "middle is brake, and right pedal is your accelerator. You push in the clutch, put the car in first, then slowly let off the clutch while pushing the gas pedal."

"I know the concept," Gemma groaned. "I've just never actually done it."

Gemma stumbled around for a second before pushing the clutch in and finding first. As she let out the clutch, the car started to vibrate.

"Give it gas!" exclaimed Chad.

"Not helping," Gemma groaned back at him as she feathered the accelerator.

"Okay, we're moving," Chad sighed. "Now, we're in Texas, so you're going to have to try and rejoin traffic at speed."

Gemma glared at Chad as she shifted into second. Chad cared not one bit. Seeing the girl flustered made him fall even harder for her. She easily found third and laid on the accelerator, signaling her intent to reenter the highway. The various commuters and commercial drivers gave her no room. She shifted into fourth, nearly matching speed with the traffic. The car rumbled and shook as it ran through the rumble strips and roadside debris.

"Easy does it," said Chad. "You have to just show them who's boss."

"Just let me think!" shouted Gemma.

She shifted into fifth and went for broke, cutting off an eighteen-wheeling hauling welding gas. She squeaked out a little scream when it blared its air horn – that kind of girly pip girls make when they're startled.

"Shift back down into fourth," Chad instructed.

Gemma did just that, her countenance showing the same determination Chad saw whenever they shared workout sessions prerace.

"Okay, back up to fifth," said Chad.

By now they were doing eighty and steadily gaining speed. Gemma impressed Chad as she kept up with the traffic, easily shifting into sixth.

"I thought you said you've never driven stick," said a shocked Chad.

"Never in my life," replied Gemma confidently. "I guess it is as easy as you say it is."

"Okay, but our exit is coming up," Chad pointed out. "Can you get it slowed down without killing us?"

Gemma kept that same determination as she signaled for the exit. She gently merged onto the offramp and effortlessly rowed down the gears.

"Okay, just remember," Chad began, "you don't need to put it in first until after you've stopped."

"Chad, this isn't my first time shifting gears," laughed Gemma.

Gemma brought the Mustang gently to a stop right on the line. She found first and indicated her turn before taking off like she had been driving like this for years.

"To the shop?" asked Gemma.

"Yeah, yeah, to the shop," Chad stuttered in amazement.

Gemma drove the rest of the way to the shop and found Chad's personal parking spot. After she pulled in, she killed the motor, only for an awkward silence to ensue. Gemma could hardly contain her excitement. She was hoping Chad would share in that, but when she glanced over at him, she was puzzled by his expression. She couldn't tell if he was amazed, shocked, angry, or disappointed. It was just that type of ambiguity that makes one party extremely nervous to continue a conversation.

"So," she began as she slapped her knees," how'd I do?"

Chad breathed in and out a deep full breath – one of those deep, refreshing breaths that completely fills your lungs and almost makes you yawn.

"That was incredible," he began, almost whispering. "You say that's your first time? Tell me you're not lying to me."

"I've never done this," chuckled Gemma, still excited.

"But now you get it?" asked Chad.

"Get what?"

"Why Nigel and I do what we do."

"Fully," replied Gemma. "I think I should schedule an appointment at the DMV."

"Would Nigel let you," asked Chad, his sense of humor returning to him, replacing the shock and awe of Gemma's natural talent.

"Funny," said Gemma sarcastically, "but I want my license now. I need power. I need a car like this!"

"Great, now Nigel _is_ gonna kill me."

And that's exactly what could have happened. As Chad walked Gemma into the lobby, Nigel appeared from the simulator room adjacent to said lobby.

"Where in blazes where you?" asked Nigel.

"Chad took me out to lunch," Gemma explained.

"I was talking to him," hissed Nigel as he pointed to Chad.

"Me?" asked Chad.

"Yes, you. Where were you, and what were you doing with my sister?"

"I just took her out to lunch," Chad tried to explain.

"Nigel, calm down," said Gemma, trying to play peacemaker. "It was harmless. He meant no harm. Anyway, I'm going to get my license here."

"Like heck you are!" growled Nigel. "You!" He was pointing at Chad again. "You leave me sister alone. Don't talk to her. Don't look at her. Don't even think about her. Got it?"

"But I…"

"Got it?"

"Nigel," Gemma pleaded, "this is really all unnecessary."

"Get in the car," said Nigel. "We're leaving."

"But Nigel," moaned Gemma. She felt like she was back in school.

"Now, Gems. Chad and I need to have a talk."

Gemma did just as she was told. She trudged out to Nigel's Aston. Nigel waited until she was gone.

"Come with me," he beckoned to Chad.

Chad's heart was beating hard, harder than ever. He could feel the blood rushing through his temples. The butterflies in his stomach had flown up into his chest, almost stinging as they radiated around inside. Against his better judgement, he followed the Brit to a secluded meeting room just adjacent to the lobby. Unbeknownst to Chad, Nigel closed and locked the door. Chad felt he had to be the one to break the ice.

"Look…"

Chad was cut off by a hard right hook to the jaw. He stumbled back into the wall. This was war then. He lunged at Nigel, but Nigel was fast. The wiry driver easily dodged Chad, sending him face first into the wall. Chad quickly recovered only to see Nigel's right hand coming for his face again. Now in fight mode, he was prepared. He ducked, causing Nigel to send his fist into the drywall.

Chad had never been in a fight before. Growing up, he had always kept to himself and stayed out of trouble. His first love, and he had a hill to climb; but if this was what it took to get the girl, then so be it. He lunged again for Nigel, but Nigel was able to use his greater height to his advantage. He grabbed Chad by the neck of his shirt and lifted him off the ground. Chad was taken by surprise at the beanpole's surprising strength. He tried to swing at the Brit, but it wouldn't do. Nigel drove Chad back into the wall, leaving a Chad-shaped impression in the drywall. Chad sunk down onto the floor, defeated.

"Stay away from my sister," hissed Nigel.

"What the heck is your problem?" asked Chad, wheezing from the blow.

"She's my sister," Nigel continued to growl. "Nobody talks to her unless I let them, especially second-rate punks life you."

"Come on," said Chad, finally regaining his breath, "she's an adult."

"She's my little sister," Nigel retorted as he picked up a chair.

Chad had barely caught his breath when he saw the heavy metal chair flying toward him. He ducked out of the way again. Before Chad could rise to defend himself, Nigel again lifted him up by the collar.

"I could easily make things difficult for you," he said through gritted teeth. "You really think you're here because you're that good?"

"Well, I…"

"Shut up. You're only here by my good graces. I could say the word, and either Colin or Lars would send you back to that small town out west where you belong."

"What the heck, Nigel?" It was Chad's turn to speak, even as he was still hoisted off his feet. "You recommended me. Are you that scared of me?"

"It's been one race, Helton. One. You got lucky. And you screwed up. We'll see how well you do in Jeddah next week. And you had better remember your place. I'm the lead driver."

"Nigel, I came to Formula One to do one thing. That's to win."

"Then I hope you enjoy disappointment, Helton. You just do your job and let me do mine."

"You are scared of me, aren't you? Does the great Nigel McKenzie seriously lack so much talent that he has to physically threaten his teammate into standing down? Seriously, Nige, where I come from, that doesn't fly. That's not racing. I'll see you in Jeddah, and I will be racing you; so you'd just better get ready. There won't be mistakes like last time."

"Just watch out then, and stay away from my sister. If I catch you with her again, it'll be worse for you."

And with that, Nigel stormed out of the conference room. Chad looked around the wrecked room. Was Nigel actually serious? Deep down, Chad couldn't fight the urge to poke the bear. What did it matter what Nigel said? He was determined to win the race and get the girl.

"*After all*," he thought to himself, "*isn't that what the good guy does anyway?*"

Chapter Twelve
Love and War

Chad slid into his pit stall for the final green flag stop. The Atlanta air was heavy with heat and humidity, but this day was going as good as any could. The team performed their choreography flawlessly and let the car down within thirteen seconds.

"Go, go, go, go, go!" screamed Larry as Chad mashed the accelerator.

It was perfect. Chad had maintained his position out front as every car still in the running pitted behind him. Could things get any better? The teal and black wrap that covered his Ford shone in the hot afternoon sun. It looked great as the car sailed around the mile-and-a-half superspeedway.

The laps began to wind down as Chad lapped the field. He made the mistake of not looking in his rearview mirror.

"Look on your six!" shouted Hawk.

Chad looked in his rearview mirror and noticed another car, wrapped almost identically to his approaching fast. It was Nigel.

"Have you been asleep, Hawk?" he shouted into the radio.

Chad moved in to block as they rounded turn four into the frontstretch approaching the final lap. Chad threw every block he could on Nigel as he took the white flag. Out of turn two, Nigel took advantage of the slingshot and swung out onto the outside lane. He had the momentum and led into turn three.

"Not today, limey," growled Chad as he inched ever-so close to Nigel's Mustang. As turn three turned into turn four, something had to give. He barely had to do anything. Nigel lost his nerve. He faltered just enough to bring his car down, down into Chad's lane. The left rear quarter panel made contact with the nose of Chad's car, breaking Nigel's traction. His Mustang swung completely around Chad's car as Chad passed the wrecking Nigel. Nigel's Mustang caught air as it slid backwards. Just when you thought it would land safely, the car was buffeted again by oncoming traffic, sailing high above the track and into the frontstretch catch fence where it burst into flames and disintegrated.

Chad brought his car back around to the frontstretch after his cooldown lap and performed a burnout that sent his own car up into flames as the heat from the burning tires and brake ignited some leaking fuel. He didn't care. It was the burnout to end all burnouts. He removed his helmet and donned the SportStream cap he kept in his car, climbing out of the burning wreck and backflipping off the window. Media crews surrounded the winner, ignoring the carnage that was once Nigel's stock car.

The surprise for Chad came in the form of Gemma. Not only did she ignore her brother who was now running around the wreck that had once been his car like a cartoon with flames consuming his rear end at the moment, she was stunning. Gone was the anachronistic British school garb she always wore for the race. She was dressed to

impress. Her sable hair was done up like she was a bridesmaid or even
the bride. Her dress even matched the car: teal on top fading to black
on the bottom. She approached Chad with a hungry look on her face.
She pulled out what looked like a single bobby pin which dropped
down the entirety of her hairdo, now tumbling down over her
shoulders almost to her waist. He didn't even have to think twice. He
threw his arms under her waist and lifted her up, passionately kissing
her for all the world to see on live television. Now this was living!
Everything was right with the world. The foe had been vanquished,
and the princess had been won.

The crowd's chants of "Chad! Chad! Chad!" rang in his ears as he
took in the warmth of Gemma's kiss, caressing her soft cheek with one
hand while the other held her aloft. The smell of her hair entered his
nostrils; intoxicating him in a way no drug or alcohol could ever
replicate.

"*Okay,*" he thought, "*this is weird.*" He couldn't figure out why, but
even his relatively easy life didn't ever seem this easy.

Gradually but still very quickly, those crowd chants of his name
turned into a single voice. The fruity smell of Gemma's hair turned to
a musky scent that he couldn't exactly place. Then all of a sudden, that
voice was muffled, followed by a loud pounding, and the scent of a
vanilla bourbon air freshener entered his nostrils. Gemma's deep
green eyes disappeared from his view as it faded into a white ceiling.

"Chad!" came the muffled voice, followed by even louder
pounding. "Green flag is in two hours."

Chad looked at his watch. It was six o'clock in the evening.

"Come on," moaned Larry outside the door of the RV, "contract
says you have to hobnob and schmooze our sponsors. Let's go."

"Give me a minute," said Chad as he stumbled over his shorts, "let
me shower."

"For what?" laughed Larry. "You'll be sweating like crazy in that
car."

"Can't let them think I smell or something," Chad excused himself. "Just fifteen minutes. I'll be showered and in my firesuit. Then I can shake all the hands and kiss all the babies they want me to."

"You know you're not allowed near that agent," said Larry.

"What agent?" asked Chad incredulously.

"We all know you have your eyes on Nigel's agent. We also know Nigel tore up the conference room putting you in your place last week."

"What Nigel don't know," said Chad, "won't hurt him. Will you just go back to the paddock and stall while I clean up?"

"What do I tell them?"

"I don't know. Talk about the car. You know, the normal B.S."

Chad stepped into the shower. It was hot and dry outside, but he preferred this environment to the humid Georgia swamp of his dream. After a quick wash and rinse, he stepped out and dried off. The SportStream firesuit had been cleaned and pressed the night before. How he wished it were a NASCAR suit, but he was here now. This was life.

He stepped out of the motorhome to a gaggle of press and media pundits all with their millions of questions. Did he really have to do this? Unfortunately, it comes with the territory. As much as he hated it, Chad was a master at trolling the media as was seen on full display in Bahrain. The mob struggled to keep up and ask questions as he made his way to the paddock. As much as sponsors and media pundits hated this behavior, it proved endearing to fans watching at home.

"How do you feel about your chances today?" asked one reporter.

"I'd say they're pretty decent," Chad replied, still walking toward the paddock.

As dogged as the pursuit was, many of them decided he wasn't worth their time and moved on. The few that were left gained his attention and respect. These would be the ones he would talk to.

"Your teammate, Nigel McKenzie, has shown some contempt for you," said another reporter, one of the lucky ones. "What do you have to say about that?"

"Nigel can think what he wants," Chad answered. "I get paid to drive a car fast and win. If he can't win without me holding back, then he has no skill."

Soon enough, press time was over, and it was time for the race to begin. Chad and Nigel had qualified front row again. All of the same prerace ceremonies took place the same as in Bahrain. Chad glared once again at Noodle as he snickered at the imam saying his invocation.

He looked over at Nigel's side of the paddock. There was Gemma busy at work. He hadn't talked to her since the incident with Nigel, but he still stole a glance or two at her when they were at work. He wondered if she was thinking what he was thinking. He wondered if she too stole glances at him when he wasn't looking, admiring him while he was hard at work, longing to speak to him. It didn't matter. Nigel would likely win and get completely plastered. Then he could have all the time he could want with Gemma that evening at the afterparty while Nigel drank himself silly.

Chad climbed into his car as the parade lap was about to begin. Jeddah Corniche Circuit is a thin, long road course consisting of twenty-seven turns completed in a counter-clockwise pattern. After two parade laps, the cars took their position on the grid. Chad looked over at Nigel to his left. Nigel could feel it too and discreetly flashed his middle finger at Chad. Chad was undeterred. The red lights went out, and the two SportStream cars rocketed forward into the 90° left at the end of the frontstretch.

Chad's strategy this week was to not take any unnecessary risk. This would be easier said than done. There were so many open doors, but Nigel closed them all. Even when they tried the same pit strategy as the previous race, Nigel still somehow ended up back out front. This week did end on a more positive note however. Instead of making a rash move and sending it into the final turn, Chad waited for a safe opportunity to pass in his last chance. Unfortunately, that safe opportunity never came, and Nigel won the race handily. Fortunately for Chad, the second-place finish garnered him eighteen points. Not only that, he had the honor of mounting the podium alongside Nigel and the Spaniard, Gerardo Lopez, another journeyman driver who had just signed with the new Auburn Racing Team out of Canada.

Chad repeated his routine at the end of this race and snubbed the reporters as they clamored around him. He attended Nigel's afterparty as well. That was one thing Nigel wouldn't take away from him. It was all about the optics. This time, he waited until Nigel was sufficiently drunk to find Gemma.

"Is the coast clear?" he asked her when he finally found her.

"I thought you'd never show up," Gemma laughed.

"It's been too long," Chad sighed.

"It's only been a week," Gemma laughed some more.

"One long week."

"What did Nigel say to you?"

"'Don't talk to my sister. Don't look at my sister. Don't even think about my sister' in that exact order," he said in a goofy imitation of his teammate. "Well, you heard that part. I personally think he watches a little too much television."

"Is that all?"

"Well, he also threatened worse. I'm guessing he meant actually putting me in the hospital. I'm sure you've seen what he did to the conference room."

"How terrible!" Gemma exclaimed.

"I feel like I'm playing with fire right now as we speak," said Chad. "He threatened to get me fired if he catches me with you. He really doesn't like me for some reason."

"Then I guess," said Gemma coyly as she walked her right index and middle fingers up Chad's chest over his heart, "you'll have to win a race to win me."

That conversation put a determination in Chad's heart for the next race down under in Australia. One of the older tracks on the tour, Albert Park Circuit is another road course, this time fourteen turns around a lake in Melbourne. Things weren't good, but they weren't exactly bad there. Chad was caught up in a mid-race pileup and had to pit and replace the nose of his car, costing valuable seconds. Through all of that, he still finished a respectable fifth place. That meant ten points.

Again, he spent the evening at the afterparty playing designated driver with Gemma. The added risk of Nigel giving Chad another beating gave an element of secrecy both found romantic, as if they were two lovers in a Shakespearian play, doomed to never reveal how they felt to the world for fear of an angry and powerful father. With every late night spent with Gemma, Chad fell further in love with her. He began to notice every little tick she had, making a mental note of it – something to think about later on to get him through the day; the way she laughed and brushed her hair back when she was nervous or the dimple that appeared in the right-hand corner of her mouth whenever she smiled at him. He couldn't tell, but he was sure Gemma was falling for him too. At least, he never saw her with any other man besides Nigel. Everything she did, the way she talked to him and looked at him, told him with what little information or experience he had that she liked him.

At Suzuka Circuit, rain impaired racing all day. It was miserable, and the FIA refused to call a stop to proceedings. Visibility was at an all-time low. Surprisingly, Nigel and Chad agreed for once and suggested that the race should not be run. One would think they would listen to two men who grew up in the rainy climates of the United Kingdom and the Pacific Northwest.

After crossing under a bridge that turns the road course into somewhat of a figure eight, the drivers brake hard into a left hairpin that turns into a large sweeper. After most of the field had cycled through pit stops, one lone gambler decided to stay out and see if he could make it a few more laps to gain distance on the hard-charging duo of Nigel McKenzie and Chad Helton. By turn nine, the hard right-hand 90° turn before the underpass, the SportStream pair had caught up to him. They made their way up to the rear of the gambler, but he fought hard for his position. The thing about gamblers, many will tell you, is that eventually their luck runs out. What they don't tell you is that when that luck runs out, it also affects other people. The gambler's left rear tire finally gave out and exploded spectacularly, sending pieces of rubber flying and tearing the rear of his car apart. Nigel and Chad were helpless to avoid the carnage and plowed into the wreck. The wet tire compound turned out to be completely useless today. The slick track surface was of very little help as they continued sliding for several more feet before they hit the gravel traps on the side of the track. Neither would score points. Chad angrily lobbed his helmet at the poor gambler still in his car. Were it not for the pelting rain, he would have marched over to the wreck and pulled the poor loser out of his car. Instead, he climbed into an ambulance and rode off to the medical center where he would watch Gerardo Lopez take the checkered flag from the monitors inside.

There would be no afterparty this week. There was no celebration. Chad missed it. He wondered over the next week if he could somehow sneak in a chat with Gemma. There was no such luck as they prepared for their trip to Shanghai.

If there were any other country for his crew to be deported from, Chad was sure it was China. They were already an embarrassment in the Arab countries. They were loved in Australia and tolerated in Japan. Noodle had already written down the jokes he would tell before they left. Fortunately, they never saw the light of day as Chad stole Noodle's cigarette lighter and burned the college-ruled notebook page.

"We are respectable Formula One people," Chad reminded them. "There will be no racist jokes. There will be no comments about how their dictator looks like Winnie the Pooh. You will speak English respectfully <u>with</u> your native accents, <u>Noodle</u>. You will not laugh when they say 'Nàgè'. They are not insulting Quizz."

The race went just about as well as Chad could expect at this point. Nigel threw all the right blocks. Even the long DRS zone before the final few turns at Shanghai helped very little. At the end of the day, it was Nigel with twenty-five points and Chad with eighteen.

Chad was becoming more and more flustered. Gemma tried to comfort him that evening, but even she couldn't sooth the beast raging inside him. Nigel was sitting in first with a hundred and three points while Chad trailed third with forty-eight. It was still early in the season, but the fifty-five-point gap still seemed almost insurmountable.

Back in Austin, Larry called a powwow with Chad. He was technically supposed to be unbiased, working for both drivers, but he knew Chad needed the pep talk.

"Look, I know you're trying," he began. "But I also know what you're capable of. I'm trying to be fair here, but I'm kinda getting tired of Nigel winning over you. Look, we're going to Miami next. That's where you first drove one of these cars. You set a track record there. This is our moment. Now get at it."

"How?" asked Chad. "He shuts me down every opportunity."

"Don't hold back this time," he plainly told Chad.

"What do you mean?" asked Chad. "I can't pass the guy. No matter what I do, he always finds a way to close the door."

"Then you force it open," said Larry. "Now, I normally wouldn't recommend this, but I think it's time you started showing a little aggression. Sure, you made a mistake in Bahrain, but that's just one time you've failed doing that in so many tries. Remember, you have more control over that car than your Mustang. You don't use the power modes like you can. If he blocks you after you've clearly got control of the turn, let him suffer the consequences."

"So, are you saying I wreck him? You know that doesn't fly here."

"You know those final three turns before the frontstretch?"

"Yeah, I know it."

"Cut them as tight as you can without losing grip."

"What's the strategy then?" asked Chad.

"We'll go with hard-compound tires in the beginning to get you some speed," Larry explained. "That'll also allow you to stay out a little longer. Then we bring you in and throw some medium tires on there. We know you'll drive the wheels off that car. You'll have all the grip you'll need to send it into those final turns and catch him off guard. Knowing how Nigel races, you'll probably have to wait to make your move until the final lap. It's a gamble, but I think it'll pay off."

"I sure hope so," said Chad.

"I might also be risking my job here," continued Larry, "so this is strictly off the record. If I give you team orders, and you have a clear shot at the win, ignore them.

"Ignore you?" asked Chad.

Larry made sure to make eye contact with Chad as he said, "Checkers or wreckers this week."

Chad left the conference room with renewed confidence. Sure, the going had been tough, but he knew he could pull off a win this time. He knew Larry knew his stuff. With this in mind, he knew he had already won.

Chapter Thirteen
Welcome to SportStream

It had been nearly three months since Chad stood in the parking lot that was used as the Miami International Autodrome. This time, it was the middle of spring. The sun grew even hotter over Florida. The breeze off the Atlantic helped a little bit as Chad prepared to head out to the grid. The parking lot had been temporarily overhauled into a multi-million-dollar racetrack. Standing in the paddock, one would never be able to tell this was once a football stadium parking lot.

As tradition now dictated for the SportStream cars, Chad had qualified second to Nigel. Were he honest, Chad would admit that he hated this arrangement. But today was not normal. The secondary team of SportStream had come with one goal: to win.

The Mercedes-Benz safety car led the twenty competitors around the track. Chad kept his eye on that safety car, not even paying attention to Nigel or whatever he was doing. As the safety car ducked into the pits, the competitors took their places on the grid. Chad kept his eyes on the starting lights. As happened many times before, the world went silent as he focused on the lights. Then out of that silence, the lights went out, and twenty engines screamed to life.

Chad's first order of business was to beat Nigel into that first turn. He held the unofficial track record here, so the plan was to run a qualifying lap. Forget what Nigel was doing. That turn would be his. He had very little time to think as he cut down into his qualifying line. Nigel flinched; the first mistake he had made all year. Chad was out front for the first time in his Formula One career by virtue of a good pass.

"How's that for a challenge?" he imagined himself saying to Nigel out loud.

Back in the 88 car, Nigel was having none of it. Chad led the first lap, but Nigel was far from done. Coming out of the wide esses on the backstretch out of turn ten, he activated DRS and beat Chad into turn 11.

Larry, watching on a monitor in the paddock, tossed his baseball cap down on the ground and let out a rebel yell. It seemed he had forgotten where he was and who he was with.

"Looks like we got ourselves a race!" he shouted to the crew.

He scanned the area, realizing what he did. It seemed almost satisfactory to see the scowl on Lars' face and the looks of disdain from the other mechanics' faces.

Over the last several weeks, the MorrisSport guys and the established crewmembers from the SportStream team had gotten to know each other and bonded over practice time and Nigel's all-night afterparties. Larry's lapse into unprofessionalism fazed nobody in that pit box.

While the commotion was still ensuing in the SportStream paddock, Chad and Nigel continued to battle it out through the final turns before the long straight. Nigel exited the 90° left-hander out of turn 16 with Chad inches from the rear of his car. Chad took advantage of the DRS. Nigel knew what Chad would do and blocked him. Closing in on turn 17, Chad appeared to be going low. He moved his car slightly to the left. Nigel mirrored the move and turned to block him, only for Chad to quickly swing to the right and fly past with his DRS advantage. Being on the outside gave him a speed advantage into the turn as well. After a couple sweepers, Chad crossed the lined first, but there were still fifty-five to go.

Gemma watched the race from Nigel's side of the paddock as well. As much as she loved and respected her brother, she was secretly rooting for Chad. Her heart skipped a beat when she watched him pull those passes on Nigel. She knew, through some convoluted way, that he was fighting for her. She had told him that a race win could earn him Nigel's respect. If that were true, then maybe he would let them be and see each other. In a way, she felt like she was the princess, and Chad was the knight in shining armor fighting the black knight (Nigel) for her favor.

Even after two months of racing Formula One, Chad still couldn't get over how these cars handled. Even the new stock cars had nothing on the torque these cars had. He could never imagine sending his Mustang into one of these corners at over 100 mph and making it stick to the ground like these cars could. As much as he missed the high-banked ovals, the speeds these cars carried more than made up for the fact he could barely pass another car.

Nigel had been taken by surprise. After his threats to his teammate, he thought Chad would learn his place, but he was wrong. He didn't expect such a challenge from the American. He was angry, but you wouldn't be able to tell just by looking. Nigel was still a professional after all; however, the conversation over the radio was a different story.

"What in blazes does this Yank think he's doing?" he yelled to Larry.

"I believe," Larry tried to explain, "he's going for a win."

"The idiot is going to get us both killed!" shouted Nigel.

MorrisSport redneck and SportStream gentleman alike could barely control their laughter.

"Keep it up, Chad," said Larry. "You got 'em scared. Just keep diggin' and hit your marks. I can see you on top of that podium already."

Chad kept his mouth shut. He wanted to stay focused. He crossed the line battling Nigel side-by-side. That was twelve down, forty-five to go. He could do this: 151 miles left. He calculated his averages in his head.

"A lap here is roughly a minute and a half. Forty-five laps, then if I do the math right, is just a little over an hour. I can do this."

Gemma had had enough of Nigel's complaining. It had gone from amusing to downright childish. Even she, who barely knew the first thing about racing, knew that you can't just win them all. Something had to give. She snuck out of Nigel's side and into Chad's. She found it refreshing. Here, everyone all seemed happy. She took one more glance at Nigel's side of the paddock and took a seat next to Larry.

"Hello," she said curtly. She had never introduced herself to Larry, and she didn't want to seem rude.

"Hey," Larry responded, he himself trying not to be rude, busy as he was monitoring the cars and drivers.

"Gemma McKenzie," she continued. "I'm…"

"Nigel McKenzie's sister," Larry butted in. "Chad's girlfriend. What brings you to our humble abode."

"Well," Gemma began, "I really can't stand it over there right now. It's Nigel, he's…"

"Pitching a huge old fit?" Larry finished her sentence.

"You could say that," replied Gemma. "I came over here, and it seems like a breath of fresh air."

"Well, we all at least try to wear some deodorant," joked Larry. "Here," he handed her a headset, "put it on and you can listen to us."

Even sitting in on Nigel's races, Gemma had never been granted such access. She gladly accepted the headset, watching Larry's screen as Chad continued to battle her brother.

"Hey, do you happen to remember what compound Nigel's running?" Larry asked Gemma after about twenty minutes.

"I believe one of the mechanics mentioned he was on hard tires," she replied. "Why?"

"Explains why they're running almost identical laps," said Larry. "Dang! These SportStreams are fast on hards!"

Chad and Nigel continued to swap first and second. Chad continued to run like he was qualifying while Nigel fought to defend his position. He was getting sloppy, and Chad knew it. It was the art of intimidation. It wasn't like he was going to hurt the guy or wreck him, but he knew he could get inside Nigel's head. Only the best drivers could do it effectively, and Chad knew he was among the best.

By this time, cars were starting to pit. Depending on the tire compound used by the teams, out times could vary. The harder the compound, the longer the tire lasted, and the faster the car went. The softer the compound, the better grip the car had at the expense of speed and longevity. Each tire compound is color coded: white for hard, yellow for medium, and red for soft with the treaded tires green for intermediate and blue for wet. Intermediates and wets would be out of the question today.

Chad and Nigel expertly avoided cars exiting the pits as they still battled their way around the track. The viewing world was shocked to watch what was unfolding. As impressive as it was for Chad to shadow Nigel in the first few races, it was even more incredible to see the two stay practically neck and neck since the first lap.

By lap thirty-eight, the hard tires were beginning to show their age. Chad would not back down, but he was also beginning to get worried. Losing a tire was how a disaster could happen. He had had personal experience with that. He did not desire a repeat of the Phoenix race.

"Come on, Larry," he thought to himself, *"call me in. 'Box, box, box'."*

Both drivers were now visibly fighting their own cars around the track in addition to each other. Approaching lap thirty-nine, Chad watched Nigel peel off onto pit road.

"Crap! Box, box, box!" shouted Larry.

Chad swerved off the track just in time to make it into the pits.

"I'm so sorry about that," said Larry. "That's my bad. Get ready, boys."

The whole twenty-man crew was standing ready in the pit box. This was their moment to shine. Like Chad, the MorrisSport transplants missed NASCAR too. There was nothing like racing against the clock, dodging moving vehicles, and jumping over obstacles while carrying heavy equipment. Now, for many, it was a small job like removing a tire, replacing a tire, or operating an air ratchet; but it was work, and they had great chemistry. They lined up tires two-by two. Nigel slid in. Two seconds, and he was gone.

Chad slid into the pits ready for his tire change right on Nigel's heels. That was it. Just a change in tire compound. They needed no other adjustments. The car was wicked fast.

"Holy crap, I think he can win this," gasped Larry. "What was that stop time again?"

He looked at the telemetry report.

"1.72 seconds!" he shouted. "That's a record! Good work, gentlemen!"

Chad rejoined right on Nigel's tail. They had retained their position.

"Go for it!" shouted Larry into the radio. "You can't lose today! Remember what I said last week: checkers or wreckers."

Chad remained silent, only listening to Larry's instructions. He was lucky he didn't see just who was sitting next to Larry when he pitted, or it would've thrown off the whole enterprise. He would admit later that had he known Gemma had now moved to his paddock, he would've been distracted by the prospect of seeing her after he race. As it was, he was chasing her brother down to earn his respect and permission to see her publicly.

Chad pushed his car hard, still keeping up with Nigel and even passing him briefly at times, but something was wrong.

"Hey, Larry," he radioed, "you sure you put medium's on here?"

"That's what I ordered," he replied. "Why?"

"I have speed," Chad explained, "but not enough to do much of anything."

"Well, everything looks good on the computer," said Larry. "Hold it just a second!"

He rose from his chair and walked to the garage opening as Nigel and Chad made their way down the frontstretch. He watched very closely at the tires.

"Shoot!" he exclaimed. "Someone's color blind. Who set out the tires?"

"What!" shouted Chad. "What tires am I running?"

"Red is soft. Yellow is medium, Noodle!"

"I'm on softs?"

"Yeah, unfortunately. Can you do anything with it?"

"I can certainly try. It's too late to come in and change them. Dang it!"

Larry smacked Noodle on the back of his head and took his seat.

"What's wrong?" asked Gemma, genuinely concerned for Chad.

"We put the wrong tires on the car. Nigel has mediums. They're balanced for grip, speed, and longevity. Chad was supposed to get mediums as well, but we put soft tires on. He's slower than Nigel, and they'll wear down quicker, but he does have the advantage in the corners.

Chad counted down the laps, miraculously keeping pace with Nigel. The Brit now had the advantage on the straights, leaving almost no opportunity for Chad to activate his DRS. At the end of these straights, Nigel would have to brake earlier, leaving a glimmer of hope for Chad to take the lead. Nigel still kept a commanding lead, though. The cornering advantage was no match for Nigel. All had returned to business as usual in his paddock as well.

They were now down to two laps within what seemed like minutes. Nigel continued to shut the door on Chad. Chad was starting to get flustered again.

"Can't this idiot slip up once!" he shouted into the radio.

"This isn't good," Larry whispered to Gemma. Then he turned his attention to the radio. "You're doing good. Keep diggin'. Just stay on him. You're almost home."

"No good, Larry," said Chad. "I have to win this. I can't keep this up. This is more than about the race." Chad's communication was coming through all of SportStream's headsets, including Gemma's. "This is about Gemma. If I can win this race, maybe I have a chance with her. Nigel will lay off, and I can actually see her without him interfering. Larry, she's all I've thought about since Daytona."

"Then shut the heck up and win this bloody race for me!" Gemma blurted into the microphone.

What possessed Chad then, even he didn't know. Instead of a distraction, hearing Gemma's disembodied voice was an encouragement. He thought for a minute that he was imagining things, but after Larry never responded, he put two and two together. With renewed determination, he positioned himself perfectly behind Nigel.

"Tell Helton to hold back," said Lars.

"Tell Chad to hold back?" asked Larry.

"Team orders," Lars continued. "He needs to give Nigel a little space."

Larry rolled his eyes behind Lars' back. The time for disobedience had come.

"Okay, Chad," Larry began, "I need you to hold back and let Nigel win."

"Let Nigel win?" asked Chad.

"You're not seriously going to…" Gemma began to protest to Larry before he cut her off."

"It's coming down from the top. Let Nigel win, and we'll have to try again. Did you hear that? Let Nigel win the race."

Crossing the line for the final lap, the two SportStream cars were perfectly aligned. Chad had little to no wind resistance. Going into turn one, he was nearly glued to the rear of Nigel's car. The same was true for two, three, four, and so on. On the backstretch, he ducked in and out from behind Nigel.

"What in blazes is this muppet doing!" shouted a panicked Nigel at Larry.

"You'd better hold on tight, bud," Larry replied to Nigel. "He's here to race."

"The devil he is!" Lars shouted before commandeering the radio. "Helton, hold back! That's a team order! Hold back!"

What Chad was doing was the old intimidation game again, ignoring team orders. Even though he could, he opted to not use DRS on the backstretch and stayed close on Nigel's rear. The two cars slowed significantly through eleven to sixteen. Coming out of sixteen, Chad decided to let Nigel have it. He activated DRS and peeked out from behind Nigel. Nigel tried to throw the block, but Chad was too fast.

Turn seventeen was fast approaching. It would be the real last chance for Chad to make a move. This time, it was Nigel's turn to make a mistake. As if it were a dream, he ducked low on his approach into the turn, not braking as hard as he normally would have. Chad ducked lower and entered the turn just as fast. Nigel's medium compound tired lost their grip and refused to turn the car, much less slow it down like it needed. Chad's soft tires carried him around turn seventeen safely. He kept his eyes on his twelve as Nigel spun into the wall, damaging the rear suspension of his car. Chad flew through eighteen and nineteen and crossed the line fifteen seconds ahead of second place. Meanwhile, Nigel cowered in his car praying the remaining competitors would see the yellow lights of the virtual safety car and take caution through his sector. Chad could hardly believe it.

"You won, you son of a gun!" Larry shouted into the radio.

Chad brought the car back around to the frontstretch and did only what he knew to do: a burnout. The frontstretch filled with blinding white smoke as he locked the front brakes and spun the rear tires. The unruly SportStream team rushed out to meet Chad on the frontstretch. A true race victory was something they had all been missing for a long time. After Chad had finished his burnouts the team all crowded on top on the car and rode it into the paddock, a tradition they had started back at MorrisSport as a sort of throwback to pay tribute to Davey Allison and Robert Yates Racing, the team that had held their number 28 for many years.

As Chad pulled the car into the paddock, he had another surprise waiting. Gemma stood near the team computers. He ran to her. She ripped off her headset and ran to him. They embraced one another.

"My knight, you've won me," she whispered to him, only half joking.

"Hey, let's get you to the podium," said Larry. "That's twenty-five points for the win and a bonus point for fastest lap!"

Any anger Lars would have held for Chad's actions was dissipated as he watched the disgraced Nigel's car towed off the track and back into the paddock. His new driver had proven himself, and his veteran had acted like a rookie. In the end, he reasoned that the loss in manufacturer's points would rest solely on Nigel.

"Congratulations, Helton," he said, extending a hand to the American. "Aside from disobeying team orders, that was a great showing out there. Welcome to SportStream."

Chad had been on the podium once already this season, but not at the top in first. He stood in the middle along with two other drivers as they were given giant bottles of champaign. Chad shook the bottle, and the cork flew off, bathing him and the other drivers in the alcoholic beverage.

Little did Chad know that down in the paddock, Nigel was brooding over his loss. This was not the end for him. Now that he knew Chad could beat him, he would be out for blood.

"I'm number one", he thought. *"I'm the primary. And my sister? How could she betray me like this?"*

He considered the information about what Gemma did. It sure felt like betrayal. The fact was that Chad would've won his respect any other day; but now that Gemma was in the middle of it, there was no way that would happen. He watched from his paddock as Chad continued his wild celebration.

"Enjoy the win, Yank," he said to himself. *"It's the last one you'll ever get."*

Chapter Fourteen
Out West

But it wouldn't be the last win Chad would get. Despite Nigel's best efforts to derail him, two weeks later, Chad would dominate at Imola. The SportStream cars would finish one and two. Nigel feigned joy as he stood in second place on the podium.

Chad and Gemma now felt safe to go public with their relationship. Nigel had very little to say on that front; at least, not to Chad's face. Chad was now introducing Gemma as "Gemma, my girlfriend". Emily was finally granted her wish of meeting Gemma. The two bonded very quickly. Whenever she accompanied Chad to Mike and Emily's house, the two women would spend hours in the kitchen and dining room carrying on conversation as if they had known each other for years. What made Gemma's heart melt was when little Kevin quickly took to calling her "Auntie Gemma".

Upon their return from Miami, Chad phoned Ace and politely let him go. He thanked the sleaze bag for his years of loyal service and wished him well. Then he hired Gemma. With the extra client, Gemma rushed to the DMV and got her American license. With her newfound freedom, she purchased a 1989 Miata. Chad thought the little roadster was perfect for her, and he said as much. Little did they know these big changes would send Nigel into a spiral of self-destruction.

It had been only three days since their return to Austin. Gemma had already met Mike and Emily. The contract to represent Chad had been signed. She had been out with Chad walking around the state capitol after dark. Nearly every waking moment she had since returning from Miami, she spent with Chad. Gemma walked in through the front door of the house she and Nigel shared; Nigel actually owned it, and he kept a room for his sister. Nigel was seated in an armchair, a glass of scotch in his right hand. He looked moody. His eyes were dark. A stoney look of rage was frozen onto his face.

"Well, look what t' moggy drug in," he slurred.

"Good evening to you, Nigel," Gemma replied politely. "Hit the booze a little hard now, did we."

"The devil were you tonight?" Nigel pressed.

Nigel had never been a belligerent drunk. He always became way too friendly when he drank. Whenever he raged, he was completely sober. Tonight was different. Tonight, he had a reason to drink.

"I said 'where the devil were you'?"

"I don't see how that's a concern of yours," said Gemma defiantly. She had had enough of Nigel's overbearing. "I'm an adult, Nigel. You don't have to treat me like Mum and Dad."

"It's totally my business," he continued to slur. "Were you with that bloody Yank? Is that what you were doing? That stupid fat American? You wish to betray me? Your brother? I took care of you after Mum and Dad died. I gave you a place to live. I gave you a job.

And this is my thanks? You go against my wishes and spend every bleeding waking moment with the likes of him?"

"Nigel, you're drunk," Gemma trembled. She was scared of her brother. She had never seen him like this. He had never acted like this.

"What does that have to do with the issue at hand?" he continued. "Are you going to go work for him too? Is that it?"

Gemma held her peace. Even through the drunken haze, Nigel was able to put two and two together.

"So this is how it is," he grumbled. "Then get out."

"What?" squeaked Gemma.

"I told you to get the heck out!" Nigel chucked his glass of scotch onto the floor where it shattered into a million pieces. "Grab your things and go live with your lover! We'll see how well he takes care of you. You never had it so good."

Meanwhile, Chad was just changing into a t-shirt and some shorts. He had barely relaxed in the last two months and finally decided to take one night to settle down. He had just moved into a modest bungalow in West Lake Hills. It was perfect for what he needed. A two-car garage housed his Mustang with room for a second car if he ever needed it. Other than that, the house was pretty standard: three bedrooms, two bathrooms, a living room, a dining room, and a kitchen.

Chad flopped down onto his sofa and turned on the big 72" smart TV. He began scrolling through the many streaming apps that came preloaded on it. He didn't have much of a chance to scroll before his phone began to ring. It was Emily.

"*Why would she be calling at this time of night?*" he thought, worried at what would come from the other end of the line. He answered quickly.

"Chad, you'd better get over here," was all she had to say.

Chad threw on his clothes and rushed over to Mike and Emily's development. He rushed into the house. There, he found Gemma on the couch, bawling her eyes out. Mascara had been saturated by tears, leaving dark streaks of black from her eyes running down her soft, tender cheeks. Her face was red from weeping. It was an awful sight for Chad.

"Did he hit you?" asked Chad through gritted teeth.

Gemma shot up off of the couch and ran to Chad, embracing him, practically hanging off of his neck. She hugged him with as much pressure as her petite biceps allowed. Chad returned the hug.

"He kicked me out," Gemma managed to sniffle.

"But he didn't hurt you?"

"No, 'e never laid an 'and on me," she cried.

Chad embraced her even harder.

"He was so angry," she continued. "He thinks I betrayed him. I never even told him I was working with you. He just somehow knew. Then he fired me and threw me out."

"She drove all the way over here," Emily chimed in. "I sent Mike to the store to get some bedding for the guest bedroom. He should be back soon."

"Is there anything I could do?" asked Chad. He was really dumbfounded. He never thought Nigel could stoop this low. It was petty, just plain petty. He had lost all respect for his teammate. It was no longer a matter of earning respect if that someone clearly had no desire to return any respect.

"Emily's taking care of me for tonight," replied Gemma.

"Gemma," Emily said as she rested her hand on her friend's shoulder, "you stay here as long as you need."

"I'm going over to Nigel's right now," Chad suddenly said. He grabbed his keys and started for the door.

"No!" shouted Gemma. "He's drunk!"

"Good, then he'll have no idea tomorrow morning where he got two black eyes from and why he's missing all of his teeth."

Gemma tried to pull Chad back, but he was much too strong for her. Her only saving grace was Mike entering through the front door – a bag of bedding in one arm and a sleeping Kevin in the other. The two men stared in confusion at one another.

"Did you tell him what happened?" asked Mike.

"Out of my way, Mike," growled Chad.

"Hold it there," said Mike as he laid his hand on Chad's shoulder.

"Get your hand off of me!"

"Come on, Chad," beckoned Mike, "do you really want to do this in front of our women? In front of my kid? Do you really think you can get through me?"

Chad backed down. He knew he was no match for a former offensive lineman. Chad took a seat next to Gemma on the couch. He put his arm around her and absent-mindedly stroked her hair. It just seemed like the natural thing to do. Gemma responded by resting her head on his shoulder.

"This has got to stop," said Chad. "How does someone not realize he can't have it all?"

"I guess," Gemma chimed in answer to Chad, "when everything comes to you so easily, you get frustrated when things get difficult."

"Okay, but I didn't disown the only family I had left," said Chad defensively.

"I didn't have you in mind," said Gemma.

"May I say something?" asked Mike.

"I don't mind," replied Gemma.

Mike took a deep breath before speaking. "Now I don't know the first thing about racing other than cars drive fast, and whoever finishes fastest wins. That being said, your brother seems like a very unreasonable man. If he can't share in the talent, he has no business racing. I hear Chad talking about how he's on a team all the time. I'm not exactly sure how a team in racing works since there's only one winner, but I would think that a reasonable person would lift up his teammates, not tear them down. It doesn't make sense."

"It's a long story, Mike," said Chad. "He has it in his head that since he's the primary driver, he's automatically entitled to finish ahead of me. Where I come from, that's not how it works. You help your team get the best finish; but when it comes down to it, your main objective is to finish first. It's an entirely different culture from NASCAR."

"Anyway," continued Mike, "that's my two cents. This Nigel guy seems like a real 'D bag.'"

Chad turned to Gemma. Her eyes had dried up. Her cheeks looked raw from the salt water that flowed over them. In that moment, he felt an immense love for her; love and pity. He fought against a tear that tried to escape his own eye. Again, he stood up very quickly.

"Where are you going?" asked Gemma.

"I know you just got here," said Chad, "but don't unpack. We have a free weekend. Let's go home."

"Home? Where's home?"

"Oregon."

"But Chad, it's so sudden. Mike and Emily just opened their house up to me, and I'd feel so rude just leaving like that to go galivanting off on some holiday with you."

"Nonsense," Emily interrupted. "You're more than welcome to come and go as you please. It'll give me a little more time to finish putting your room together."

The next day, the couple found themselves on a jet bound for Portland. Chad had neglected to tell his parents he was coming home, much less that he was bringing a girl. As they pulled into his driveway late Thursday night, Gemma was out cold in the back of the rideshare. Chad nervously tapped on her hand to wake her.

"What?" she groaned through a yawn. "Where are we?"

It is often said that no matter how good your English is, when you're drunk or tired, your true accent comes out. To Chad, Gemma's Lancastrian accent was barely intelligible. It took him a couple seconds longer to process what she was saying.

"We're home," he finally answered.

Gemma slowly lifted herself out of the car. The driver already had their luggage unloaded from the trunk. Chad could tell he was ready to leave quick, fast, and in a hurry. He handed the driver a $100 bill and promised a five-star rating before ushering Gemma into the house.

Chad hadn't been home since January, but the house was shining clean. He paid a cleaning service to come by every week and keep it spotless just in case he had the urge to visit home during the racing season.

"Let me show you to my bedroom," said Chad.

"You're not going to sleep with me, are you?" mumbled Gemma.

"No! Heck no!" laughed Chad. "Not until there's a ring on your finger. I'll crash on the couch."

Chad led Gemma upstairs to his bedroom. The full-size bed looked inviting to both of them. Chad wanted it. The temptation was there. The thought was exciting to him.

"*What harm would one night do?*" he thought before his inner voice scolded him.

He hugged Gemma and left her in the room. After changing into his t-shirt and basketball shorts, he made up a bed on his sofa.

The next day, Chad was awoken by a piercing shriek to the most wonderful smell: bacon. He followed it to the kitchen. There was Gemma making breakfast. A tea kettle had just gone off. He felt a little embarrassed walking in on her; she was already dressed in her brown sweater, white blouse, and dark brown skirt, an apron tied around her waist, while he was still in his t-shirt and shorts. She had done her makeup and already styled her hair; Chad sported a five-o'clock shadow, and his hair was a mess. Chad was mesmerized with his girl, as if she was ready to be the housewife God had created her to be.

"*So, she is wifey material,*" said his inner monologue.

Besides the bacon, Gemma had decided to treat Chad to a traditional English breakfast. She had run into town long before Chad woke up and picked up some bread, baked beans, and some Earl Gray, along with a tea kettle.

"Good morning," said Chad.

"Oh, good morning," Gemma responded. "I thought I'd get started on breakfast. I've done some grocery shopping. I hope you like beans on toast. I know it's not something you'd be used to. Just try it. I also bought some bacon."

"Oh, that's all fine," said Chad. "I'm starving as it is."

As they sat down to eat, Chad started laying out plans. Their first order of business was to run down to Lebanon to say "hi" to the parents and introduce her to the family. Chad had mentioned his girl to the folks, but he knew they wouldn't believe him until they saw her with their eyes. If they had time later, Chad suggested a trip to the Coast. Sunday would be filled with church. Gemma had never set foot in a church, except for an Anglican Church. The way Chad described the different worship style of an Independent Fundamental Baptist church intrigued her – two hours in the morning and one more in the evening.

"Just to let you know," he said as they were making final preparations, "everyone is going to grill you with questions. Don't worry. My siblings do it to everybody. They'll love you. I promise."

Reality was better than Chad's predictions. When Chad rang the doorbell of his childhood home, his mother answered. Kate Helton was the daughter of a Sicilian businessman and an all-American housewife. In her late 50s, her thick dark brown hair was graying. She still exuded a motherly warmth that made anyone let down their guard. Upon seeing the girl next to him, she quickly put two and two together, screamed a blood-curdling scream of delight (a special talent she had), and hugged Gemma, nearly suffocating her.

"I wish you had told us you were coming," Mrs. Helton said as she led the couple into the living room where Chad's father was sitting in his favorite recliner watching some hunting show. "Bill, you'll never guess who's home!"

Bill Helton powered the television down and stood up from his chair. He shot Chad an approving glance. That was validation enough from his understated father. Beyond finding a good occupation, if there was one thing that would earn Bill Helton's respect, it was for his sons to find a good woman, marry her, and raise as many grandchildren for him as possible. Bill Helton was an old grass seed farmer, the fifth in a long line that started almost immediately after arriving on the Oregon Trail. Now in his early 60s, his golden hair was also graying, much like his wife's. He was quiet and understated. He was a man who enjoyed the simple pleasures of life. If he was excited, the only indicator was the understated smile that snuck out from time to time.

"You came just at the right time," Mrs. Helton continued. "Tom and Jana are in town, and we're all having a big supper here tonight. I can't wait for you to meet everyone!"

Mrs. Helton then took Gemma by the hand and started leading her away toward the kitchen. Gemma shot Chad a glance of shock as if to say, "What the devil is going on? Help me!" Chad's glance back at her was one of reassurance as if to say, "It's alright. She just wants to get to know you." Mrs. Helton had a habit of doing this with all of her daughters-in-law-to-be. She would take them to the kitchen and find out all of the latest tea.

Chad sat down on the couch as his father resumed his hunting show. On the screen, some guy with a southern accent wearing camo in the middle of Idaho drew his compound bow and expertly pierced a mule deer through the heart. Chad wasn't as interested in it as his father was, but just being with him brought back fond memories of his childhood here.

"You picked well, son," Bill said out of the blue.

That made Chad even happier.

At dinner, all five children were gathered around the big table with their spouses and significant others. The grandchildren were sequestered to a corner of the large dining room at their own table. After Mr. Helton said grace, the chatter started as the various food items were passed around. As much as the evening was about Jana and her husband visiting, much of the conversation revolved around Chad and Gemma.

"So, where are you from?" asked Chris.

"Blackpool."

"Where's that?" asked Todd. "Somewhere near Astoria?"

"It's in the north of England."

"What do you do?" came a question from Vickie. "Are you an influencer? If you are, we <u>need</u> to talk."

"No," Gemma chuckled. "I'm a sports agent. Chad just hired me after he won his race in Miami.

"So, I guess we should've led off with this question," said Jana, "how did you two meet?"

Gemma looked at Chad as if she wanted him to answer a question for once. When Chad didn't get the message, she elbowed him and discreetly cleared her throat. That got through to him.

"Well," he began, "I met her in Daytona back in February. I was racing against her brother. After MorrisSport closed down, she recommended me to SportStream to drive their second car, and I got the job. I would see her every day at work, and we'd spend the afterparties after the race talking until it was time to drive all of the drunks home. From then on, it just snowballed to where it is now.

"So, when are you going to put a ring on it?" asked big brother Will.

"William!" scolded Will's wife. "Please excuse my husband's big mouth."

"No, it's perfectly alright," chuckled Gemma nervously.

She reached under the table and squeezed Chad's free hand tight. She hadn't considered that, and it scared her. It wasn't that she was averse to the idea of marriage or a family; it just wasn't anywhere on her radar at that point. Everything with Chad was still so fresh and new.

The ride home was silent. Chad knew something was up, and he was pretty sure what that something was. The silence was only broken once he had pulled his Ford GT into the garage.

"My brother, Will," he began, "likes to talk."

"What are your intentions with me?" asked Gemma. She figured if Chad was going to open the conversation, she'd get right to brass tacks.

It caught Chad off guard. He struggled to formulate anything that resembled an English sentence. Gemma stared at him with saucer eyes – big green eyes that demanded an answer. Chad felt embarrassed to answer, because he knew what he felt the last three months. He knew what he was thinking the last three months. Would it even be appropriate to tell her that he had envisioned their entire life together: the good and the bad? Would he tell her that he saw the proposal, the wedding day, the birth of their first child, the birth of their second child, the birth of their twelfth child, his retirement, spoiling their oodles of grandchildren, her holding his hand as he drew his final breath? He finally decided that honesty would be the best policy. He took her hand and stoked it as he spoke.

"My intentions," he began before taking a huge breath, "is to spend the rest of my life with you."

"Does that mean…" she began as she reached up to stroke his cheek.

"I have never been with a woman," Chad continued. "I wouldn't have pursued you if marriage wasn't my end goal. I wasn't raised like that."

"I don't know what to say," said Gemma.

"Is there something wrong?"

"No," she answered, "everything's alright."

Gemma began to weep. This time, they were tears of joy. Chad opened her door and initially tried to sweep her off her feet and carry her across the threshold. After an awkward glance from her, he decided against it and just ushered her into the house. That could wait until they were married.

That night, they sat close together on the couch as they watched *Pride and Prejudice*. He would have preferred the version with zombies, but he deferred to Gemma. Chad still couldn't get past the sappy love story presented onscreen even as he lived out his own. He paid little attention to the film and more to Gemma's reaction to it. He felt warm as he watched her bright green eyes brighten and her lips curl into a comforting smile. As the movie ended, she rested her head on his shoulder and fell asleep to the ticking of his grandfather clock, his trophy from his win in Martinsville. If this was what life with her would be like, then this unofficial proposal was worth it.

Chapter Fifteen
Monaco

On a normal Memorial Day weekend, Chad would have found himself in the pits at Charlotte Motor Speedway preparing to take on NASCAR's longest race: the Coca-Cola 600. Instead, he was in the Mediterranean paradise of Monte Carlo, Monaco preparing for the Grand Prix.

One of Formula One's most storied and challenging circuits, the Circuit de Monaco is a course laid out on public roads every year at the end of May. The narrow track, though filled with many twists and turns, provides little opportunity for passing. The only choices, then, are to either qualify well or take risks. Chad already knew what he was going to do: both.

After his back-to-back wins at Miami and Imola, Chad now found himself second to Nigel with only a twenty-one-point gap. The relationship between the two drivers had gone from lukewarm to cold to flash freezing. It then may have been a blessing in disguise that Chad was sent to the back of the grid for a gearbox change after qualifying on the pole. He knew he had a rough road ahead of him; but he also knew he had a world class team behind him.

The Monaco Circuit starts on the Boulevard Albert 1 er in Monte Carlo. The frontstretch ends abruptly on a 90° right-hander. The track then follows the Avenue d'Ostende before making a sweeping left turn before correcting into a long right-hander that passes the Monte Carlo Casino. This is followed by the tight right-hander known as Mirabeau Corner. Exiting out of this turn, the cars then head downhill before encountering the Fairmont Hairpin. What used to be a great passing zone is now only left to mad men like Chad Helton. After the hairpin, the cars encounter another right-hander at the bottom of the hill called the Portier. They then race through a tunnel before encountering the Nouvelle Chicane, the only real place to safely pass. After the chicane is the left-hander Tabac corner. Exiting Tabac, the field drives along the marina, encountering the Piscine Chicane. Soon afterwards, they turn away from the marina with a hard right-hander called La Rascasse. This leads to the final turn: Virage Antony Noghés, a hard right. The cars then pick up speed through the sweeping front stretch and do it all over again. Nineteen turns in all, and barely anywhere to pass. It would be nearly impossible for anyone to come from twentieth and win.

Chad lowered himself into his car. Before he had a chance to put his helmet on, Gemma climbed over the side and pecked him on the cheek for good luck. He was unsure of how he felt about that. Having come from a strict conservative household, the mere thought of dating was frowned upon. As the kids aged out of the house, the Heltons became laxer with their standards. Though he was given more leeway than any of his siblings before him, Chad still felt some reservations. He had decided that he would save a kiss on the lips for their wedding day, whenever that actually came. For now, a quick kiss on the cheek would do.

Gemma jumped back down off of the car and stood back as Chad donned his helmet. She stood there with her hands folded and pressed close to her sternum like a wife watching her husband going off to war. She knew how to play the role well, and Chad was all for it.

Once the command was given to start their engines, Chad was cut off from any other sound except whatever came through his radio. As the parade laps drew on, Chad squinted to see Nigel's car on the front row. After what seemed like hours, the field finally came to a stop as they took their places on the grid.

"I'm coming for you, McKenzie," Chad said as he pointed toward the first row.

Chad had never started in the back. He had never had to deal with traffic at the start of the race. The moment the light turned off, the back rows sluggishly began to move. Here, people were impatient. As they picked up speed, the leaders braked hard going into Sante Dévote, the first corner. This caused an accordion of cars that ended many peoples' day not twenty seconds into the race. A caution and virtual safety car were immediately called for that sector.

Chad was smart enough to hang back when the lights turned off. He slowly completed the first turn as he passed the ruins of what used to be multi-million-dollar race cars.

"That was a blessing," said Larry. "You're up to thirteenth."

"How lucky," Chad mumbled as he passed the Casino and picked up speed for Sector Two heading into Mirabeau.

Being in the position he was, Chad had elected to play it safe in these first few laps and let everyone else make mistakes. They had seventy-eight laps to complete this race. It was tempting though. Chad wanted to make a pass, but there was no safe opportunity. He felt like he was on the freeway stuck behind two eighteen-wheelers in a 62 MPH drag race.

"Forget it!" Chad thought audibly.

Going into Fairmont, Chad faked right, causing his competitor to move to the right to block, only for Chad to go left and hold on a little longer before braking hard for the hairpin. Chad exited the turn in twelfth.

"What the heck are you doing?" shouted Larry.

"I'm sorry," Chad apologized. "Guy was driving like a granny."

"Don't be stupid," Larry chastised Chad. "You can't afford to mess this up."

Gemma sat next to Larry in their paddock listening to the whole conversation. She rolled her eyes at Chad's lame excuses. It was almost endearing to her.

Chad advanced to eleventh through the chicane, and by the time he reached turn 19, he was sniffing out tenth. The first sector was still yellow when he crossed the line for the second lap. The last of the wrecks was being cleared away. Next time by, it would be all out. If he was close enough to another car, he could activate his DRS on the frontstretch, the only DRS zone on the circuit.

"No more risks," said Larry, "at least not until the race winds down. Just play it safe and be patient. We got one pit stop, and you have the fastest pit crew in Formula One."

By the time he reached Fairmont, he had caught up to the tenth-place driver who was himself battling for ninth. Chad fell in behind him. He hated to play follow-the-leader, but team orders were team orders. Upon reaching the tunnel, their downforce was hampered due to the lack of wind inside. There was no way Chad could even think about going for a pass here. The short seconds-long section seemed to take all day. Upon emerging from the tunnel, Chad saw an opening in the chicane and took it. As straight as he could keep the car without going off-course, he cut ninth and tenth off.

"He never listens," Larry whispered to Gemma.

Up front, Nigel was running away with the lead. Already a third of a lap ahead of second place, he would have already popped open a victory champaign if he was allowed to. Four laps in, and he already had lapped thirteenth place. Larry seemed unnerved, even though overall, he was in charge of the show.

By lap twenty-five, drivers began peeling off for the pits. Nigel opted to stay out on his hard tires. Chad was on mediums, and they were beginning to show their age. Chad nearly lost it going through Fairmont.

"Larry, this car is becoming a bear to control," he radioed as he flew into the tunnel.

"How long do you think you can hold it?" asked Larry. "Those mediums should last you at least until lap thirty."

"I honestly don't know," replied Chad. "I'm not sure if you saw it, but I almost ate it in the hairpin."

"Shoot!" Larry shouted. He had become accustomed to cameras and censors over the years and knew when and where appropriate places for profanity were. Here, on live television with live radio chatter was not one of those places. Larry crunched some numbers as Chad held on for dear life through Tabac. "We can spare a lap or two. Just hold on until I radio back. You got this."

Chad reluctantly obeyed. The next few laps would be all about survival. Chad was losing time as he slid through every corner. Lap twenty-six saw a three-second increase. Meanwhile, Nigel was still running away with the lead.

Larry kept his eye on his computer, closely monitoring the lap times. Chad passed by them again to begin lap twenty-seven. It looked bad as he was visibly fighting the car into Sante Dévote.

"Head's up, guys," Larry addressed the crew, "we're throwing hard tires on the 28 and adjusting the wing. We're gonna make this car fly."

Chad was running along the marina now. As he approached the Piscine, a steward showed him a blue flag. He checked his mirrors and breathed a sigh of relief. It was someone he had already passed on fresher tires. He could live with that. Soon, Virage Antony Noghés came into view.

"Box! Box! Box!" came the command on the radio.

Chad coasted into his pit box. Without any issue, the car was improved within three seconds. Chad bolted out and back onto the track.

"I've got good news and bad news," said Larry.

"Let me guess," said Chad. "I'm still on the lead lap, but Nigel's closing in."

"How did you guess?" asked Larry.

"What else could it be?"

"Well, I would use those fresher tires to your advantage," said Larry. "He hasn't come in yet."

"Do you think he'll go for a pass?" asked Chad.

"I don't know what good it would do," replied Larry. "You're P8, by the way. Someone else just retired, and it looks like you'll be P7 soon. We have someone else slowing down in Sector 2. They may call for a VSC, so watch it."

Larry was a clairvoyant. The seventh-place competitor came to a stop off-track inside the Nouvelle Chicane. Chad could barely see the nose of Nigel's car come into view as he exited the tunnel. The two cars drove with caution until they hit the start of Sector 3 leading into Piscine. He used his fresher tires to his advantage, leaving Nigel in the dust.

Now it was Nigel's turn to pit. The team prepared the red-letter tires.

"He's going for grip?" Gemma asked Larry.

"Yeah," Larry replied, "Chad will have a speed advantage. He's good at holding on even with hard tires. Not only that, but those tires won't last him until the end."

"What do you mean?"

"To be honest, Gemma," Larry began, "I don't even think our hard tires will last us until seventy-eight. He'll have to pit again sometime before the end."

Chad was now the fastest car on the track. He soon caught up to sixth and handily passed him in Nouvelle. On the frontstretch, he activated his DRS and beat another driver into Sante Dévote for fifth. Despite all the passing, he was still many seconds behind Nigel.

Around lap seventy, Nigel prepared to pit his car in one last time. Gemma watched the team again as they prepared soft tires. Soon, Nigel appeared at the entrance to the pits. Chad wasn't far behind, trailing in second, a feat within itself.

"Box!" cried Larry. "Softs all around," he instructed the crew. "We're going to do this back-to-back again like we did in Miami. Make sure they're the right ones this time."

Nigel slid into the pit box. His stop started out normally. All four tires came off. All four new tires were mounted. Three lug nuts were fastened in under a second. The fourth lug nut positioned on the right rear of the car did not go on. The tire changers air ratchet had jammed, costing valuable time. It was enough time for Chad to enter the pits and make up some ground. Quickly, another crew member tossed the poor tire changer another ratchet, and he torqued the wheel on. Nigel peeled out with about a meter to spare before Chad slid to a stop. Now they were on the same playing field. He was now three seconds behind his teammate.

"You got him now," said Larry. "Keep diggin'. You got good tires and eight to go."

Neither Chad nor Nigel was stupid. They knew not to take unnecessary risks. Where Chad passed recklessly in the hairpin, he followed Nigel slowly. When they came to Nouvelle, he attempted an overtake, but Nigel knew it was coming and blocked him easily. On the seventy-first lap, Nigel was unable to repeat his block in the chicane, and Chad passed him for the lead.

"If he wants to play," thought Nigel.

The next few laps were a cautious game of cat and mouse, the lead constantly changing whenever they encountered the Nouvelle Chicane. On the seventy-seventh lap, Nigel once again passed Chad in the chicane.

Crossing the line one final time, the gloves came off. Chad used his DRS to pass Nigel on the outside. He outbraked him in Sante Dévote. It was almost too easy. Now it was Nigel's turn. He crowded Chad out of the Casino turn and retook first. Chad was having none of that. He rode right up onto the rear of Nigel's car in Mirabeau. The right rear tire rubbed the edge of Chad's front wing. The crowd cringed at what could have easily turned into a disaster. Chad never flinched. He crossed behind and beat Nigel into the Fairmont Hairpin. He then crossed over in front of Nigel and blocked him in the Portier. They raced through the tunnel, the V6 mills echoing off the walls.

Nigel was livid. This was impossible! Nobody starts in the back and makes his way to the front, especially at Monaco. Yet, here was Chad beating him. Nigel barely let off the brakes as he flew through the chicane and retook first. He didn't care anymore. Through Tabac and the Piscine, he made his car two lanes wide. Chad again rode up on Nigel's rear. It was time to play intimidation. Chad's front wing again made light contact with Nigel's rear wheels, lightly damaging the wing. Going into La Rascasse, Nigel seemed like he was going to take it all.

What happened next would be played and replayed all over the world for generations to come. More than Chastain's Hail Melon or Hamilton's seventh championship, this moment would become clickbait for millions if not billions, especially due to SportStream's involvement. Going into Virage Antony Noghés, Chad pushed too hard. Nigel hit the brakes as you do, but Chad braked too late. It was impossible to avoid the inevitable. Nigel was right in Chad's path when Chad's machine rode up underneath Nigel's rear wheels. The two cars were carried by their momentum away from the turn and straight into the wall at 90 MPH. Their vehicles totaled, the two teammates could only helplessly watch as Gerardo Lopez caught the lucky break and safely made it around the corner and on to his second win of the season.

Chad and Nigel climbed out of their cars. Both drivers were furious at each other. Chad removed his helmet and approached Nigel. He was angry, but he also knew that there had to be a diplomatic solution. Nigel did not agree. He, rather, used his preferred method of decking his competition. Chad's reflexes had improved since their last encounter, and he ducked. He spun around and lobbed his helmet straight at Nigel's face.

Initially, the cameras were trained on the winner and the other two top three finishers on the podium. That lasted all of twenty seconds as one by one, the crowd noticed the brawl taking place in turn nineteen.

By the time race stewards made it to the turn, both Chad and Nigel were bloody and bruised. Despite this, they were still throwing punches. They were so close to victory, and it was taken away by a mutual act of recklessness.

The pit crew also rushed to the scene to break up the fight, but that instead had the opposite effect. What started with Noodle grabbing for Chad somehow ended with a different crew member's fist in his face. The stabilizer returned the favor. Now the brawl had gotten out of hand. The stewards could no longer control the chaos. Soon, the police arrived. They meant business. Many crew members were led away in cuffs to cool off in the police van.

SportStream cut their broadcast short as Colin Singleton watched the disaster unfold. That mattered little to the millions of subscribers as they logged onto the internet and found videos already posted of the undignified act.

In the police van, Chad was handed an ice pack for his left cheek. Larry, who had wisely stayed out of it, hopped in and took a seat next to him.

"We're screwed," he told Chad after a long silence. "You know that, right?"

Chad stared at him like it was a no-brainer.

"I didn't start it," said Chad.

"No," said Larry, "but you didn't have to get out and try and talk to him either."

"What are you? My dad? Where's Gemma?"

"Talking to the reporters. Trying to clean up your mess."

"She's the one," groaned Chad through the pain.

"You really don't want your woman cleaning up after everything you do," said Larry. "Anyway, this is probably too big for her to clear up. I have a feeling we're in for a lecture." Larry sighed after this. "Well, at least it was a good race. We at least know you can come from the back at Monaco and win. Well, obviously, you didn't win; but you could have."

Just then, Gemma showed up at the van. Gone was the sweet angelic face of a homemaker watching the love of her life head out to battle. What replaced it was a look of disdain and fury that Chad found oddly attractive.

"Hi, babe," he said as he waved his free hand.

"I'm not cleaning up your messes when we get married," she sternly told him.

"Told you," joked Larry.

"You think this is funny? I had reporters asking me all sorts of stupid questions. 'Why aren't you representing your brother?' 'Why did he throw the first punch?' 'Why did Chad Helton get out of the car and approach him?' 'Could they have done anything different?'"

Chad felt for her. He really did. He even felt bad for being so attracted to her at this moment. He tried his best to keep a stern face on as well. This was serious. He may have not thrown the first punch, but he was in many ways responsible whether it be for reckless driving or just not avoiding it altogether.

"Anyway," continued Gemma, "Mr. Singleton called me. There's a mandatory all-team meeting on Tuesday."

Chad and Larry looked at each other knowing what this meant.

Chapter Sixteen
The Big Boss

Colin Singleton was a busy man. In addition to running the SportStream app, he owned a hotel chain, part interest in a diesel-electric truck startup, and an international airline. The SportStream Formula One team was just one of the many sports subsidiaries of the SportStream conglomerate, and he owned all of it.

SportStream held all-team meetings every Tuesday that followed a race. Usually, Lars Ströh would chair the meetings, being the team principle. If Mr. Singleton attended, it was always by video call. He was a busy man.

This time, Mr. Singleton was there in the flesh long before the first employee arrived. He meant business today. There was no denying that. He was solemn, but behind the mask was a man holding back a torrent of rage.

Chad took a seat between Larry and Gemma. Gemma took Chad's right hand as a show of support. He knew he was in trouble. He could only take solace in the fact that Nigel was also in trouble and probably worse.

As the last few employees trickled in, Mr. Singleton stood up. His short stature seemed tall compared to those who were just humiliated this past Sunday.

"Formula One," he began, "is seen as a gentleman's sport. Drivers take their quarrels out on the track and solve them with their skills. So it completely escapes me why the two greatest talents the sport has ever seen would act so recklessly at the tour's most storied and dangerous track. That's bad enough, but you know what was the icing on the cake? Those same drivers then started a donnybrook like two young schoolboys. On top of that, their crews decided it would be a good idea to join the fun. Did I also say that this was being filmed live and streamed all across the world to millions of televisions? Because it was."

"On behalf of the crew, I would like to…" Nigel began but was cut off.

"Zip it," snapped Mr. Singleton. "I'm talking. When I'm talking, you listen. I only want to hear 'Yes, sir'. Understood? If you want to act like schoolchildren, then the least you could do is raise your hand."

Nigel, who never showed intimidation was shattered. Chad and Gemma had never seen the look of shock now plastered on Nigel's face. He sunk back in his chair, almost cowering from the mighty presence of Colin Singleton.

"We were livestreaming three major racing events on Sunday," he continued. "For the first time in years, the Monte Carlo race was outdoing the Indianapolis 500 and the Coca-Cola 600. We were getting exposure. That was our team being shown on twenty million screens. I would have loved to say we were beating out Indy and NASCAR."

Mr. Singleton paused here. The whole room quickly figured out what this meant.

"In what universe on God's green earth or whoever deity you do or don't worship is it acceptable to leave your wrecked vehicle and start brawling? When the whole world is watching, I just want to know what possesses you people to do something like that. Grown adult men forget they're not animals. Are you animals? I don't think so. This isn't some good ol' boy stadium stock car race in the middle of Kissin' Cousin, Alabama. I would only slightly, but only a miniscule amount, expect that from Chad. That's his background. I know they have a 'boys, have at it' policy in NASCAR. But you, Nigel, no. A professional driver who has worked his way up and has proven himself in Formula One? It's beyond ridiculous."

Nigel sunk in his seat even further at being publicly called out for his transgressions. There was only so far he could sink in that chair. It would only get worse form here.

"Nigel McKenzie, I hired you because you were top talent. You've won multiple championships across FIA competition. I'm paying you top dollar to race in my equipment because the results speak for themselves. I see that. You've proven your talents time and again. However, Lars here tells me you've got it in your brain that because you're the primary driver that you're entitled to every win. That's not how this works, and a professional like you should know that. I hired Chad because he's top talent. He gets results. He's a quick learner. On top of that, you spoke very highly of him not three months ago. Then, I hear that you wrecked my conference room after beating the living daylights out of him. And for what? Because he likes your sister? Listen, I don't care that you beat him. No offense, Chad; I'd be overprotective of my sister too. But you did $7500 in damage to my personal property. It was $7500 that you didn't have to pay. It's $7500 I could've invested into this team that now has to go to repair a conference room because my drivers can't keep their hands to theirselves."

Chad gave Gemma a knowing glance.

"And you, Chad," Mr. Singleton now turned his conversation toward the secondary, "you take too many risks with my equipment. I know I'm not there every week or know the technical ins and outs of these cars, but I know you can't go beating and banging them around. They're fragile, and they cost a fortune which you don't have to shell out every race. Do you know how I got my money? It wasn't from wasting it on replacing and repairing equipment every week, I'll tell you that."

Gemma squeezed Chad's hand even harder. Mr. Singleton had seemed such a pleasant man to talk to three months before. Now, he genuinely scared her. Even so, she could tell that he was going relatively easy on her boyfriend.

"Chad, you caused that wreck on Sunday. You made contact with Nigel twice on that final lap. He was racing clean. If you can't make a clean pass, then don't make one at all."

Now came time for the real meat of the monologue.

"Sunday was to be a day of triumph for our team. We would've won Monaco. To top it off, we could've potentially had a car come from the back and win at Monaco or at least take second. That never happens there. Instead, you two turned SportStream into the laughingstock of the motorsports world. I have other sports teams I sponsor questioning whether or not they want our logo on their kit after the race. I've been on the phone constantly reassuring them I didn't hire a bunch of jackwagons to run my racing team. You guys want to keep it up? Fine. Do it. I have two great Formula Two drivers dying to make a break into the big leagues. I can ruin anyone in this room, and that's just the fact. I will bury you so low that you won't even be able to get a job running the family fun center go-kart attraction."

Mr. Singleton then sat back in his seat.

"But I'm fair," he continued. "I'm benevolent. I believe in second chances. You think I want you gone? The FIA is asking me to take care of the problem. Were it up to them, you'd already be gone by now. They hate you at this point, but I don't. It helps to be their biggest broadcaster. I have some sway with them. You will both race at Montreal. You will lay off each other. Understood?"

Chad and Nigel nodded in agreement.

"I would suggest you pack for a couple weeks more," he continued, "because you will then be heading out to Le Mans. I've managed to get our company livery onto a Toyota Hypercar. There, you will learn how to work together and play nice."

Nigel raised his hand at this.

"Yes, Nigel," Mr. Singleton addressed him.

"Do you mean to tell us we're racing in the 24 Hours of Le Mans?"

"That is correct, Mr. McKenzie. You will learn to work together as a team. I expect nothing less than you guys standing atop the podium at the end of the day."

It was Chad's turn to raise his hand. Mr. Singleton nodded at him to speak.

"Who's the third driver?"

"Oh him? You'll be happy, Mr. Helton. He's from your neck of the woods: a Clint Larson. He's fresh off a winning streak in the WRC."

Chad was visibly excited. Besides having to share a car with Nigel, he couldn't see how this was punishment. Nigel could see the excitement on his face.

"Well, if that's all," Mr. Singleton picked up the conversation, "then I guess this meeting is adjourned. Gentlemen, enjoy Canada. I'll see you in Le Mans in two weeks."

As Mr. Singleton left the room, the team members stood up and began milling around. Many were still shaken from the tongue lashing, even if it wasn't directed at them. What further scared another part of the crowd was the way Mr. Singleton calmed down and politely answered questions of his drivers, even if they had little or nothing to do with that actual point of the conversation.

Chad and Gemma ducked out of the room. The room was starting to feel stuffy and claustrophobic. They were keen to get out of there to start making plans for their trip to France. Nigel caught up to them.

"No," said Chad with his back turned to Nigel.

"'No' what, Helton?"

"Now is not the time."

"I just need to know."

"Need to know what? No, I'm not sleeping with your sister."

"No, I know you're too much of a man for that."

"Well, at least we agree on something."

"Why are you so excited about this Clint Larson bloke?"

"Who says I'm excited?"

"I saw it in your face."

"Yeah," Gemma said, "I saw it too."

"I grew up going to dirt track races and church camps with him. He's a great guy. His dad used to race out at Willamette Speedway. He died in a freak accident. Well, that's what they thought until they found the car had been sabotaged. Chad won a rally race about a year later and was picked up by Toyota."

"How good is he?" asked Nigel.

"I'm not sure. I've never raced him."

"He'd better not drag us down," Nigel said bluntly. And with that, he climbed into his Aston Martin and drove off.

"Well, that was different," said Gemma. "He didn't threaten you or try to kill you."

"Still hates me," replied Chad.

"All the same," Gemma added, "I think he's sufficiently afraid of Mr. Singleton. He'll keep his hands to himself."

"Do you really believe what he said?" asked Chad.

"About what?"

"All the threats he made if we didn't shape up. Will he really make it that hard to find a job if we screw up?"

"I guess he has the billions to back it up."

"Great," Chad groaned.

"But I wouldn't worry about that," Gemma continued. "It's really more or less Nigel causing all the trouble. I would say you need to be more careful."

"You know, you're not the only who keeps reminding me."

"Maybe spend a little more time in the simulator, love, and less time, what do you call it, macking."

"I don't think that's possible," said Chad, raising his eyebrows suggestively.

"Look, I love you," said Gemma slightly embarrassed, "but you're not that smooth."

"So, France," Chad changed the subject. "Anything to do there?"

"I guess we could drive around the countryside," said Gemma. "We're about two hours from Paris, so I don't think seeing the Eiffel Tower is in the question. Anyway, Paris is rubbish. It's literally covered in rubbish."

"So, no real sightseeing?"

"Chad, like it or not, you're being sent to Le Mans as punishment. I don't know how that would be seen as punishment outside of having to share a car with my brother, but there you have it."

"So I'm just going to sit around for a week and stare at a racetrack?"

"Heck no! I am going to schedule interviews every waking hour when you're not behind the wheel. It's time the world got to know Chad Helton. No more snubbing the reporters. They're humans too, despite their behavior."

Chad pouted. He didn't really like the bossy side of Gemma, but he hired her. He was dating her. He didn't really have much of a choice.

"And stop pouting," she scolded him. "It's so off-putting. You have a job to do, so do it. No more excuses."

And with that, Gemma walked to her side of the Mustang. She stood by the door tapping her foot, her arms crossed and an impatient look on her face as Chad stalled. She cleared her throat. When Chad failed to move, she cleared her throat louder and at a higher pitch. That got his attention. He rushed down and opened the passenger door for her.

"I'm so sorry," he said. "It's been a long day."

"I know, sweetheart," she said.

"Sweetheart". That melted his sweet heart.

"It's been tough for all of us here," she continued. "I'm only pushing you because I know you can do it."

"I love you," said Chad as he stared into her eyes.

"Get in the car," she giggled as she closed her door.

Chad walked across to his side, tossing his keys in the air and catching him. He truly felt lucky. He felt as if he had hit the jackpot on the first try.

Chapter Seventeen
Old Friends

The SportStream private jet landed at a Le Mans Arnage Airport just outside of the City of Le Mans. Chad had made it a point to stay on his side of the plane as they made the trans-Atlantic flight from Canada to France.

Nigel kept to himself, peering over to the other side of the jet to make sure Chad and Gemma were on the up and up. He still felt some sort of protective duty over his sister. He himself had imagined over the past few months Chad taking advantage of Gemma, only for him to rush in and kill him; then he would carry his little sister home to his protection. He still dreamed of that even as they were estranged, even as that was his own doing.

As they debarked, a limousine awaited them on the tarmac ready to take them to the track. There would be no rest for them. The airport was nestled right up against the Circuit de la Sarthe, the 8 ½-

mile track the 24 Hours of Le Mans is run on. Upon their arrival, the three were led into the paddock as cars were making their test runs. A representative from SportStream Japan met them. He was about a bit shorter than Chad and carried himself with pride. He bowed as he introduced himself.

"Greetings," he said, "I am Tadashi Nahara, team principal for SportStream Japan. We are very excited to have our two brightest stars here in Le Mans to race for us."

"*Really laying it on*", thought Chad.

"If you wait a few minutes," Mr. Nahara continued," your teammate will be back around with our newest prototype: the Toyota SS020 Hybrid."

"Wait," said Chad, "did you say prototype?"

"Yes," replied Mr. Nahara, "SportStream will be the first team to pilot the new Le Mans Hybrid from Toyota."

As if on cue, the roar of a twin-turbo V6 echoed through the frontstretch as the new car appeared around the corner. It slowed down and entered the pit road, coasting to a stop in the SportStream pit box. The driver door opened, and out of it emerged a driver about Chad's height, just an inch or two shorter. He tore off his helmet, and Chad immediately recognized him.

"That was great," said the driver. "She takes those corners like a champ. She may need some more suspension adjustment in the front though. It feels a little light on the straight. Just see what you can do." Then he recognized his old friend. "Chad Helton!"

"Clint!" Chad shouted.

The two ran to each other and embraced as long-lost friends.

"I hear you're running the race with us!" said Clint.

"That's about the size of it," replied Chad.

"And who are these nice folks?" asked Clint, gesturing at Gemma and Nigel.

"That's my girlfriend, Gemma," replied Chad, "and next to her is her brother and my teammate, Nigel McKenzie."

"I see," said Clint.

"Gemma's the hot one in the dress in case you were confused," said Chad.

"Honestly, with the way things are these days, I'd be glad for that confirmation," joked Clint.

They were suddenly interrupted by another team member. At least, they thought it was a team member.

"Clint!" a female voice shouted.

The owner of that voice ran past the McKenzies and into Clint's arms. The was petite, about 5'2". She rushed so quickly past the three of them that all they caught of her was her wavy honey hair as she ran to embrace Clint.

"This is Eden, my wife," said Clint as she let go of him.

"You never told me you were married!" said Chad.

"We've barely talked since you left," laughed Clint as he wrapped his right arm around Eden's hip.

"So, are we going to look at this car or what?" Nigel interrupted. "We've a race to win, and I personally don't want to waste time strolling down Memory Lane."

Clint shot Chad a knowing glance. Their feelings about the teammate were mutual.

"If you have your gear," said Clint, "you should hop in and give her a spin. You have been around the Sarthe before, haven't you?"

"A year or two back," replied Nigel. "It'll all come back to me after a couple laps."

Within ten minutes, Nigel had changed into his firesuit and helmet. Clint grabbed his personal seat cushion out of the car. Each driver generally has a personalized seat that perfectly conforms to the driver's body shape and personal comfort level. In endurance racing, the car is shared between multiple drivers, necessitating the use of personal seat cushions that perform a similar duty. Nigel threw his seat cushion in and climbed into the car. He fired it up, and the crew closed the door for him. As quickly as he could make it, he was off.

"Ever race here?" asked Clint.

"Only in the simulator," replied Chad.

"I'm trying to get them to make adjustments to the front," Clint explained. "It feels like it's catching air in the Mulsanne Straight. You've seen what happens here, right? Cars flip backwards and cartwheel across the track."

"I'm sure Nigel will find the same problem then," said Chad.

As the two drivers talked racing, Gemma stood behind. That was until Clint's bubbly wife made her acquaintance.

"You must be Chad's wife," said Eden.

"Girlfriend," Gemma corrected her. "Girlfriend and agent."

"I'm so sorry," said Eden. "I just missed your arrival."

"I'm not bothered at all," said Gemma.

"I hate to pry," said Eden, "but how long have you known Chad?"

"About four months," Gemma replied.

They were again interrupted by the roar of the Toyota as it blasted down the frontstretch.

"See?" said Clint as he pointed at the car. "There! Look at that, Tadashi. See how the front is lifting?"

"Oh my!" exclaimed Tadashi. "Nigel," he called into the radio, "take it easy on the straights and box next time by."

"I concur," said Nigel over the radio. "This thing handles like complete rubbish on the straight. It should be doing at least three hundred klicks, if not more. Can't risk a blow-over before the race."

"I take it I won't be driving for a bit," said Chad.

"Well, hopefully we can get the suspension worked on," replied Clint.

Nigel safely made it around and brought the car into the paddock.

"I agree with Clint," he said as he climbed out. "The car can't take the straights. Front suspension needs lowered. Maybe more downforce up front or less in the back. I don't want to see the sky through my windscreen come race day."

"Well, while we're waiting for them to work on the car," said Clint, "who's ready for dinner? Eden and I have been wanting to try this nice little café in town."

"I'm a bit famished," said Chad. "We've barely eaten since we left Montreal. How about you, love?" He turned to Gemma.

"I could go for a bite," she replied.

"How about you Nige?" asked Chad. He tried to offer his future brother-in-law an olive branch.

"No," replied Nigel. "We're here to work, not to go galivanting off playing tourist."

"Suit yourself," said Chad.

"Helton," said Nigel, "if we screw up on race day, it'll be all you."

"That's a risk I'm willing to take," said Chad.

And with that, the two couples left Nigel in the paddock, waiting for the crew to finish their adjustments. Nigel watched in frustration as his two teammates seemed to abandon him for what he saw as trivial compared to their mission. He was determined, as always, to win and to get back into Colin Singleton's good graces.

Chad had never taken a moment to try the local cuisine in his recent travels. After traveling halfway across the world, both Chad and Gemma were famished and would have eaten just about anything. Even here at the café, the food consisted mainly of sandwiches. Wine was offered, and though all four were of legal age, they all abstained, Gemma mainly just not to be the odd one out.

"So, Chad," said Clint as he started picking at his sandwich, "Nigel is…"

"Interesting," Chad finished the sentence. "It's a long story."

"Well, we're here to listen," replied Clint.

"Do you know why SportStream sent us in the first place?" asked Chad.

"Someone said it was a team-building exercise?"

Chad let out a mocking laugh. It was loud enough to draw attention from the other patrons. He waved an embarrassed apology and continued.

"'Team-building exercise' is putting it mildly," he replied. "No, did you see the race in Monaco a couple weeks ago?"

Clint nodded in the negative.

Chad continued, "Long story short is I raced a little too aggressive…"

"'A little', he says," interrupted Gemma.

"I'm telling the story here," he chuckled. "Anyway, I roughed Nigel up trying to pass him on the last lap, and we wrecked coming out of turn nineteen. One thing led to another, and we ended up in an old-fashioned Daytona brawl on live television."

"Aren't you guys teammates?" asked Eden

"Well, they are," Gemma answered, "but my brother hates Chad."

"Why?" asked Eden.

"A couple reasons," said Gemma before taking a dainty sip of water. "First, Nigel feels threatened on the track. He feels that because he's the primary driver, he should just get the win over Chad. Second, he's an overprotective brother. He did Chad up a few months back. He doesn't like us being together."

"So yeah," Chad picked up the conversation, "basically, Mr. Singleton sent us over here to learn how to work as a team. What you saw back at the track was Nigel on a good day. That's the Nigel we want. He'll play ball if it gets him back on the boss' good side."

"I'm sure everyone has asked you," said Eden, "but how did you two meet?"

Chad and Gemma recounted the story they had repeated several times to family and friends over the last month or so. After repeating the narrative, they took each other's hand and stared into each other's eyes like they had been married for fifty years.

"Oh, they're so sweet!" Eden gushed.

"Enough about us," said Chad. "What has the great Clint Larson been up to these last few years?"

"Work," Clint replied.

"Forgive Clint for being so short with his answers," said Eden. "He's never been one to answer questions."

"He and I both," laughed Chad.

"Anyway," Eden continued, "Clint's been rallying for Toyota since the beginning of 2024. I just had our baby, so this is my first trip since then. I left him with my family so I could visit Clint here."

"You enjoy rally racing?" asked Chad.

"Never thought that's what I'd be doing," Clint replied. "Brian and I always thought we'd make it to NASCAR with you."

"Maybe it's best you didn't," said Chad.

"As much as I miss living in the States," Clint continued, "I love the travel I get to do. So many places I never thought I'd see."

"You and me both," Chad replied.

"You know, Chad, I honestly think it's for the best that our paths changed. Looking back on the last couple years, I wouldn't change a thing."

"No regrets?"

"Well, there's a limit to it. If we go back far enough, Eden and I have some major regrets. We wasted a year not talking to each other." He took his wife's hand here. "In the end, it all worked out, but it's a year we both wish we had back."

"Gemma," Eden jumped in, "if Chad ever misses a phone call, there's probably a good reason."

"So, change of subject," said Chad. "I guess we could actually get some work done while we're here. Might make Nigel happy. What can you tell me about the car? About the track? I mean, I've only done Le Mans on my PlayStation."

"Well," Clint began, "our car is a Toyota SS020 Hybrid. It's got a 3.5-liter twin-turbo V6 mounted in the middle and mated to a seven-speed sequential transmission that sends power to all fours. No clutch. It's a paddle-shifter like your Grand Prix cars. It's good for 700 horses. The hybrid motor can power up to 300 horsepower. She's good in the corners. In the straights, she still needs some work.

"Here's how the Circuit de la Sarthe works," Clint continued. "We start headed north on the frontstretch. There's a wide right-hander followed by two 90° turns left and right. There's the Virage de Chapelle, which is kind of like a wide left and then a right. That ends at a hard left followed by an even harder right. After that is another hard right-hander at the Virage du Tertre Rouge. This opens up into the wide right-hander at Courbe d'Antares. You'll fly down the Mulsanne Straight and hit the Daytona Chicane to the inside about a third of the way down and then the Michelin Chicane two thirds. The straight ends with hard braking into a hard right-hander at Virage de Mulsanne. The track opens up with some more straights and a wide right turn. It's followed by a mid-right-hander and then left at Virage d'Indianapolis, which you can guess where they got the name. Then there's a 90° left at Virage d'Arnage, a wide left, and then a series of esses leading to the final two chicanes right before the frontstretch. It's a little under 8 ½ miles and should take your around three minutes and twenty average."

"So, what you're saying is we need to get as much seat time in as possible?" asked Chad.

"Well, Nigel wasn't exactly making a bad decision staying behind," replied Clint. "We're pushing that car to its limits for over three thousand miles over an entire day."

"Three thousand miles?"

"And most of that time," continued Clint, "is at full throttle. You've done Daytona a few times, right? Well, it's kind of like that."

"All that for a day and night?" asked Chad.

"Exactly," replied Clint. "Likelihood is we'll each split six four-hour shifts between us. That gives us each eight hours. Although, from what I've already gathered about Nigel McKenzie, he'll probably do the fourteen-hour limit if given the opportunity."

"I wouldn't put it past him," said Chad. "He seems pretty desperate to go above and beyond."

"You'll also be racing at night," said Clint. "Now, I know you've done night races, but that was with a lit track. This car has headlights. It's a whole different story racing with headlights compared to big overhead stadium lights."

"Well, I kind of want to get behind the wheel now," said Chad.

"There'll be plenty of time for that," said Clint. "You should really rest this evening. Tomorrow, we'll head to the track, and we can get the car dialed in. I'm sure Nigel's fine with having the car all to himself tonight."

Nigel was not fine. He cursed Chad under his breath with every lap he took. As much as he loved testing the car, he felt betrayed by his teammates for abandoning him to do all the work. For several laps around the 8 ½-miler, he fought the car, trying to even keep it on the ground. He suffered a scare more than once.

In 1999, Mercedes-Benz debuted the CLR. They entered three of them at Le Mans that year. The cars had a short wheelbase compared to their bodies, giving them a massive overhang. This turned the cars, which already had a very low profile, into massive wings. Throughout the race weekend, two of the three cars caught air and backflipped spectacularly along the Mulsanne Straight. Though nobody was hurt, Mercedes-Benz wisely withdrew the remaining car before a real disaster happened.

With that in mind, Nigel took to the Mulsanne Straight with trepidation. Approaching top speed, he could feel the car shake and his front tires lose grip as the wind started to get beneath the car. It was no good. Their car wouldn't last a minute out here like this, much less twenty-four hours. Adjustments needed to be made. It took several passes and several visits to the paddock to dial in the suspension and aero before he finally had the confidence to take the car over 300 klicks, or around 185 MPH. After several adjustments and test laps, the hard work finally paid off. Nigel took the Toyota out and put the hammer down going down the Mulsanne Straight. As the speed climbed, the car stayed glued to the track. This was how a Le Mans car should handle. Once he hit 300, he tried for 330, or 205 MPH, the average top speed on the Mulsanne. The car topped out at 330 by the time he reached Daytona. Satisfied with his achievement, he brought the car in and retired for the evening.

Nigel spent the night alone in his hotel room. He sat in his bed, a bunch of pillows propped against the wall as if they were a car seat. He sat there, playacting a lap around the Sarthe. The race was all he could think about. He didn't need friends. They were a distraction. He needed focus. At this point, the 24 Hours of Le Mans was the most important race of his life, and he was for sure not going to let anything get in his way of winning this race.

"If Chad screws this up," he thought as he drifted off to sleep, *"he'll pay dearly. I'll make sure of it."*

Chapter Eighteen
24 Hours

Chad, Nigel, and Clint spent the whole week testing and familiarizing themselves with the car. With the suspension adjustments made by Nigel on day one, the car handled like a dream. Chad babied the car around the track the first two laps, but as soon as he familiarized himself with the track, he started posting lap times comparable to Clint and Nigel.

Three days before the race, practice sessions were held. Not only did they test the limits of the car, they also tested each other. Each driver would perform three flying laps. After the third lap, they would bring the car around, switch, and repeat the process. The goal was to get driver switches down as much as possible. This process should take less than a minute. With an additional practice later that evening and two the following day, the SportStream Toyota team had become a well-oiled machine

Nigel took the car the day before the race for a one-hour qualifying session. If any of the three drivers had the experience to put their car on the front row, it was him. Clint and Chad also reasoned that if he messed up, they'd be off the hook. Anyway, Nigel had spent so much time setting the car up, it only seemed fair and right for him to be able to set the qualifying laps. With a fastest lap of 3:25.21, he easily made it into the top eight of the Hypercar class, which would go back out again for another half hour for the Hyperpole Session. The Hyperpole Session set the pole position. Nigel, a perfectionist, came close to making pole. At 3:22.945, he had set a blistering pace, but a Ferrari beat him by three one-thousandths of a second.

Nigel stormed into the paddock and tossed his helmet onto a workbench. Chad and Clint stared at each other in amazement. Nigel never acted like this, even after a rotten qualifying lap in Formula One.

"He's taking this way too seriously," said Clint.

"He's that desperate," replied Chad. "I believe he actually thinks his job is on the line if he loses. I mean, all he has to do is stop being a jerk wad."

"So do we just roll out the red carpet for him tomorrow?" asked Clint.

"I don't know," said Chad, "but we need to talk to him before we race."

"Team meeting," Clint said bluntly. "It'll keep you off the hook for having to awaken the beast."

That evening, Clint convinced Tadashi to call an all-team meeting. Here, responsibilities, mainly driving, were divvied up.

"Regulations state that no driver can do more than eight hours," said Tadashi. "That being said, we will start with four-hour sessions per driver to cut down on time in the box."

Nigel raised his hand. Tadashi gestured at him to speak.

"So, are we being limited by team policy to eight hours?" he asked.

"Why do you ask?" Tadashi questioned.

"If I can do the full fourteen as allowed by the organizers, I would prefer to do so."

"Brown noser," Chad whispered to Clint through the corner of his mouth.

"It all depends on how the race goes," said Tadashi, "but for the time being, you will take the first shift, then Clint will relieve you. At the eighth hour, Chad will relieve Clint. That brings us to the halfway point where we will repeat the process. We keep it straight and simple. If any issues come up, Nigel, we will throw you in the car if you have time."

"Hope that seat cushion is soft enough for you, McKenzie," laughed Clint.

Nigel just sneered at the American. He wondered why they all were like that. He wondered why they couldn't take this seriously.

The next day, Nigel took the car out for a fifteen-minute warm-up session. It wasn't as if he needed it. He had already logged so much time in the new car that he knew every inch of it. If there were any untoward sound, he would be able to detect it and diagnose it in a heartbeat.

The race started at 4 PM that Saturday. A parade lap was held as the various teams put their work on display for the cameras. As with their Formula One and NASCAR efforts, SportStream put special cameras and telemetry devices in their car for subscribers to see in real time. As one of the many nameless and faceless celebrities waved a French Tri-color in lieu of a green flag, Nigel mashed the accelerator, leaping past the pole-sitter upon crossing the line.

Nigel wanted to stay out and away from any mayhem that may or may not happen behind him. He sailed through Dunlop Curve as the destruction he predicted happened mid-pack. As the field slowed for the turn, some drivers failed to brake in time and plowed into their competitors. Just like that, months of development, training, and practice were gone in less than thirty seconds.

Nigel made it safely through the Dunlop Chicane and expertly piloted the Toyota through the Esses. He maintained radio silence. His goal was to focus on the car and the race at hand. He blocked out any thought of what Chad and Clint might be doing. He reasoned whatever it was would only upset him. He flew off of Tertre Rouge and arced around the corner until it straightened out into the Mulsanne Straight. Here is where he met his first challenge. That Ferrari that started in first had caught up. He lined up perfectly in Nigel's slipstream. Nigel knew he would use Daytona to his advantage. He gauged the driver's intentions perfectly and threw in a block at the chicane. One down, one to go. The two hypercars powered down the Mulsanne Straight, accelerating to 205 MPH. The Ferrari tried to outbrake Nigel at the Michelin Chicane, but Nigel had raced against Chad enough to know that trick.

"I taught him well," laughed Chad as he and Clint watched the feed from the paddock.

There was one more short straightaway before they reached the hard right-hander at the village of Mulsanne. It would be like a game of chicken, only the two cars ran parallel to each other, and it was a game to see who would brake first. The Ferrari surrendered, and Nigel kept his lead as they cornered in Mulsanne.

"He's racing like it's the last lap," Clint commented.

"Did you expect anything different?" asked Chad.

"I guess not, but he needs to save some racing for the rest of us. He's liable to make us look bad."

Soon, the two drivers heard the roar of their car echo through the paddock as their Toyota appeared in the final chicanes. Nigel tore through the frontstretch with the Ferrari trailing a second behind.

"Looks like he's building his lead," said Chad.

"Well, it's only the first lap," said Clint. "We've got," he looked at his watch, "twenty-three hours, fifty-six minutes, and thirty-two seconds left."

"So, what do we do for eight hours?" asked Chad.

"Me?" Clint began to respond. "I have a little under four hours. I might go sit with my wife. After my session, I'll get eight hours before my second session. I suggest for us both to get as much sleep in between sessions."

Chad thought for a second and began to speak, but Clint cut him off as soon as he opened his mouth.

"Your cot is in the back room," he said.

"Have fun with your wife," said Chad.

"Oh, I will," replied Clint, "and I'll say 'hi' to Gemma for you."

Chad found the cot and laid down. He held up his phone over his face, dropping it on his nose once or twice. He seriously considered video calling Gemma, but changed his mind when he realized she would barely be able to hear him. That mattered little to him. She had sent him selfies of her and Eden on the front row of the grandstand. He held his phone over his heart as he drifted off to sleep.

Over the last few months, Chad had a pleasant recurring dream of living the rest of his life with Gemma. By now, it had become more real and less of a boy's fantasy. The dream seemed to always end in the same way. Gemma would speak his name over and over only to be replaced by someone else calling for him.

"Chad," Gemma whispered.

"Chad-san," came the replacement voice.

"*Who is it this time?*" he thought.

Chad opened his eyes to a frantic Tadashi.

"Chad, it's your turn!" he exclaimed. "Clint is bringing the car in after this lap. Do you have your helmet and seat cushion?"

Chad felt like he was in no shape to be driving, but he had very little choice.

"I'm on my way," he mumbled.

Chad bent back and stretched as he stood up. It seemed like every joint in his body had seized while he was sleeping. He slowly walked into the paddock with his helmet already on. He reasoned that it would be an issue if people could see how tired he was. It wasn't needed. The smell of the track invigorated his senses, and he walked outside to wait.

It was dark. That's the way things normally are in France at midnight. The headlights of the various competitors broke through the darkness of the chicane as they blended with the stadium lights on the frontstretch. Within two minutes, Clint reappeared with the Toyota. It was Chad's turn. As Clint hopped out of the car, crew members jacked the car up and set to work changing the tires and refueling.

"We're P3," said Clint as he high-fived Chad. "Make up that time, and don't tell Nigel."

"Ten-four," said Chad as he closed the door.

With the car serviced, Chad tore out of the pit box. He wasted no time picking up speed on the out lap. He cared very little where the other competitors were. His philosophy was to just set the fastest lap times. If he did that, then they should add up to a win. This would be difficult as the stadium lights disappeared as he set out on the main parts of the track. The Mulsanne Straight was well lit, but the forested section after the village was covered in shadows. At nearly 200 MPH, the prospect of a wreck appearing out of the dark was very likely.

By the time Chad made it to the Ford Chicane, he had caught up to second place. That Cadillac ducked into the pits, leaving only one car for Chad to pick off in the next four hours.

As the world slept, Chad slowly reeled in the Glickenhaus. By 3:30, he was on his fellow American's rear bumper. This driver had not raced against Chad. As they flew down the Mulsanne Straight, Chad brought his Toyota to within a centimeter of the Glickenhaus' rear. Chad watched for the brake lights as they approached Daytona. Within milliseconds of the brake lights shining red, Chad pulled out from behind and waited a second longer to apply his brakes. He darted past the Glickenhaus and sailed around Daytona, leaving a very startled and confused Glickenhaus driver in his dust.

By this time, Nigel had woken up. He watched the move on the paddock monitor and grinned in approval. It cheered him to see Chad use that move on someone other than himself for a change. Nigel had seen what he needed to see. He approached Tadashi.

"Mind if we switch early?" he asked. "It looks like he's running low on fuel."

Tadashi looked at his monitor. He crunched some numbers and determined there would be little chance of Chad making it to 4 without a pit stop.

"Box this time by," he radioed. "Nigel is ready to switch."

Chad kept the Glickenhaus in his rearview as he brought the car into the pits. The Glickenhaus followed.

"This is too easy," he thought.

As Chad climbed out of the car, he said not a word to Nigel. Instead, he ran into the paddock to grab his phone to see the latest message from Gemma. That's what he thought about the entire time he was out there. That was his motivation.

Chad laid back down on the cot. It was still stupid o'clock in the morning, and he began to feel the shock of his sudden arousal four hours prior. He fell asleep before his head hit the pillow.

Light came pouring in through the windows at 8 o'clock. Chad woke up naturally. He took a moment to reacclimate himself. As he sat up, he heard the noise of the pit crew as they prepared themselves for another pit stop. Again, he bent back as he stood up, every joint cracking and popping from the cramped conditions of the car and paddock. Following the noise, he found Clint embracing his wife as they waited in the paddock.

"Where's Gemma?" Chad asked, expecting his girl to be hanging out with her new best friend every chance she got.

"She's somewhere around here," said Eden. "I think she was getting breakfast when I came in to see Clint off."

As if on cue, the Toyota made its way down the pit road. As soon as it stopped, Clint pecked Eden on the lips and ran out to the car. Nigel climbed out visibly exhausted.

"How are we doing?" Chad asked Tadashi. Nigel looked like he had just come home from a warzone.

"Still P1," said Tadashi. "Mr. McKenzie is putting up a fight. Those Glickenhaus cars are much faster this year."

Clint rushed past Nigel, throwing his seat cushion into the car before lowering himself down inside. While he buckled himself in, the pit crew set to work refueling and changing all four tires. The pit stop ended with a crew member tearing a clear layer of plastic off the windshield, an ingenious way to quickly clean the windshield during the race.

As Nigel disappeared into the back of the paddock, Gemma appeared through the side door with breakfast in hand. Chad rushed to her and embraced her, nearly making her drop the croissants and coffee she had brought them. He felt like he hadn't seen her in years, though it was only about sixteen hours.

"Brought you breakfast," Gemma told Chad as she regained her balance from his bear hug. "Sorry it's not bacon and eggs, but c'est la vie."

Chad gratefully scarfed down the croissant, forgetting how hungry he actually was. He hadn't eaten since noon the previous day. He only paused to thank Gemma after he finished the croissant.

"Long night?" asked Gemma as she sat down on the bench next to him.

"I was only in that car for three and a half hours," said Chad. "Nigel really wants as much seat time in that car as possible. I'm almost more than happy to let him have it."

"Where is he anyway?" asked Gemma.

"You just missed him," Chad replied. "He's in the back sleeping. He kept that car up front for four and a half hours."

"So, is he done?"

"Technically, yes. Well, according to our original plans. He's allowed fourteen hours behind the wheel. He's had eight and a half. I'm supposed to finish the race for us and take the checkered flag, but I feel like I should give Nigel that opportunity."

"What's possessed you to do that?" asked Gemma.

"Call it 'Christian charity' or just a pacifier," replied Chad, "I just feel like it's only right. Of the three of us, he's put in the most time behind the wheel. He's taken ownership. Come what may after this race is over, I really think it's the right decision."

"While I think it's sweet that you're doing this and all," Gemma started, "are you sure you want to do this? I'm speaking as your agent, not your girlfriend. Do you understand the ramifications of this?"

"I do," said Chad. "I think given all that's happened between us, I think it's only right to give way when possible. It's one race that has no points ramifications for us. I can take it. Anyway, it's only fair."

"Your loss," said Gemma. "Just remember that my brother can tend to be an ungrateful sod."

"That's not the point, Gemma," urged Chad. "I don't care about his gratitude. I think I'm far beyond that point. I got over it the moment he threw the first punch."

"If this is what you want, you had better tell Mr. Nahara then," said Gemma, "before Clint brings the car back in."

Chad stood up and walked to Tadashi, glancing back at Gemma every three or four steps. Gemma watched as the two exchanged words, inaudible to her over the distance and roar of the competitors flying by. It was settled. Nigel would finish out Chad's four remaining hours if he wanted. Chad returned to sit back down next to Gemma. She rolled her eyes disdainfully at him, unable to believe he would throw away a chance at that kind of glory.

As noon approached, Clint began to falter. Miraculously, he kept P1, but his Glickenhaus rival was on his tail. Tadashi had woken Nigel up around 11 to make sure he was sufficiently ready to make the switch. He didn't need to ask twice. Nigel sprang off of the cot and was up and about as if he had consumed a whole pot of coffee. Gemma secretly scowled at her brother as he paced around, mentally preparing himself.

"Box anytime now," Tadashi said to Clint.

"With pleasure," said Clint. "Track feels like crap. Car feels like crap. Driver feels like crap."

Chad observed Nigel waiting on the edge of the pit box for Clint to bring the car around. He almost pictured his teammate as a young child waiting on the curb for the school bus on his first day of school. Nigel could usually be described as lacking a personality. He was just Nigel, calm and cool Nigel. The anticipation for this opportunity was visible. As Clint brought the Toyota to a stop, Nigel wasted no time jumping the wall and bolting across the car to the door. He was there before Clint had an opportunity to open said door. Nigel set a personal record for buckling himself as the team continued to service the car. He would later describe an itching sensation as he waited. It only went away the moment the crew let the car down. He tore out of the pits P4. Not a good look, but could improve depending on pit strategy.

By one o'clock, the field had dwindled down quite a bit. Of sixty-five entries, only thirty-eight remained. Whether by accident, collision, or mechanical trouble, to keep a car running at full throttle for a whole day is a nearly-impossible feat. Many cars that enter are just simply not up to the task. What did this mean for Nigel? It meant less obstructions. It also meant less obstructions for his competitors. This in turn meant more opportunities for his competitors to close in on him.

By two o'clock, Nigel had made it to P2. Chad was still waiting in the wings for Nigel to decide to throw in the towel. It never happened.

As much as he wanted to be behind the wheel, he felt he had seen enough of the Sarthe and had told Gemma as much. Gemma, for her part, still felt Chad was making a stupid decision no matter how much Chad reassured her it was the right call.

With one hour to go, Nigel had P1 in his sights. He wanted that win. Second wouldn't do. He had come here to show Mr. Singleton that he wasn't just being handed advantages and wins. He had already proven that he could play nice, even if it was just lip service. None of that would do. He had to pass that Glickenhaus.

Trouble appeared on the horizon with thirty minutes to go. Nigel shifted down into second at the end of the Mulsanne Straight. The only problem was when he hit second, the only thing he got was the loud grinding of gears. He now had two neutrals. He said not a word, but everyone in the paddock could tell something was wrong.

"Talk to me, McKenzie," said Tadashi into the radio. No answer. "You're falling off."

What makes you think that?" Nigel finally yelled into the radio. "Bleeding second has gone entirely."

Tadashi uttered a four-letter expletive. Realizing what he had just done, he quickly checked to make sure his mic wasn't live.

"Do you think you can make it last?" asked Tadashi. "You're full throttle through most of the lap. It's less than ten to go."

"I came here to win," said Nigel. "Sod the gearbox! I'm going for it. I think I know what I can do."

Nigel flew by the paddock, now picking up speed.

"*I can do this,*" he thought. "*What's eight or nine laps?*"

"Crazy mongrel!" exclaimed Clint. "He's not going to do what I think he's going to do."

"What's that?" asked Chad.

"If he's thinking like me, he's going to drop it into first and then just powershift from first to third. He's basically going to force it past second."

"Is that possible?" asked Chad.

"I don't know," said Clint. "We'll find out. If it is possible, I'm not sure how long that gearbox will stay in one piece. That's a lot of abuse over seventy miles or so."

Clint read Nigel's mind perfectly. The Mulsanne chicanes were usually second-gear turns, but Nigel could manage them in third. The biggest problem came at the village turn. Here, Nigel would usually have to shift down to second, almost to first. These final few times by, he would force it down into first. His speed low enough to safely make the turn, he would then mash the accelerator, revving the engine nearly to redline before hitting the clutch and tapping the paddles twice to force it into third. It wasn't a perfect system, but it worked.

With fifteen minutes to go, the Glickenhaus was back in Nigel's sights. He had also put some distance between himself and a Cadillac and Porsche that were battling amongst themselves.

The Glickenhaus led Nigel across the line for the final lap. Nigel was now right on the Glickenhaus' rear bumper. The Glickenhaus was not going down without a fight. Her driver knew how to make his car two lanes wide.

"He's got him!" exclaimed Gemma.

"Now's he's just gotta pass him!" said Chad.

"Not just pass him," added Clint. "He has to put a few yards on him to be safe."

"Why's that?" asked Gemma.

"Because we started ahead of them," Clint explained. "If two cars finish in a dead heat, the car that started further back is the winner. That's how they screwed Ken Miles out the win here in '66."

Nigel must have had this in mind as he trailed the Glickenhaus down the Mulsanne Straight. Without that lower gear, these full-throttle high-speed sections were their Toyota's bread and butter.

"Muck it up. Muck it up. Just once, you nilly," he said to himself.

Nigel performed his powershift routine one more time as they approached Mulsanne. He was glad to leave it behind as he forced the car back up into third. He heard a faint grind as he left third for fourth.

"Bugger!" he exclaimed. "Tadashi, I think we've got another problem."

"Don't tell me you've lost another gear," groaned Tadashi as he shot a knowing glance at the other two drivers.

"I think I can manage," said Nigel. "I just need to find a line and try to make it faster than it is."

"You've been quite the magician so far this week," Tadashi encouraged his driver. "Go for it if you can."

Nigel regained his speed and closed the gap again. It wouldn't be easy. Upon entering Indianapolis, he could feel the strain as he shifted down into fourth. Halfway through the turn, he heard the grinding as he lost the gear. No problem. He shifted up into fifth.

"There goes fourth," he announced, still somehow on the Glickenhaus' tail.

He took Arnage wide in fifth. The engine coughed at the low speed, but it held on. Besides the final chicane, that was the last of the slow hard turns. It was here that Nigel started to make his move.

The Glickenhaus would not give him space. When Nigel moved right, the Glickenhaus mirrored him. When he went left, the Glickenhaus mirrored left. In the winding turns nearing the Ford Chicanes, the Toyota made slight contact with the Glickenhaus, though not enough to affect any outcome or trigger a penalty. It was enough to shake up the driver of the Glickenhaus though.

Nigel kept moving in and out. The SportStream crew left the shelter of their paddock and crowded the pit road, waiting to see their car appear around the corner.

"Hang it all!" Nigel thought audibly as they approached the Ford Chicanes. He hung as far out as he could to the right as if he was going to enter pit road. At the last possible second, he veered left, cutting across the turns and overtaking the Glickenhaus, never once leaving the track limits, never once shifting out of seventh. He exited the final chicane close to the outside barrier.

The sound of the SportStream celebration drowned out the applause of the crowd as Nigel took the checked flag three car lengths ahead of the Glickenhaus. A loud clunk emanated from the car as it coasted toward Dunlop.

"There goes the gearbox," laughed Chad.

Track officials rushed to the dead Toyota as Nigel emerged from it. Gemma observed that Nigel had never been overjoyed at winning. This time was different. Normally reserved, he howled and shouted like it was his first time.

The three SportStream drivers stood top and center on the podium as the post-race ceremonies took place. Chad and Nigel had accomplished what they came here to do. It was time to go home, but first, a celebration.

Nigel had ordered his normal tab of alcohol in anticipation of a massive afterparty at the hotel. Clint had plans with Eden.

"We're going into Paris just to see the lights and maybe have some dinner if you want to come," Eden invited Gemma.

Gemma glanced back at Chad longingly. She had admitted to Chad earlier in the week that Paris wasn't all that great, but she couldn't resist going to see it at night with everything lit up.

"I'm down with it if you are," said Chad. "I'm not playing designated driver tonight."

Chapter Nineteen
Hot Coals

Chad carried Gemma's bags to the lobby. For being so understated in dress, her bags were still heavy.

"There is no way she packed this much," he thought to himself before he dropped the bags hard on the ground.

"Careful!" Gemma scolded him.

"What's so fragile in there?" asked Chad.

"I still have perfume bottles," said Gemma with a roll of her eyes.

"Perfume is not that heavy," Chad argued. "How much perfume do you need? It's not like you bathe in it. You're not a seventh-grade boy."

"Funny," said Gemma, but she did not find it funny. "I also have a curling iron in there."

"So, perfume and curling iron. Got it."

"Thanks for carrying my bags for me though," she told him as she batted her eyes.

"Say, do you know where Nigel is?" Chad asked her as he drew out his credit card.

"No," Gemma replied, "but wasn't he supposed to be down here? We're all supposed to take t' plane back to Austin together."

"You don't think he…" but Chad trailed off. "I'll go check his room. See if the jet can wait, please."

Chad bolted to the elevator and rode to Nigel's floor. It was quiet. He found Nigel's door and knocked. No answer.

"Nigel, it's me, Chad."

He waited a second. Still no answer.

"Cripes," he Christian cursed. "Dang it, Nigel! We have a plane to catch."

Chad wasted no time. He drew out his phone and dialed Gemma.

"Hey, ask them if they can make up a key for room…" he paused to check the number on the door, "205. Tell them who I am. I'm on my way down."

As Chad exited the elevator, Gemma was in a fierce argument with the clerk. Apparently, it was against policy.

"What seems to be the trouble?" asked Chad.

"It is none of your business, Monsieur," the clerk snapped back.

"Actually, he's my boyfriend," Gemma snapped at the clerk, "and it is his business."

"Criminy," groaned Chad. "Look, we need a key for Nigel McKenzie's room. This is his sister. We're trying to get out of here. He's nowhere to be found. Has he checked out? It's that simple."

"But as I told the madame, it is against 'otel policy," replied the clerk.

"I don't have time for this runaround," Chad complained as he slapped down a €100 note on the desk. "There's another €100 when I get back if you just make me a room key."

The clerk sighed. "Alright, I'll do it."

"Thanks," said Chad. "You've been a great help."

The clerk handed Chad the key card.

"I'll be right back," he told Gemma. "Did you get ahold of the pilot?"

"Yes, they can wait as long as we need. But please, do hurry."

Chad again bolted for the elevator. Even through all the trouble he had gone through to get the key, he still tried knocking. After two attempts with no answer, he tried the key. As the light on the lock turned green, he slowly turned the knob.

The room smelt horrible, like alcohol and urine, mainly urine. Empty bottles littered the floor. The remains of a cigar lay half burnt in an ash tray, still lit but not in use. The curtains were drawn, only letting a small amount of light in. The room was a dark haze. Chad's gorge rose as he anticipated the worst. What he found wasn't the worst, but it wasn't good either. There, in his bed, lay Nigel, out cold and lying in a puddle of urine. Chad pulled out his phone and rang Gemma.

"Might want to take a seat," he told her. "It'll be a few."

"What is it?"

"Let me answer your question with a question. Is this what it's like to drive him home from an afterparty?"

"He's spent a few pennies, 'asn't 'e?"

"If that means he's piddled all over the front of his pants, then yes."

"Bloody Nora! I'll come and help."

"No!" Chad almost shouted. "I got this, sweetheart. Just stay there. I'll take care of him."

"Please, Chad, you're not going to hurt him?"

"I won't harm a hair on his head."

"Please take good care of him. He's still my brother and maybe soon your brother-in-law."

After arguing over who would hang up first, Chad finally hung up and set to work. He went into the bathroom and drew a shower – cold. He found the ice bucket and filled it with the freezing water. He had waited so long to do this.

"Wakey, wakey!" he shouted as he splashed the ice-cold water on Nigel's face.

"Wha' the devil," Nigel mumbled as he slowly regained consciousness. "Turn off that bloody light. Who the devil are you anyway?"

"It's your old buddy, Spring-heel Jack," said Chad sarcastically. "I've come to haunt you. Also, it's time to get up and go home. Look at this place. How many people did you have here tonight?"

"What do you want, Helton?"

"I want to go home. We're waiting. Get up."

"I feel like rubbish."

"Well, yeah, that happens when you drink yourself to sleep. On a real note, how many people were here? It looks like it was quite the party."

"Just me," Nigel mumbled.

For some reason, this broke Chad's heart. He already felt some bit of compassion on Nigel seeing him in this condition; but knowing he celebrated his big win by himself hit Chad even deeper.

"No one came? Nige, I'm sorry. Here, let me help you up."

He extended his hand. With Chad's help, Nigel sat up. He groaned in disgust at himself as he felt the damp from his diaphragm to his knees.

"Uh oh," Chad said in a gruff cartoonish voice, "Nigel made a peepee. It's everywhere. Oopsie."

"That was good scotch too," Nigel complained.

"It doesn't matter," said Chad. "You have clean clothes. I'm sure you can go without these ones. I drew you a shower."

The running water did look inviting. Nigel struggled to stand. Chad let his teammate rest on his shoulders. As Nigel stood over the shower, a massive throb of pain hit his head, and he fell in.

"Bloody Nora!" he shouted. "This water's so bloody cold!"

"That's the best kind," laughed Chad.

Nigel pulled back the curtain and started throwing articles of clothing out at Chad. As often as he had taken care of his drunk crew members, this new experience was more amusing.

Chad wasn't wrong. As Nigel acclimated himself to the water, he found the cold soothing and invigorating. He wrapped himself in a towel and stepped out of the shower. The headache was gone for the most part, but he felt he'd need some shades all the same. When he stepped out into the room, Chad tossed him a pair of briefs.

"Sorry, Nige," he chuckled, "I couldn't find your polka dot boxers."

"That's rich," mumbled Nigel.

"I think I've got all your stuff packed," said Chad. "I left out a shirt, some jeans, some socks, and everything else essential."

"Shades?"

"Right here," Chad replied as he held up some aviators.

Nigel sat down on the edge of the bed and started dressing himself. The two teammates sat in awkward silence as Nigel fitted his t-shirt over his head. Nigel could barely take it and spoke first.

"Why, Helton?" was all he said.

"Why what?"

"Why are you still here?"

"Because I wanted to make sure you made it to the flight."

"But not just that. There's more to it. You helped me out of bed, drew me a shower. You packed my bags for me and set out some decent clothes. I didn't ask for it. And especially from you, it's the last thing I would've expected. I mean, you really gave me the royal treatment."

"Nigel, we're teammates," Chad began. "Teammates are supposed to build each other up. I know the last three months have been tough. I genuinely want to be your friend. Up until this point, I've kind of just given up on it, but something inside me this weekend just told me to give you what you wanted – to treat you with respect. You earned it. You played nice. You worked your butt off all week."

"'If thine enemy be hungry, give him bread to eat; And if he be thirsty, give him water to drink: For thou shalt heap coals of fire upon his head, and the LORD shall reward thee.' I believe that's in Proverbs."

"I never took you for someone to quote the Bible," said Chad.

"We didn't attend regularly, but you can learn a bit in the Anglican Church," Nigel replied. "And you've done it thoroughly."

Chad was in awe. He didn't know what to say. He opened and closed his mouth several times before Nigel got the message and continued talking.

"I've seen how you look at my sister."

"*Here comes the bad part,*" Chad thought.

"I have never seen a man look at her the way you do. Chad, she's had several men come for her. They've all been trouble. There was one at Oxford who successfully asked her out. I knew him. He already had a girlfriend. I knew it would break her heart to lose him, but it would've broken her heart even more if she found out what he really was. I scared him away from her. I could see the look in their eyes as if they were undressing her in their minds. They were savages, Chad. Not you though. I mean, I'm sure you've pictured it. You can't lie to me. I'm a straight male. We all get curious. But I've seen something else in your eyes that I never wanted to admit."

Chad winced in his heart, still not sure where Nigel was going with this.

"You adore her," Nigel told Chad. "The way you look at her when she's not looking. It's not this hungry look like some animal about to attack. It's love. You are the first man who's ever truly loved her."

Chad breathed a sigh of relief.

"I didn't want to admit it to myself. Ever since our mum, dad, and nan died, it's just been us. I've felt like I had to protect her. If this trip has told me one thing, it's that my job is done. As soon as we land in Texas, you need to go to a jeweler and buy a ring. Seriously, buy that engagement ring and marry her. I know you don't need it, but you have my blessing."

"I, I don't know what to say," stuttered Chad.

"You don't need to say anything," replied Nigel as he stood up off the bed and donned his shades. "I need to apologize though. You've been nothing but patient and merciful these last few months. From this point on, we're teammates and brothers. Let's build each other up. If we work together, there's no way they can catch us."

And with that, they left the room. Chad carried Nigel's suitcase down. He found a cart and loaded all of their luggage onto it to push out to the limousine.

Gemma could see the change in countenance between the two. When Chad took her hand as they sat in the limousine, she noticed Nigel had no visible reaction. He just sat there as if it were normal.

"*What happened between these two?*" she wondered.

They boarded the plane back for the States. As they took their spots, Nigel no longer kept himself a stranger. Aside from the three-hour nap he took to sleep off the remaining hangover, he spent the lion's share of the flight with them. If Gemma were honest with herself, she kind of found his presence annoying.

Chad, on the other hand, was happy to finally have a friend in his teammate. Mr. Singleton's experiment was successful, probably more successful than he expected.

As they parted ways at the airport late that night, Nigel shook Chad's hand before he left. Gemma was puzzled at this sudden change in attitude.

"What did you do?" asked Gemma as soon as Nigel was out of earshot.

"I guess a little compassion and mercy go a long way," replied Chad.

Gemma rolled her eyes and lowered herself into her Miata. She looked back up to Chad as he squatted down to eye level.

"Is it over?" she asked.

"I love you so much," said Chad to Gemma, staring into her bright green eyes. "And Nigel knows it too. He loves you. He wants the best for you."

"You're the best for me," said Gemma.

"He knows," replied Chad as he placed a hand on her cheek. "Get some rest. I'll see you in the morning."

Chad watched Gemma's taillights as she disappeared into the night. He leapt up into the air and shouted for joy.

"Yes!"

He won the girl and the blessing of her brother. Even after the long flight home, he was wide awake when he walked through the door of his bungalow. Everything seemed new and refreshing to him. He lay in bed for three hours looking at engagement rings online, narrowing down his choices by her favorite color and overall fashion sense. He finally settled on a modest rose gold double band studded with small diamonds and an aquamarine rock in the middle. Everything was coming together perfectly.

Chapter Twenty
The Team of His Dreams

The next race was at Barcelona. It would be long stretch over the summer with the race in Spielberg, Austria following up a week afterwards. Silverstone, Nigel's home race, followed a week after that. That would be followed by the Hungaroring in Hungary and Spa in Belgium before a refreshing three-week break before heading to Zandvoort in the Netherlands at the end of August.

Chad and Nigel no longer held back during qualifying. Nigel knew Chad was coming for him and vice versa. Striving to beat each other's times, they broke the track record at Barcelona-Catalunya, meaning when one set a record lap, the other would break the record, then the other one would break that record.

No longer rivals trying to tear each other down, they faced a new enemy together: Gerardo Lopez of Team Auburn. Relentless, if neither Chad or Nigel were leading at the end, it was he who took the checkered flag. Throughout the summer, one could expect to see the podium populated by any combination of these three drivers.

Due to their tense rivalry over the first third of the season, they never paid much attention to the Spaniard. Now that they were working together, it became more evident. It was even more evident when they both beat him at his home grand prix. Third at home was not good enough. What was worse for him was he held no power to make any moves at SportStream, being an outsider. He would have to beat the two SportStream drivers on the track fair and square.

It wasn't like the rivalry between Chad and Nigel was gone either. They were friendly, even close, off the track. They started hanging out together. They would watch other races with each other and teach each other new strategies they picked up from their viewings. Even on track, they would help keep each other in front, but that would all change when it came down to the line. Neither of them wanted to finish second to the other; but instead of a cold indifference or even rage at the outcome, it was always a handshake and a compliment of a race well-run from the loser.

Though Nigel led in wins, he did not lead in consistency. Like Chad, his stats showed a "checkers or wreckers" mentality. Both drivers agreed this would need to change. Lopez led them. They had the speed, but they did not show the ability to finish and get points. Gerardo Lopez finished no worse than third all season, save for a fourth-place finish at Imola. The fight was still close, and if they kept up their consistency, they projected they could be fighting for the championship come the season finale at Abu Dhabi in December.

The constructor's championship race was a different story. The other Auburn Driver, Aldo Rosselli, struggled to crack the top ten most weeks. This left team owner, Mark Auburn, in a tough spot. After Austria, Rosselli was out and replaced by one of their Formula Two drivers, Josue Cardinas, but he failed to make much of an impression.

With consistent wins and podiums for both SportStream drivers, they led the rest of the constructors over leaps and bounds. With the team dynamic better than ever, they knew that consistent podiums, along with consistency from only half of Auburn, would win SportStream the constructor's championship; and they'd possibly even clinch it weeks before season's end.

After dominating in Austria, Chad found himself closer to second in points at Nigel's expense. He knew that the next race was at Silverstone, Nigel's home race. Though he couldn't care less about how Gerardo felt about not winning his home grand prix, he decided to let off just a little to allow Nigel win. Second place would have to do.

Chad, Nigel, and Gemma traveled to England early. A series of mixed emotions plagued Emily as she said good-bye to her new friend, and Gemma moved back in with Nigel. Rehired by her brother, she enjoyed the income of two clients.

Their first order of business was to visit Westminster. Apparently, some members of the royal family were racing fans. Nigel had already been awarded an OBE years ago when he first took the racing world by storm. Now, they wanted to honor him with a knighthood. On camera in front of millions of viewers, the king himself conferred upon Nigel the title of Sir Nigel McKenzie. Later, at the celebration dinner, Nigel's American future brother-in-law could not help but tease him for the title. As much of an honor as it was for the driver, he eventually just told Chad to call him "Nigel" or "Nige" and left it at that.

After their day in London, the trio traveled north to spend time at the McKenzie Estate near Blackpool ahead of the race at Silverstone. The McKenzie Estate was a sprawling 18th-Century stonework mansion. Financed by the initial successes in Nigel's career, the McKenzie family hardly stayed here, generally traveling around the world building Nigel's budding racing career. Kept by an army of groundskeepers, it was always kept ready just in case Nigel or Gemma decided to pop in.

"You never told me I was marrying a rich girl," Chad whispered to Nigel as they entered the foyer.

"What did you think I did with all this brass," chuckled Nigel.

Each of the occupants was given their own room in which to stay. Nigel was relieved that Chad was more than willing to wait until the honeymoon to share a bed with his sister.

This portion of the trip also served as a birthday celebration for Gemma. Nigel spared no expense on a large birthday dinner for his sister. Chad tried to chip in, but Nigel would not have it.

Their first full day in Blackpool, Nigel busied himself in the shop he kept on the grounds, tinkering on an old Ford Sierra he had kept since his sixteenth birthday; at least, he pretended to be busy. As Nigel worked, he watched out the window. He and Chad had discussed some plans the previous evening, plans that were to not reach Gemma's ears. As Nigel watched, Chad walked Gemma around the grounds. He was never one to stop and admire the beauty and architecture of a place. He was always on the move, but today, something felt just right about it.

Nigel peered out the window. When he caught sight of the couple, he quietly opened the door and pulled out his phone and turned on the camera app. Chad and Gemma stopped in front of a fountain that was the centerpiece in front of the palace. Chad took Gemma's hand and started stroking it. Even from different vantage points, both Chad and Nigel could tell Gemma was catching on.

"Gemma," Chad began, "I know I made a commitment to you when we went home to Oregon." He paused here to gather up courage to speak and not say something cheesy or stupid. "But I think it's time we made it official in front of God and man." He knelt on one knee here. This is the part he didn't think through as the gravel dug into his knee. He ignored the pain though as he said, "Gemma Charlotte McKenzie, will you marry me?"

Even though she was picking up the hint long before, the full realization hit her all at once, and she covered her mouth with her free hand in shock. Nigel still hid behind his shop door, taking a video of the event on his phone. Nigel admitted to himself that hiding and taking video like this made him feel like a creep and a voyeur; something he had intimated to Chad.

"I hope it's worth it then," Nigel half joked to Chad.

It was worth it. Gemma began to cry tears of joy before giving her answer. It was an emphatic "Yes" from her, followed by more emphatic yeses. Chad slid the modest ring on her finger, stood up, and embraced her. He swept her off her feet and spun themselves around in celebration.

There was something about the engagement being official that felt different to Chad. It felt good. He couldn't place it.

With the engagement secured, it was time for Chad and Nigel to clear their minds and race. Silverstone is built on the site of a World War II-era RAF base. The track partially follows the three runways with some additional track surface to complete the circuit. This year, it marked the end of the first half of the season. With help from Chad, Nigel won the race handily, though Chad collected the bonus point for the fastest lap. He wouldn't let Nigel off that easy.

Chad and Nigel found some respite with the two-week break before th next grand prix. Gemma spent her free time planning the wedding. Emily was more than happy to help. Chad and Mike tried to help, but eventually, they ended up in the living room, each doing their own thing. You could not find two more opposite men.

The one-two punch dynamic of Chad and Nigel's teamwork efforts gave Chad his fifth win of the season at the Hungaroring in Mogyoród, Hungary near Budapest. Gerardo remained consisted, finishing third. Chad was reeling in Nigel for second place. It was still anyone's season.

Nigel was able to create a little breathing room between Chad and himself at Circuit de Spa-Francorchamps in Belgium. Gerardo, on the other hand, was slowly inching his way back toward second, and a DNF would put both Chad and Nigel ahead of him. Chad felt some minor disappointment at not winning at Spa. This was one of the tracks he had remembered playing in his simulators. He enjoyed the sweeping roller coaster turns of the track, dipping down for a wide turn at full throttle and exiting that turn uphill.

"Well, there's always next year," he reasoned to himself.

Gerardo Lopez would finally lose his lead to Nigel McKenzie at Zandvoort. Though not a bad showing, his fifth-place finish lacked the consistency. So far, it was his first and only finish outside the podium. Chad would dominate the race, collecting first and the fastest lap. By now, the top three drivers were all separated by two points between each position. Rarely was there a points battle this close.

Formula One went to Monza next for their second Italian race of the season, the other being Imola. The third purpose-built track ever built, the original layout included an oval, something Chad was keen to try out. Unfortunately for him, the grand prix would be held on the road course. The frontstretch still partially followed one of the straights of the old oval, which was of some consolation to the former stock car driver. Chad dominated the track. It was one of the first tracks on the circuit that reminded him of the road courses he raced in NASCAR. He soared in the points, leading for the first time all season. To Nigel's chagrin, he was relegated to third in points after finishing P3.

"Hey, don't sweat it," Chad comforted his friend, now probably his closest friend, after the post-race festivities died down. "We were separated by what, four points? You're only, like, six down from me.

You can make it up at Baku. I mean, I'm not going to let you, but you can try."

Nigel slapped his friend's back and burst into laughter.

"Bet," was all he had to say.

Nigel returned to his winning ways at the street circuit in Baku, Azerbaijan. He overtook both Chad and Gerardo. By this point, the trifecta was miles ahead of the competition. Though over a hundred points separated third and fourth, a poll taken by fans showed they much preferred this three-way battle than just one driver dominating the entire season and clinching the championship three or four races before season's end.

The dynamic shifted again after the night race at the Singapore Street Course. Both Chad and Nigel were suffocating in their cars, even in the open air. The humidity of the equatorial city-state had barely dissipated as the sun went down. Dehydrated, the two SportStream drivers struggled to keep their cars up front. Even through his own suffering, Gerardo Lopez managed to finish in first. Chad and Nigel eked out second and third respectively. Gerardo was back on top with Chad and Nigel tied for second.

Chad and Nigel were drawn into wedding prep during their nearly month-long break between Singapore and Circuit of the Americas. A win at their home track was all they could both think of as they helped Gemma sort through engagement photos to use for the invitations. Being busy with racing, Chad had put off selecting his groomsmen. He knew Nigel was a shoe-in for best man. He made calls to his brothers and Clint, all of whom agreed to be a part of it. Gemma, on the other hand, had to carefully select from her friends back home, many of whom she had very little contact since leaving Oxford.

The close proximity of COTA to the SportStream headquarters made the trip to the track very short. The team all arrived on track in their personal vehicles. Chad and Nigel showed up determined to dominate. Chad was certain, though, that he would win. He knew this track. He had raced here a few times before, even won in a Cup Series car.

It was still hot in Texas in late October. The long summer had dried up all the humidity, though, making the heat somewhat bearable. That was the only gift the drivers would receive. The race was a slog. The circuit starts at the end of a long uphill straight. At the end of that straight is a tight acute-angled turn. At the beginning of the race, a pile-up is bound to happen. This turn continues to be a hazard throughout the remainder of the race. Speeds remain mid throughout the first half of the course as the cars navigate through a series of esses before hitting another tight turn. This leads into a long DRS zone. That DRS zone ends in a series of approximately-90° turns before a wide right-hander and two more tight left turns before ending up back on the frontstretch. Mistakes were made that day.

Chad fought all day to keep his car up front. He had help from Nigel. The Brit pushed his teammate around the track. He had not forgotten the favor back at Silverstone helping him win his home grand prix. Though Chad had never told him his intentions, he knew Chad could have done better. He felt he needed to return the favor. The SportStream cars crossed the finish line one and two after fifty-six laps. An exhausted Gerardo Lopez crossed the line in third, his own car barely holding together. Chad had now built an eight-point lead over the tied Nigel and Gerardo.

Chad would maintain his points lead by one point over Nigel, even with Nigel's win at Autódromo Hermanos Rodríguez in Mexico City. Gerardo would be relegated to third and trailing Nigel by ten points; that deficit only shortened by the bonus point he received for the fastest lap. Though he dominated all day in Mexico, Gerardo faltered with two to go, allowing th SportStream duo to get past him.

Nigel would get his first back-to-back victory since his threepeat at the beginning of the year at Interlagos in São Paulo, Brazil. He would overtake Chad in points, and Lopez would trail even further behind.

Chad would win in Lusail, Qatar, cutting Nigel's lead to just two points. Gerardo finished in third again, sinking further back. All three drivers were miles ahead of the competition. All three still had a chance at winning, and only these three had the opportunity to win this year.

It was this week that Gerardo would go on the offensive verbally. He was now in a must-win situation going into Sonoma in three weeks. Twenty points behind Chad, another SportStream win would make him mathematically ineligible to win the championship. In interviews with the press, he railed against Chad and Nigel. He complained that their strategy was unfair.

On the jet ride back to Texas, Chad was watching one of these press conferences on his tablet.

"Sounds like we've ruffled some feathers," laughed Nigel.

"He's saying he's going to protest," said Chad. "Can he actually do that?"

"It's too late in the season for that," said Lars. "You two have been doing it almost all year, and there's nothing in the rulebook against it."

"It's because," added Nigel, "he doesn't work with his teammate. He falls into the same trap I fell into. He's the primary, like me." Nigel still had to remind Chad that he was number two from time to time, just to get a little under his skin and light a fire under his friend's behind. "He has a struggling teammate, but he's so focused on being the most important man in the paddock that he doesn't develop the help he needs. Bloody Nora! Could you imagine a four-way battle?"

"It'd be like Atlanta in '92," said Larry. "Six men were mathematically eligible to win the Cup that year. They say that was the best NASCAR race in history."

"Well, as much as I'd hate it," Chad laughed, "I guess we'd better let Gerry win Sonoma so we could have the greatest Formula One race ever."

"You sit back then," Nigel joked, "I'm going for that win."

"Bet!" shouted Chad. "I've got more seat time there than you do."

The spirit at SportStream had never been better. Gemma watched the interaction of the team from behind the book she was reading, wearing a smile invisible to the men. There was cohesion among these people. SportStream was now living up to Colin Singleton's dreams.

Chapter Twenty-One
Thanksgiving

The Qatar race had been moved up by three weeks. In its place, the third American grand prix of the season was moved to the first weekend of December. This race was then moved from the Las Vegas Strip, after much protest from locals, to Sonoma Raceway in California.

This left another three-week break between races. Chad decided it was time to take Nigel back home with him and Gemma. Emily and Mike tagged along. This time, Mrs. Helton knew they were coming and opened up a room for Gemma. Chad had thought ahead this time, and asked his mother to furnish a guest room in his own house for Nigel, which she was more than happy to do.

Their first weekend in Oregon, Emily and Chad's sisters threw Gemma a big bridal shower ahead of the planned February wedding. The amount of doting and attention they gave her was almost suffocating. Growing up, her family had been limited to Nigel and her parents, occasionally spending time with her grandmother. Even with them, they were never this close-knit.

Chad and Nigel were more than happy to not be invited to the shower. Instead, they stayed at Chad's place and watched the NASCAR finale at Phoenix. Chad watched in amazement as the Rick March Racing Chevrolet, the team that bought MorrisSport's charter, crashed out in 40th before the end of the first stage. As he found out later in the broadcast, that team never finished on the lead lap all season. By Phoenix, their sponsor had left them. A not-so-surprising announcement came before the checkered flag dropped that they were closing up shop. As deserved as it was, it still somehow hurt Chad's heart to hear that news.

Chad's brothers wanted to throw him a bachelor party, but they wanted to wait until February. Nigel already had something in mind for Chad's bachelor party and was working it out with Will and Chris. He understood that alcohol was not to be permitted, though the two brothers would break taboo and let some celebratory stogies slide for one night only.

Nigel was able to experience the Heltons' church as Gemma had months prior. Sunday School was a foreign experience to Nigel. The college and career class had flourished since Chad had left. A group of young single girls took up a whole row. That morning, they paid more attention to the newcomer than they did to the lesson. After Sunday School, Nigel was in for another surprise: a full worship service capped off with an expository sermon. He decided he preferred this to the dry liturgy of the Church of England. He stayed for two hours after the morning service talking to the pastor, who was more than happy to wait for lunch to talk to his visitor.

This time around, Chad was able to find time to take Gemma to the Coast. Nigel tagged along but kept his distance. They started on early Monday morning and drove Chad's other Skyline, an R33 Sedan, up Interstate 5 to Highway 26, which led out to Astoria. From there, they drove down the 101 until they reached Brookings. From there, they found the closest eastbound road and found their way back to the I5 Corridor then back north, making it back home on Wednesday in time to clean up and head to Wednesday night church services. Chad celebrated his birthday the week after the Coast trip.

In honor of Chad finally (in their eyes) getting engaged, the Helton family decided to hold Thanksgiving at his house. The modest kitchen had never seen so much use. With so many people in his house, Chad wanted to just disappear to his shop, but the line of family members with an even longer line of questions never ceased. He would have even sat down and watched the football game with Mike if he could get away. Gemma stayed in the kitchen all day with the women, learning all there was to know about cooking for Thanksgiving.

With four o'clock nearing and dinner still not ready, the game was over. Mike had brought his football and was itching for a pick-up game. Chad and Nigel reluctantly obliged – Chad indifferent and Nigel with no idea what to do. Two teams of six lined up on either side of a makeshift line Mike had set up. A cousin of Chad's made some calls and hiked the ball. Nigel had lined up directly opposite to Mike. The former offensive lineman thought it would be easy pickings. He was wrong. Nigel was used to taking hard hits. Not even knowing what to expect, his reflexes and muscle memory kicked in when Mike clobbered him. The wiry Brit surprisingly stood his ground until the end of the play.

"Where did you play?" panted Mike.

"Nowhere," Nigel replied.

"You should seriously walk into an NFL camp and do that. They'd sign you in a heartbeat."

"Maybe in another life," laughed Nigel.

The game went on for another hour until Chad's mother called everyone in. The sun was sinking, and it was getting cold, but everyone was hot from the exertion.

"Have you ever had turkey?" Mike asked his new best friend.

"Never," replied Nigel. "I've never had a Thanksgiving dinner."

Once everyone had taken their seat, they all bowed their heads, and Mr. Helton asked the blessing. As soon as he said "amen", the loud conversation resumed. Plates were passed around. Gemma and Nigel had never seen so much food. Even after traveling the world, they had never seen such a feast. The traditional American foods were foreign to their British taste buds, a dry turkey replacing the greasy goose they were used to. Nigel watched as Chad dowsed his turkey slices in gravy and copied what he did.

Throughout the dinner, children from the kids table popped over to ask a parent a question. The interruptions ranged from asking to be done to asking for more food. At first, Nigel felt a little annoyed at the constant distractions, but he quickly got used to it, even going so far as to let little Kevin sit on his lap after he was finished with his dinner: a single yeast roll and a couple bites of turkey that Emily was finally able to get him to eat. To Kevin, he was now "Uncle Nige". The family just kept growing.

Soon came time for pie. When Mrs. Helton stood up to go to the kitchen, Gemma stood up with her.

"I've got something special for you," she whispered to Chad.

Soon, she emerged behind her future mother-in-law with a chocolate pecan pie.

"Your mum told me it was your favorite," she told him as she set it down on the table.

Chad looked at his fiancé in wonder. Nigel observed the look in Chad's eyes. He made the right call. This man appreciated and adored his sister. He trusted him fully. He knew he would treat her right and that his job was done.

After dinner, the men retired to the living room while the women cleaned the kitchen. Mr. Helton would play this game every year where he would insist on helping clean up only for Mrs. Helton to refuse him. She had her way of doing things in the kitchen, and she didn't want him putting the mixing bowls where the plasticware went.

"I don't come barging into your barn demanding to help," she joked every year.

After the women were done clearing the table and kitchen, they joined the men in the living room. Another Thanksgiving tradition for Nigel and Gemma to experience for the first time, everyone went around the room and said what they were thankful for. Some hemmed and hawed for a few seconds before reaching for something random. Others got emotional and very specific.

"I'm thankful for a good harvest this year," said Mr. Helton.

"I'm thankful we got that development in Austin finished," said Mike.

"I'm thankful that I hit half a million followers this year!" exclaimed Vicky.

"I'm thankful," said Chad, "for my new job and my beautiful fiancé." Here, he took Gemma's hand and stroked it, staring into her green eyes as they sparkled back at him. The family all let out an obligatory "aww".

"I'm thankful for Chad," said Nigel. "I know that might sound queer, excuse me, weird. Sorry, the dialect sometimes escapes me still. I know that might sound weird, but I never thought anyone could love my sister more than I did. I'm not sure if any of you outside of Mike and Emily know our history, but it wasn't always like this. I hated him at first. I was jealous, and I felt threatened. I thought he was coming for my job and my sister. Well, he was at least coming for my sister, but that's a different story. He proved me wrong and humbled me. In fact, you all have. Mr. and Mrs. Helton, you raised a good man, and I'll be proud to call him my brother-in-law."

From then on, the remainder of the family members struggled to top what Nigel said. After they were done, people started to leave. It was getting late. By 11, Mrs. Helton was ready to go. She had a bear of a time trying to tear Chad and Gemma apart, but she was finally successful.

"Three months," said Chad, "then we won't have to do this anymore."

Chad watched the taillights of his dad's F-450 disappear into the night. He already missed her. He went back inside and plopped down on the couch. Nigel grabbed two Mexican colas from the kitchen and handed one to Chad.

"To a job well done," he said, toasting with his glass bottle.

"I am never hosting Thanksgiving again," said Chad.

"Not in this house you're not," laughed Nigel. "Next year, you'll be in a big estate house like me."

"Why, so the state can gouge me even more on property taxes?" laughed Chad. "Do you know how much the State of Oregon charges for property taxes? Shoot, I don't know how people afford it and also manage to make payments. Anyway, I think we'll be happy here. It's not like we'll be in this house much anyway."

The two friends laughed more. It was just an all-around good feeling between the two. It was the end of a long day that went just right.

"Is this really all there is?" said Nigel, changing the overall mood with a sigh.

"What do you mean?" asked Chad.

"I mean, for me. Is this really all there is to do with my life?"

"Nige, I'm not sure I follow."

"I had the time of my life today," Nigel explained. "I experienced a close family. I watched them all up close. They're all happy, even when they're mad. Your brothers and sisters all love their spouses, even when they get, how do I put this, quirky, like your sister, Vicky.

The kids, they get on my nerves, but I can't help but want to hear what they have to say. That little child of your cousin's, Kevin. He worships the very ground you walk on.

"All my life, I've done nothing but racing. From the time I could drive a go-kart, I've been on t' track. I've always looked out for me. It's always been a race to the top. Heck, even when my parents died, I still went back to work the very next weekend. I've done everything there is to do in Formula One. I've got two championships under me belt, even more wins. I've helped build a rather successful team. Outside of that, I've won Le Mans. I have a NASCAR win. I even tried rally once. You might say that I've lived a full life.

"After seeing your family, I've come to the conclusion that that's not it. My life is far from complete. I want what you have. I want what Mike has. I want what your brothers have. They're all happily married and have kids. You're about to get married, and knowing how much you love my sister, you're going to have a whole nation's worth of kids. I want a little Nigel Junior running around one day. I want a family. No trophy could ever be as good as that. So, what, I've won races and championships. What am I leaving this world, Chad? It can't just be that."

"Why don't you ask someone out?" asked Chad. "There's loads of girls at the track every week. Many more would want to go out with you."

"Chad, you don't understand. You got extremely lucky with my sister. Somehow, you know it. I've been with many women. You've seen them every time I've thrown an afterparty. I've even spent the night with one or two. At the end, I barely even remember their names. I don't want just any woman. I want a relationship. I want someone to go to bed with and then wake up every morning knowing I love her even more. I want someone to mother my children. I am not complete, Chad. I'm not asking you to hook me up with someone."

"You haven't seen how some of those girls at church were looking at you last week," Chad added. "Maybe you should stay here a little while."

"Perhaps," Nigel pondered. "Or perhaps it's time to move on from racing."

"Nige, you can't be serious," pleaded Chad.

"I told you I've done everything there is to do. I've won every trophy. I've broken every record I could. I'm twenty-seven."

"It's not that old," said Chad. "The whole 'marry them young' thing was only pushed on us when Will got engaged. My dad was twenty-nine when he married my mom."

"After Sonoma, I think I'm going to put in my resignation effective as soon as I beat you and win the championship," said Nigel as if he were ignoring Chad.

"So, never then?" joked Chad.

"As if.," laughed Nigel. "I don't know if it'll be a permanent retirement. Maybe I'll just sit out a season and sign with someone else. All I know is I need to make some changes. Chad, I feel like I've wasted so much of my life. You know, you're my first friend I ever made. Yeah, all these years working with people, and I've only made one friend."

That hit Chad hard somehow. Sure, he considered Nigel his friend, even his best friend; but to know he was Nigel's only friend cut him deep.

"What'll you do?" asked Chad.

"I have so much disposable income," said Nigel. "I like your church. It's funny, my nan used to always tell me I needed to be in church and that I'd find a nice girl there. I think she's right. I think I might actually move here. Like you said, there's plenty of good women to meet in your church."

"Are you sure you want to do this?" asked Chad. "What am I going to do next year without you?"

"Train the next driver," said Nigel. "I'll still be around. I still need to make sure you're treating my sister right."

The two friends laughed at this. They stayed up late watching old races archived on SportStream. Neither of them actually went to bed, and they woke up bent out of shape on the couch. They never spoke of Nigel's plans again for the rest of the trip. The next Monday, they were back on a jet headed for Austin.

Chapter Twenty-Two
Sonoma

Sonoma was Chad's official home track. Though the Grand National Series raced in Portland, the Cup Series kept it off their schedule, instead racing in St. Louis that weekend. In his NASCAR days, Chad was closest to home here. It was here he visited with his family when he was five years old. He still kept the picture of himself standing next to a blue Chevrolet Impala with red flames, a neon yellow 24 on the doors and roof. It was here that his journey into racing began. It was truly like coming home for him.

Sonoma has had many layouts since its opening in 1968. The main course, which Formula One would be using this weekend, consisted of twelve turns. A short straight composed the frontstretch with the start/finish line right in the center. Turn one was a wide and flat left-hander. This opened but then very quickly closed in the uphill turn two. Two and three are unique in that there is negative camber in the turns. Instead of the track banking into the turn like any normal hard turn, the vehicles lean out of the turn, providing a unique challenge. This would be where the majority of the wrecks would happen as traffic always bottlenecks here after that initial burst of speed on the start. Turn three is similar to turn two. Turn four is a hard right-hander and back to positive camber. This turn starts a long downhill section called the Carousel. Turn five is another right-hander, though it is wider. This is followed by a banked left-hander into a straight that uses part of the surface of the infield drag strip. Turn seven is a hard right hairpin. The track then opens into a series of esses, which are all turn eight. Turn nine is a wide left followed by the right-handed turn ten. The section between ten and eleven is the only place for DRS on the track. Turn eleven is notorious as it is the second slow-down of the track. It is a flat hairpin just after the opening of pit road. This opens into another short straight and into the final left at turn twelve.

Chad had never raced this configuration before. From the time NASCAR started at Sonoma in 1989 to 1997, and again from 2019 to 2021, they used this configuration. However, from 1998 to 2018, a modified layout of the track was used. This involved bypassing turn four and heading into a soft right-hander that sent the course straight downhill into turn seven. This shortcut was called the Chute. By the time Chad had made it to the Cup Series, the old Sears Point layout had again been abandoned in favor of the Chute.

This was the first time Formula One had ever visited Sonoma, but it seemed a fitting place to go. The track owners had dumped millions of dollars into the track over the summer to raise it to a Grade 1 track, making it eligible for Formula One racing. This included adding more runoff and spectator seating as well.

Chad had never been to Sonoma during this time of year. The NASCAR race is held in June. By that time of year, the grass is dry and yellow. It looks like the middle of the desert. By the fall, the grass has turned green again, transforming the track dramatically. Chad hardly recognized the place.

Chad nailed practice and qualifying, and Nigel trailed not too far behind. Gerardo Lopez played third wheel yet again. He would have to fight hard against a SportStream front row if he wished to remain in the title fight at Abu Dhabi.

Friday and Saturday were clear and dry. The breeze coming in off of San Pablo Bay was enough to clear anyone's sinuses. Everybody in attendance was more than happy to drink in the late fall vitamin D. Then late Saturday night, the mighty Pacific reared her ugly head. Were it daylight when this change happened, the sky would have darkened within seconds. A heavy thunderhead rolled in. The stormfront battered the coast outside the bay, the twin peninsulas of Marin and San Francisco sheltering the bays contained behind them from the brunt of the storm. The rains were a different story. The track was soaked. By the time staff started showing up at the track, the rain had not let up. It was almost zero visibility, the impact of the water on the ground deafening around them. Team members started showing up around 9 in the morning. Even in early December, daylight is generally past by 7. Today, it felt like it was twilight.

Chad and Nigel sat in their paddock arm wrestling to pass the time. They had found this a beneficial pre-race exercise, preparing them to fight a steering wheel for two hours. Their competition was interrupted by an announcement from the higher ups. There was to be a drivers and team meeting in the Turn 11 Building at 10. Hopefully, they'd get some news.

Anticipation filled the air as drivers and team members filled the conference room. By 10, it was standing room only. The chief race steward stood up before the crowd and spoke.

"We have decided that the race will go forward as scheduled today," he said. "The people have paid good money for this, and we do not want cheat them out of it. We go green at noon. Do we have any questions?"

Almost immediately, the crowd began talking over each other, everybody trying to get their question heard as if they were the most important one in the room. The chief steward called on Nigel, the only one who actually waited and raised his hand.

"Um, yes," Nigel began, "Have we taken into consideration the safety of the drivers and fans? I thought I heard some thunder last night."

"Good question," the steward replied. "We have no lightning in the forecast as of this time. In fact, they are predicting it to clear up by 1."

"Then wouldn't it be wiser to postpone the race until 1?" asked Nigel. "Or possibly even until 2 so they can dry the track?"

"We feel," the steward explained, "that it is the best call and most beneficial for us to run the race at noon. There are so many moving parts, and we need to be able to work our schedule in with other parties. Do you have any more questions, Mr. McKenzie?"

"No, that's it," replied Nigel.

Chad could see the look of dismay on Nigel's face. It wasn't like him to not want to race. He had never let the rain stop him before. He knew he had to talk to his friend once they returned to the paddock.

"Brother," he addressed his friend and future brother-in-law, "you're not yourself today."

"How so?" asked Nigel.

"When have you ever not wanted to get out on the track as soon as possible?"

"I don't think it's safe," replied Nigel directly. "We've never raced here, rain tires or no. I mean, you know how this track is. We have no idea how these cars will handle in the rain."

"There's tons of run-off, Nige," Chad tried to explain. "It's not like you'll go flying into a wall or something like that."

"Yeah, but it's fast," Nigel argued. "You pick up a lot of speed on those esses, and the only place without runoff is at the end of that section. I don't know how much good that SAFER barrier in turn 11 will do when you're flying at 230 straight into it."

"Then we take it easy," said Chad. "Look at it this way. We know they'll pile up bad in turn 2. Doesn't matter what discipline, it always happens there. A couple of laps in, there'll hardly be any competition. We'll trade first and second and take the podium together. Then we'll take the fight to Abu Dhabi."

"And when have you been one to just do this for show?" laughed Nigel. "I know what you're planning. You'll make it look like you're holding back and then run away with the win."

"I would never," Chad feigned.

"Go spend some time with your fiancé," laughed Nigel. "She's probably worried sick."

"Hey, I'm serious though," said Chad. "Are you sure you're okay with racing today?"

"Whether I am or not is not for me to decide," said Nigel. "It's what I get paid to do. I signed the contract. It needs fulfilled. Like you said, when has a little rain ever stopped me?"

"Well, then break a leg," joked Chad.

"You too, brother," laughed Nigel. "Hey, whatever happens, I'm proud of you. Thank you for making this the best year of my life."

Chad spent the next hour with Gemma. She had caught onto her brother's change in mood. He hadn't told her his plans to hang up his helmet at the end of the season. If he had, she likely would have flipped and convinced him to do no such thing.

"I really don't know what's gotten into him," she told Chad. "The man has changed. Ever since we got back from Oregon, he no longer has that same ambition. He doesn't have that fire that he used to have."

"I really think he's bored," said Chad. "He's jealous. Maybe I shouldn't say 'jealous', but he told me he wants what we have."

"He has girls all the time," said Gemma.

"No, not just any girls," Chad explained. "He wants a wife. He wants kids. He wants a family. Did he tell you anything?"

"No, he didn't. Chad," her tone filled with concern, "what did he tell you?"

"He mentioned he's thinking about resigning after Abu Dhabi."

"No, he is not!" she almost shouted.

"I know, I know. I tried talking him out of it, but he seems determined to be done, at least for now."

"And what does he think he'll do?"

"He told me he likes it back in Oregon. Honestly, more power to him. I'm thinking about letting the house out to him if he does. Not like I get much use out of it."

"He is not retiring," Gemma said sternly. "I need to talk to him."

She stood up from her seat and set her eyes toward Nigel. She was ready to walk over and give her brother a piece of her mind, but she was stopped by the announcement from the officials. All teams were to line up and prepare for opening ceremonies.

Much like the countless NASCAR races and the two American grand prix Chad attended, the ceremonies began with *The Star-Spangled Banner* and ended with a flyover. The rain was still coming down. It was still dark. After the ceremonies, the drivers climbed into their cars. It was time to race.

As Nigel fumbled around with his equipment, he found some difficulty getting the HANS device tethered to his helmet. The old Nigel appeared momentarily as he physically let out his frustration on his helmet.

"Everything alright?" asked Larry.

"Yeah, boss," replied Nigel. "Bloody HANS won't tether. I think I got it."

"Make sure it's on good," said Larry. "Your neck alone can't support your head."

"Yes, boss. Thanks, Larry."

Chad and Nigel got the feel for a wet Sonoma for the first time during the parade laps. Water sprayed high off of their tires as they swerved in and out at low speed. With the safety car tucked away behind the pit wall, the SportStream cars came to a stop at the front of the grid behind the start/finish line.

Sonoma had not been fully retrofitted for a Formula One race. Still very basic, it was missing the arch above the start/finish line that housed the starting lights. Instead, like in a stock car race, a steward was perched above the start/finish line and would wave a green flag to start the race.

The moment Chad saw the green, he put the hammer down. Even with it pouring rain, his time from start to turn 2 was quicker than his old Mustang. He led Nigel up the hill and through the blind corner. Behind him, the predicted melee began. From P12 on back, the sudden slow and blind corner caused a bottleneck, and the resulting mix of speed and lack thereof caused a massive pileup. It was an easy choice for the stewards to make: red flag. Chad and Nigel brought their cars to a stop before entering the Carousel.

The stewards made quick work of removing the nine wrecked cars. As soon as a safe path was made, the race went green again, though they kept a virtual safety car in the first sector for the next three laps. Nigel was not looking forward to dealing with seventy-six laps of this garbage. That was three down now, seventy-three to go; and they had just got started with the real racing on lap four.

Nigel kept behind Chad. The plan today was to preserve the cars as much as possible and keep them in the lowest power mode possible without losing track position. The rain would aid that, since anyone would be a fool to be aggressive enough to overtake just anywhere at this track in this type of weather.

Gerardo was busy in third fighting his own battle. Josue Cardinas was actually competitive this weekend, no thanks to his teammate. Defying team orders, he decided the best option was to battle Gerardo for third. The Spaniard was livid that his Mexican teammate was actually racing him.

"Josue, you need to hold back," their team principal radioed. "Let Gerardo have the position."

"Tsk-agghh," was Josue's response. As if by magic, it shut the Auburn principal down right away.

On the other end of things, Gerardo was unleashing a tirade of curses and insults in Spanish, words that while to most people reading would have no idea what they were would still be too inappropriate to print.

"Gerardo, calm down," the team principal told him. "You're on live radio. The documentary crew is here."

To those still in the paddock, it was like a repeat of the early weeks of the season where the rivalry between the SportStream drivers was heated to the point of pure rage at each other. Larry watched as the Auburn team struggled to calm Gerardo down so he could actually make up ground on the SportStream duo. He laughed and shrugged at the mirror of what he used to be.

By the thirtieth lap, the rain had stopped, but it was still overcast. The pleasant ocean breeze from Saturday was still a billowing wind that buffeted the cars around the track. As the race was nearing halfway by this point, a few teams decided to pit and switch to intermediates.

"Do we come in?" asked Chad.

"You do not," replied Larry. "That track is still a lake, and those wets are still keeping their grip. I'll let you guys know."

"Well, let us know soon," said Nigel. "We're getting bored out here. I'm tired of looking at Chad's taillight."

Larry couldn't help but laugh at that. For the first time all season, he was thoroughly enjoying himself. He never thought a team could have perfect chemistry, but here they were.

All of a sudden, Larry watched the Auburn pit crew scramble to their positions. That was not normal. Usually, they were all prepared a lap before, taking their time to make sure they were in perfect position. What he didn't notice was the conversation happening over the radio.

"I'm bringing it in," Gerardo radioed. "This car is slower than [bleep]." The broadcast caught that expletive before it could make it out to the millions watching.

"Three more laps," the principal argued.

"No, now," said Gerardo. "I'm bringing it in now. I need intermediates or something."

And that's when the scramble happened. The team principal saw Gerardo's car leaving the track and heading down pit road. They found their positions just in time to avoid disaster. Two seconds stopped, and he was gone.

Larry could see the exhaustion on the Auburn principal's face.

"That guy won't last long here," he thought.

Back out on the track, Chad and Nigel were building an impressive lead. The next car behind them was Josue Cardinas, but Gerardo was closing in on him. Josue was fast, but he was still on old tires, and they were rain tires.

"Okay," said Larry, "Nige, I need you to drop back about four seconds behind Chad. We want to do this as safely as possible. Both of you will box this time around."

"Finally!" Chad shouted into his radio. "I'm sorry, but this car is handling like crap."

"Intermediates all around," said Larry. "You guys all know what to do. Gloves come off after this."

The cars appeared at the entrance to pit road. The team readied themselves. Each tire carrier prepped two tires together, one next to the other. With Chad three boxes away, they lifted the vinyl protective covers off of them. Josh Lopez stood in Chad's path, ready to jack the front of the car.

"Be ready," said Larry. "Here's that first one. Three, two, one."

Chad slid to a stop. As soon as he was let down, he bolted out. Nigel followed directly in his path. It was the same story. They reentered the track inches from each other.

"Miss Gemma," Larry addressed the drivers' agent, "did you get a time."

"Um, Larry," she started, "you're not going to believe this." She held up the timer.

"Holy crap!" he shouted. "That's a record, everyone! Nigel was 1.25 seconds, and Chad was 0.98. Good job everyone! Let's get down to business now! Take off your gloves and get at it!"

With permission granted to actually race, Chad and Nigel did just that. Chad was not going to let Nigel get off that easy though. Like his friend, he was here to race and win. Either way, either of them had a chance at the title once they got to Abu Dhabi. What they didn't want was interference next week from Gerardo Lopez. He was in a must-win situation. The stress drove him to anger. He pushed his car hard. There were still thirty-five laps to go.

Nigel activated DRS for the first time on lap forty-three. He switched to high power and effortlessly passed Chad before switching back to mid at turn 11. Chad was wise enough not to make a move until after turn three. He began sniffing around for an opening once they reached the Carousel. No matter if he was leading or competing, Chad loved the rush down the Carousel. It saddened him that he missed doing it in NASCAR by only a few years.

Chad found his opening between turns 6 and 7. He used the short straight to get into Nigel's wake and slingshot around him into turn 7.

He led through the esses and into turn 11. The two SportStream cars would trade off the lead several times over the next thirty or so laps.

Gerardo was closing in now. He had shaken off his teammate who finally decided to pit. He was of little concern now. He needed that win. Lap by lap, he reeled the SportStream cars in. While Chad and Nigel duked it out for the lead, they never saw the competition coming. In their defense, neither did Larry.

The mood inside the SportStream paddock was electric. Crew members were already congratulating themselves for the miracle they had just pulled off. Nobody had their eyes on the monitors until it was too late to warn Chad and Nigel.

"Shoot!" Larry shouted when he noticed. "Boys, you got a bandit on your six. Be advised. Work together. If he wins today, he's still in the running. Do whatever is legal. Someone may have to be a sacrificial lamb. I know both of you want this win."

Larry needed say no more. Chad and Nigel took their attention off of each other and turned it to Gerardo. Chad was leading, but he kept his eyes on his mirrors. Nigel dropped back a little to block. His car was now three lanes wide. They crossed the start/finish line and flew around turn 1. By now, Gerardo knew he had to back off hard in turn 2. The slowdown gave Chad and Nigel a little breathing room heading up the hill and down toward the Carousel.

Gerardo was back to cursing his way around the track. Every block Nigel threw was a new name Gerardo created. The insults became nastier and nastier. Eventually, the Auburn team turned their radios off. If this was his attitude, they determined, then he could fly solo.

Chad continued to build his lead. Nigel was putting up a fierce battle keeping the Spaniard out of the lead. He reasoned that eighteen points was still enough, and he could turn around and whip Chad at Abu Dhabi, win the championship, and retire a happy man.

"Keep diggin'," said Larry. "You guys are almost home."

By this time, the sun was out. Areas of the grounds had already begun to dry. The cars still sent up a massive spray as they circuited the track. A few times, Chad noticed the rear of his car kick out a little bit in the high-speed turns. He questioned with himself if he could hold on and win this thing.

Little did either of the three competitors know that the rest of the field was catching up. They were still a ways behind, far enough to where they weren't visible in the rearview mirrors. Tire wear was becoming a major factor for Nigel and Gerardo as well. Both were now struggling to keep their cars pointed where they wanted to go in the turns.

"Keep diggin'," Larry repeated as Chad crossed the start/finish line. "Lap seventy-five. White flag next time by."

Gerardo was on Nigel's heels. He brought the car within inches of the rear of Nigel's as they climbed up turn 2. It was do or die for him now. If he couldn't get past Nigel on this lap, he most certainly wouldn't make it past Chad on the next for the win. Not only were the gloves off for the Spaniard, but now he had donned the brass knuckles.

Chad held onto his lead through the Carousel, oblivious to the events behind him. His only job now was to win. He had picked up on Nigel's strategy a couple laps ago. He zoomed around turn 7, nearly losing it, and flew down the esses.

Gerardo found his advantage on the straight before turn 7. Using the same trick Chad had used earlier in the race, he found the opportune moment to slingshot out of Nigel's draft and overtake him in turn 7. This time, he wasn't as fast as Chad. He won the inside of the turn, but Nigel had the speed on the outside. Gerardo entered the turn too fast and faltered. His car wiggled, and the result was a miniscule collision. It was enough for Nigel to notice. Gerardo's front wing barely caught part of Nigel's right rear tire. Though they both felt the impact, it didn't seem major, more or less of a glancing blow;

but the damage had already been done. Had this happened in a stock car, it would have never crossed anybody's radar. They flew down the esses neck and neck. That's when disaster struck. The impact from Gerardo's front wing had weakened the sidewall of Nigel's tire. Nearing the end of the straight, the tire gave out, sending Nigel into an uncontrollable spin. The wet surface was of no help. He came to rest straight across the lanes of travel. Those trailing competitors soon caught up. With the spray off of the track still obscuring their view, there was no time to react to Nigel's stationary car. The fourth-place competitor slammed into the side of Nigel's SportStream. The car went airborne and disintegrated, the fuselage being buffeted again by another competitor unable to avoid the wreck. As the fuselage came to rest among the scattered pieces of the car, the engine, still attached to the fuselage, caught fire.

Chad, unable to hear much over the roar of his engine, was oblivious to much of the action as he took the white flag. For all he knew, Nigel and Gerardo were still trailing behind him and could never catch up.

"Nigel, you okay?" Larry called through the radio. No response. "Nige, talk to us, buddy."

"What goes on?" came Chad's voice. Larry had accidentally transmitted to both cars.

"McKenzie wrecked," said Larry. "VSC is out for Sector 3."

"So, I just need to beat Gerardo through the Carousel?" asked Chad as he exited turn 3.

"It looks bad though," said Larry, his tone filling with worry. "I can't get ahold of Nigel. Shoot! SportStream 88 is on fire! Someone get a fire crew out to SportStream 88!"

Chad's heart beat hard, and he pushed his car even harder. He drifted through the Carousel like a street racer on a Japanese touge and only slowed down as he entered the esses. If Chad hadn't had so many vivid descriptions of Hell preached to him growing up, this was how he would have described it. As he crawled through the sector, he saw the remains of Nigel's car ablaze. He took a double take and noticed his teammate, friend, and brother-in-law-to-be was still in the car. By now, the engine compartment was engulfed in flames. Those flames were closing in on the cockpit. There were still no crews aiding Nigel. He stopped his car and jumped out. Confusion from all parties involved followed.

"Wait," said a commentator, "it appears the leader, Chad Helton, has stopped his car and is rushing to aid his teammate. We've yet to see movement from the SportStream 88. He's reaching into the car!"

Gerardo cruised through Sector 3, passing Chad and Nigel as if he were on a Sunday drive. He mockingly waved to Chad as he sailed by. Chad was oblivious to his rival.

"And Lopez passes Helton for the win! He will be competing for a championship alongside McKenzie and Helton at Abu Dhabi next week! What's this though! Helton is reaching into McKenzie's car! Ladies and gentlemen, this looks bad. As Helton is waving over to the stewards, we may need to cut away. That fire is getting bigger. It looks like the stewards are approaching the car as well to aid Chad Helton in extracting Nigel McKenzie from his car."

And that's when the fuel cell exploded.

Chapter Twenty-Three
Living the Dream

It was a sunny August afternoon at the Helton house. It was the Chad Helton house, to be specific. It was one of those summer days that screamed summer – a day that unlocks all of those core memories from growing up. The concrete driveway and footpath leading up to the house were cooked under the hot Northwestern sun. Off in the distance, combines beginning the grass seed harvest could be heard working the fields. Mike, Chad, and Nigel were kicking a soccer ball around. Mike was actually enthusiastic to play a sport other than football. Kevin was sitting on a picnic blanket, racing a model grand prix car around in circles. At varying intervals, Chad or Nigel would leave the game to run over to a combination smoker and grill to check on the steaks.

With all of their energy exerted, the three men took a seat on the lawn furniture. It was then that Gemma appeared from the house. In one hand, she held a pitcher of artery-clogging, diabetes-causing sweet tea. In the other arm, a baby. Chad watched his wife in awe as he had millions of times as she poured him and his friends their tea. Gone was the efficient anachronistic business wear and the red-carpet dresses. Now, she wore a floral sundress and sandals. How would he describe her? Domestic? She looked domestic to him. They were an established family enjoying the normal ho-hum of everyday life – just boring everyday people; and they liked it that way. Chad worked full time, providing for his family, and Gemma stayed home, raising and nurturing said family.

Gemma set their child down to play with Kevin, the toddler showing his new cousin how to drive a racecar, or at least his version of how to drive a racecar. Little Kevin soon grew frustrated as Chad and Gemma's son only wished to eat the model cars rather than actually play with them.

"Son," said Mike, "be nice and share. He doesn't know."

Kevin crossed his arms with a huff.

"Maybe Mom needs to put you down for a nap."

"No! No!" cried Kevin.

It was funny to Chad. Years ago, he would have found the interaction annoying.

"So, how long for the steaks?" asked Mike.

"Nige, did you turn them?" asked Chad.

"I'd say about five more minutes," replied Nigel.

"Rare, right?" asked Mike.

"I'm British, not a psycho," laughed Nigel.

"Aren't those the same things?" joked Mike.

The three men laughed at the joke. Chad almost fell backwards out of his chair. They were enjoying the final few minutes together before company arrived.

"Nigel," called a voice from the house, "could you help me?"

From the house appeared Nigel's wife, one of the girls from Chad's college and career class. Nigel had made good on his plan to retire after the season. He took up residence in Chad's house while he hung out around the area and got to know people. He ended up volunteering as much time as he could at the church. This caught the eye of many of the young women in college and career, but one caught his eye almost immediately. She was a perky blonde with blue eyes and golden curls that tumbled down well past her shoulders. She carried a tray of Texas toast. Nigel rushed over to her. Now six months pregnant, she was beginning to feel the exhaustion of growing life inside her. Nigel, ever the perfect husband, gladly lifted her burden and carried the tray to the large picnic table they had set up. Now a few years removed from the fast life, Nigel had finally settled down to start his family.

As Nigel set the tray down, the first of many guests arrived. Chad's parents pulled right up to the garage. Having been orphaned as a teenager, Nigel never had any parental figures when he needed them. Owing to the fact that his sister was now their daughter-in-law, the Heltons took Nigel in and loved him as if he were their son. It was already enough for Nigel that Chad always called him "brother", but this was a new humbling experience for Nigel. Once the elder Heltons arrived, the stream of visitors never stopped.

"You've got the tires, right?" Nigel asked Chad.

"They should be here anytime," replied Chad.

"I'm just thinking," Nigel continued, "Millie wants the reveal at a certain time."

"He said he'd have them here by four," Chad explained.

The occasion: the gender reveal for Nigel and Millie's baby. Nigel, sticking to his roots, had convinced Millie to let him do a burnout in his Aston Martin. The tire smoke would billow either blue or pink, indicating the baby's gender. The problem: the specialty tires for the stunt were still not here, and the time was closing in.

"I'll at least get the car jacked up," said Chad. "You still have my impact?"

"Right on top of t' toolchest," replied Nigel.

Chad retreated to his shop. True to Nigel's word, his impact gun was on top of his tool chest. He soon reemerged with the impact, a socket, a floor jack, and two jackstands. As the party went on, he set to work, jacking up the rear of the car. He then loosened the lug nuts and pulled the original tires off. With that out of the way, it would be quick work throwing the special wheels on and getting them torqued down.

"Oi! Dinner's ready!" Nigel called out.

Chad rushed to the gathering spot. Nigel and Millie took their place of honor, sharing the head of the table. With the family gathered, Bill Helton said grace, and they started passing around the food items like it was Thanksgiving. Nigel had become fully Americanized. Aside from the accent, he had embraced the culture. After discovering spices, he had become a grilling connoisseur. The steaks were perfect and tender. They nearly cut with a fork.

"So, Nige," said Bill, "what are you thinking? Boy or girl?"

"I'm thinking a boy," replied Nigel.

"He wants a 'Nigel, Jr.'" giggled Millie.

"Well, we better hurry up," said Chris. "I need to know if I'm gonna be an aunt or an uncle."

"That's not how it works," groaned Chris' wife.

"It's 2027," joked Chris. "I can be whatever I want."

"I hope," said Will in a low mocking voice, "your first child is a masculine child."

"Please, Will, not here," scolded Will's wife. The two brothers were on a roll today.

"I hope it's a girl," said Vickie. "I can't wait to spoil her and be to cool auntie."

"Then I think we'd better steer clear of you," laughed Nigel. "All jokes aside, I'd be happy with whatever God gave us. You see, this is the life I've always wanted."

Chad's ears perked up when Nigel said this. It was going to be that same speech Nigel had delivered him right here at this house all those years ago.

"As you all know," Nigel continued, "I lived the fast life, literally and figuratively. I had a successful career in Formula One, but that was all I had. I could have had any woman I wanted. Some nights I did, but they always left me empty inside. Until Chad came along and stole my sister away from me, that was my only pursuit. I haven't really expressed this to anyone, but Chad won me over because I saw the way he adored my sister. I wanted that. No, Chris, I didn't want Chad to adore me, you nilly."

Chris laughed at this, his wife shrinking in embarrassment.

"I wanted a family. I wanted a life – a real life. I wanted something that no trophy in the world could ever win. I told Chad that first Thanksgiving I visited that I was going to retire and actually start living. I think I made the right choice. I never would've met Millie. I never would be a dad, but here I am."

Chad nodded along, but something was off. He couldn't place it. It all seemed normal, but at the same time, it wasn't normal. What was it? Nigel? He's English. When did he change to a Southern accent in the middle of his speech. Chad was becoming distressed.

"Are you okay, love?" Gemma asked, grasping his hand.

Chad turned to his wife, only he wasn't sure she was his wife. He knew Gemma. She had striking green eyes, luscious, tumbling raven hair, and soft, tender cheeks. Her eyes were now blue. No, they were purple. Brown? Her tumbling raven hair was lightening with every blink he took. One moment, it was brown. Then it was red. Her cheeks began to harden, becoming more angular. She was changing, but not really settling on any one appearance.

Nigel's speech was interrupted by the sound of a truck backing up. The alarm was piercing. Somehow, the only one it affected was Chad. He stood up. It was the tire truck.

"Where are you going?" asked Gemma, now a totally different person.

"I, I," stuttered Chad, "I need to go meet the tire truck and get the tires on Nigel's Aston."

"Okay," said Gemma. Her voice had changed. That prim Oxbridge accent was replaced by a lazy urban New York accent. It was almost off-putting to Chad. "Don't be gone too long, doll."

Chad approached the tire truck. In reality, it was just a Freightliner M2 box truck. Chad met the driver, and the truck started to back down the driveway. He stood next to the Aston as the truck closed in on him. There was something else very funny about this. The truck wasn't a truck anymore. It was a Plymouth Voyager, one of those boxy minivans from the 1980s.

"*How are they making big deliveries in that?*" he wondered.

The backup alarm still blared as the Voyager slowly approached. Was it still a Voyager? It now took a new shape: a 1967 Beetle. Still blaring, the backup alarm became louder the closer it got to Chad, its steady rhythm matching his pulse. That was weird too. His heart was beating to the same rhythm as the backup alarm. Funny how that worked.

The Beetle inched closer. The backup alarm blared louder. Before the car had a chance to stop, it disappeared, but the alarm still sounded. The world, Chad's house, his family, and cars, they all blurred and disappeared. He was left alone. It was cold and dark. That was until he opened his eyes.

All he saw was a white blur. That was it. It was a white blur. But wait a minute, was that an overhead light? It was. Chad blinked again as his vision focused. He jumped a little as he turned his head. Buried in his right arm was a needle. Attached to that needle was a tube. Chad followed that tube to an IV bag. That was attached to a whole array which included a heart monitor, still making that obnoxious beeping sound.

Chad stirred and groaned. He was lying down. He knew that. He turned his head the other way and saw Larry sitting in a chair against the wall.

"What the heck," he mumbled.

Larry jumped up. "Goodness! You're awake!"

"Where am I? Where's Gemma?"

"Can we get a doctor in here!" shouted Larry ignoring Chad's questions.

"The heck is this?" asked Chad, still mumbling and nearly incoherent.

"Doc, he's awake!" exclaimed Larry.

"Who is this?!" shouted Chad. "Where am I?" He was starting to make sense.

"Yes, no sign of concussion," said the doctor as he flashed a small flashlight in Chad's eyes.

"Where the heck am I?" Chad asked more forcefully. "Where's my fiancé?"

"You're at the Sonoma Valley Hospital. It's 4:30 PM on Sunday," the doctor answered. "Seems you got hit pretty hard."

"Hit pretty hard?" Chad repeated. "What's he talking about?"

"Car explosion," the doctor answered. "You took a car explosion to the face. It knocked you out pretty good, but it doesn't look like you're seriously injured. That firesuit and helmet saved your life."

"Car explosion? What car explosion. Larry, make sense of this. Where's Gemma? Where's Nigel? What the heck is going on here? Come on, these are simple questions I'm asking you."

The doctor gave Larry a knowing glance. As if they were communicating by telepathy, the doctor just nodded and left the room, closing the door behind him.

Larry stood there for a second, unable to say a word. Chad waited. In his heart, he felt he knew the truth, but he didn't want to believe it. Larry sighed.

"Chad, Gemma's meeting with a chaplain."

"A chaplain? Why? Why are you beating around the bush?"

"Chad, what do you remember. Tell me how far back you remember."

"I took the white flag at Sonoma," he began. "Nigel and Gerardo Lopez were fighting for P2. You told me Nigel had wrecked, and I came around and saw his car."

The gears were turning as he remembered the event.

"I stopped and got out because it was burning, but nobody was helping. It was bad, but I had to save him. Larry, is the chaplain for him?"

"Chad, I don't know how to tell you this," answered Larry, "so I'm just going to give it to you straight. I can't keep it from you. Wouldn't be right. Chad, Nigel's gone."

Chapter Twenty-Four
Gone

Chad's heart skipped a beat upon receiving the news. His teammate, his best friend, his brother-in-law-to-be was gone – snapped into eternity. Despite his efforts, there was nothing he could have done.

Chad tried to rise out of his bed, but Larry was quick to put a stop to that.

"No, you need to rest," he told him.

"I need to see Gemma," Chad argued.

"I'll call her up," Larry said. "Just lay back down."

Chad obeyed his crew chief. He threw his head back on the pillow.

"Gemma will be back soon," Larry explained. "Your mom and dad are rushing down here as we speak."

"Do we at least have any TV?" Chad asked.

"Probably wouldn't be a good idea," said Larry as he pulled out his phone.

"Why not?"

"Because the news station can't get enough of the story. Never mind the fact that Gerardo Lopez just kept his head above water to stay in the championship fight. No, they'd rather replay a fatal racing incident."

"How did it happen?" asked Chad.

"I don't think you really want to know," Larry argued.

"No, I do. For all I know, they were fighting for second as usual, and you told me Nigel had wrecked soon after I took the white flag. I just want to know how it happened."

"Well, from what I understand from the multiple angles," Larry explained, "it started in turn 7. Gerardo had the advantage in the corner, but Nigel still carried some speed. Nigel was on the outside of the turn, but Gerardo wavered and made slight contact with Nigel's tire from the front wing of his car. That caused some damage in an already well-worn tire, and the tire blew. He kept control of the car pretty well, but the traffic behind didn't see him until it was too late. The next thing that happened was you came along."

"So, Gerardo Lopez crowded Nigel?" asked Chad.

"Basically," answered Larry. "The stewards ruled it a racing incident, but I don't believe it for a second. I watched the footage. He turned into Nigel. It was just overaggressive racing."

Chad's countenance changed. Larry saw it. His features darkened. There was murder in Chad's eyes.

"Now before you go blaming Gerardo," said Larry. "Lord knows we all want to. You need to understand that he was racing to stay in the championship fight. Nigel was in the way. At that point, he had everything and nothing to lose. You can't tell me that you or Nigel wouldn't have raced the same way if you were in the same position."

"Difference is we didn't get people killed," retorted Chad.

"No, you didn't. But he had no idea either."

"I hate that guy," Chad muttered. "What I'd give to see the FIA strip him of that win."

"Is that all?" said Larry.

"I literally have no words, Larry. He killed Nigel. He got cocky and thought he could get aggressive. Doesn't matter if it's a racing incident. The fact is he wasn't careful, and now a man is dead because of him."

"Then I shouldn't tell you his reaction," said Larry.

"Enlighten me, Larry. What was that Dego's reaction?"

Chad was usually slow to use racial epithets. Normally, they were reserved for gatherings among his diverse crew when everybody was roasting each other. Even then, he was never wanton with the slurs. He usually stuck to making jokes about the stereotypes. If he was flat-out throwing out racial slurs at someone, he was beyond furious.

"I guess it wouldn't hurt to show you the interview," said Larry as he handed Chad his phone. "Don't go browsing after the video. Just hand me back the phone."

"Larry, I'm twenty-two," said Chad as he took the phone. "You don't have to protect me like I'm your little boy."

"In a way, you are my son," said Larry.

"You're old enough to be my grandpa," chuckled Chad.

"Isn't your dad older than me? Anyway, watch the video, but like I said, only the video. It'll tick you off enough."

Chad hit the play button on the phone. There, on the screen, stood Gerardo speaking into a microphone. Rage started to boil up inside Chad.

"What about that limey?" the Spaniard started. "Racing is racing. If you don't have the skill to race, then you shouldn't be on the track. It could get you killed. Obviously, Nigel McKenzie lacked the skill to be on the track."

Chad shut the screen off and handed the phone back to Larry.

"If I get my hands on him, I'll wring his neck," said Chad.

"And that's why we have you here," said Larry.

"What kind of human being delights in someone's death?" Chad thought out loud. "This Lopez guy is a total sociopath."

"It sure seems like it," Larry agreed. "That isn't normal, nor is it right. And yet, you know how this world works. Sure, he'll lose fans, but the die hards will just say he's competitive. Happens every time these guys go around putting their ringworm-laden feet in their mouths."

Chad threw himself back down in his bed.

"Are they sure he's dead?" asked Chad.

"*What kind of question was that?*" thought Larry. "*Of course, he's dead.*"

"Yes, he is," answered Larry. "You don't suffer a basilar skull fracture and survive. Well, not exactly. You may get lucky and survive, but you'll never be the same."

"Basilar skull fracture?" Chad repeated.

"That was the official cause of death," Larry clarified. "Need I continue?"

"I'm a grown man, Larry. I know what a basilar skull fracture is."

The basilar skull fracture is a common injury in motorsports. At least, it was until the advent of the head and neck support, also known as a HANS. When a racecar was brought to a sudden stop, the driver's body would keep moving. Being buckled in, the driver's body would also stop moving quickly. This would throw the driver's head forward. The force of the impact could cause a fracture in the base of the skull. The telltale signs of a basilar skull fracture are bruising behind the ears and around the eyes as well as bleeding behind the eardrum. Oftentimes, the injury can cause a leakage of cerebrospinal fluid as well. The resulting trauma is almost always fatal. Following a series of basilar skull fractures in the 1990s and early 2000s which ended with the death of Dale Earnhardt, Sr. in 2001, NASCAR mandated the use of a HANS device by all drivers. Since February 2001, there has never been a fatality in any of the top three national NASCAR divisions thanks to the HANS device.

Before Chad could fully process the fact that Nigel had suffered a basilar skull fracture or what the aftermath looked like, Gemma entered the room. She had clearly been bawling her eyes out. Mascara streamed down her face. Behind that, worry was painted all over it.

"Chad!" she cried as she rushed over to her fiancé. She reached down, never mind the IV and other monitors hooked up to Chad, and embraced him.

"I think I'll leave you two alone," said Larry. "The guys are all in the lobby. They'll be glad to hear you're okay."

"I'm sorry, Gemma. I'm so sorry," cried Chad.

"No, you're alright, my love," she comforted him. "You're okay. You're safe. I'm so glad you're okay."

"Gemma, I'm so sorry," Chad continued to cry.

"Chad, it was nothing you could do."

"Gemma, I tried to save him," Chad tried to explain, choking through the tears. "I couldn't get him out before the car exploded."

Gemma stood up and adjusted herself. She then took a place on the side of the bed and took Chad's hand, stroking it like they both always did when they knew the other felt uneasy.

"Chad," she began, "listen to me. It's not your fault. There was nothing you could have done."

"Love, I could have pulled him out," Chad argued.

"It wouldn't have done any good," Gemma replied.

"I was almost there," Chad continued.

"Chad, he was gone before you even got to the car."

"No, he wasn't," Chad argued back. He was starting to get frustrated.

"Chad, the tether on his HANS device failed," Gemma explained. "When that first car hit him, it caused the basilar skull fracture."

"No, he wasn't," said Chad more forcefully.

"Baby, I know it's hard, but he was long gone."

"He was alive!" Chad cried. "I could hear him screaming. 'Help me!' Gemma, that doesn't leave you. My gosh, I can hear it now! Dead men don't scream like that. He was alive! He was screaming for me to help him! He was!"

Gemma pierced his heart with her green eyes. She squeezed his hand. She was unsure if she should continue, unsure of how he would react to her explanation.

"Chad," she started, "Nigel was dead before his car went airborne. Please don't interrupt. That was not my brother screaming, my love. It was you."

The realization hit Chad like a freight train. Him screaming out like that?

"Chad, you did all that you could," Gemma continued. "You were screaming in fear or pain. I don't know what. You called for the stewards to come and help you get Nigel out of the car. He was unresponsive because he was dead. Before the stewards made it to the car, the fire reached the leak in the fuel cell. The force of the explosion threw you back."

"How do they know?" asked Chad.

"The coroner said the fatal injury could have only occurred before the explosion," Gemma went on. "You're practically sitting on the fuel cell in those cars. The fatal blow came from the side. You are not to blame, Chad."

"Why did he go through with it?" asked Chad.

"With what?"

"Why couldn't he just call it quits?"

"Why would he?"

"He didn't want to do this race," Chad explained. "You were there at the prerace conference. He didn't think it was safe."

"When did you ever know Nigel to actually shy away from a race?" Gemma managed to choke out. "If he were here right now, he'd thank you. He'd thank you for being his friend. He never really had any friends until you came along. You changed him. I can't imagine how much more hurt I would feel knowing he died an angry man and all alone. Thank you."

Chad embraced his fiancé. He felt her body tremble as she heaved out a sob.

"Anyway, I think you're okay to turn on t' telly," she said as she recovered.

She picked up the remote and turned on the flatscreen hanging from the ceiling. She found the local news channel. She kept the volume low for the unrelated stories being broadcast at the time.

"What are you doing?" asked Chad.

"The FIA president is going to issue a statement," Gemma replied, still wiping tears from her eyes. "They haven't officially announced Nigel's death yet."

Soon, the local news stories were over. The scene turned to a live feed from London. It was the wee hours of the morning there, but representatives of the sport all turned up. The mood was somber. It was clear no announcement would actually have to be made, but they would do it all the same.

"It has been just over three hours since the disaster at Sonoma today," the commissioner began. "We would like to start with some good news. We have just received word that SportStream driver, Chad Helton, has just woken up and is doing fine. He has suffered from cuts and bruises, but apart from that, he has no major injuries. He should be given a clean bill of health and cleared to race within the next two or three days."

Gemma took Chad's hand again.

"On a sadder note," he continued, "there is some news I must deliver that I never wanted to ever deliver. As of 2:45 this afternoon, we have lost Sir Nigel McKenzie. A preliminary investigation has shown that he was killed instantly from the first impact on his number

88 SportStream. We will be further investigating the cause and repercussions. As of now, we will be postponing the final race in Abu Dhabi by a week. We will deliver more news as it comes out."

Gemma turned off the television. She looked back toward Chad. The sadness in his countenance had once again turned to malevolence.

"They're investigating the cause," he mocked. "We already know what it was! Freaking Gerardo Lopez clipped him! It blew his tire, and they couldn't see because the track was wet. He told them it wasn't safe, but they pushed it anyway. Now look! He's dead because of them.

"My love, listen to me," said Gemma. "Listen to me. As much as I hate to admit it, Nigel chose to go out and race. He knew the risks better than anybody. He wanted you to get that win. He was doing what he loved."

"He was going to retire," said Chad. "He was going to move out west and start a family. He had so much ahead of him."

"I know," whispered Gemma. "And that's why we need to make every day count. Chad, I need you. I have so much to do. I have statements to make, documents to file. I need your help."

"Of course," Chad replied, settling back down. "We haven't said our vows yet, but I made you a promise."

Gemma looked down at her watch.

"Bugger! I have to go!" she said.

"No, please!" cried Chad, reaching out to her as she stood up. "Stay here. Don't leave me alone. As much as you need me, I need you."

"Chad, I have appointments," Gemma protested.

"Please, stay!" Chad cried. "I need you!"

"Okay, I'll stay," she replied in a soft, motherly tone, sitting back down on the edge of the bed. "I'll stay. Nothing is more important than us. I'll stay here. I won't go anywhere."

Chapter Twenty-Five
Black Stripes

Chad was discharged the following day. His parents visited him for a couple hours. Mrs. Helton was relieved her baby was okay. Chad could only remember the look on his father's face. Bill Helton said nothing, but his expression said, "See what happens? You could have a nice, comfortable life if you just stayed at home and worked the farm like everybody else." Beyond that, the whole visit seemed like a blur to him. Chad was ready to be out of California and back home in Austin.

Chad and Gemma chartered a flight back home. When they arrived, Gemma almost immediately returned to work, fielding calls from every inquiring mind that thought it needed to know. It was only Tuesday, and she already had three weeks' worth of work.

Chad reported back to SportStream as well. The atmosphere at headquarters was all melancholy. The black team colors were joined by more black that covered the SportStream teal décor. Everyone wore black armbands. Few words were said. In fact, nobody really knew what to say. It's not every day a team on the top of their game loses their star.

Chad forced himself to sit down in the simulator, but that's all he did. When the sim started, he did nothing. The seconds began counting up as he just stared at the screen. The confines of the simulated Formula One fuselage felt claustrophobic. A minute after entering, he left. He couldn't bring himself to do it. He found Gemma in her office and sat down across from her at her desk. Papers were already stacking high. She was all business as she answered questions.

"Look, I can't guarantee anything," she said in her one-sided conversation. "There's a lot to go through, I'm sure you understand. Yes, I'm sure you did. Just send in the paperwork, and I'll take care of it."

"For crap's sake," he thought, *"that was her brother. Why can't they just let up?"*

Chad picked up one of the folders and thumbed through it. Inside were pictures of a model. He thought he recognized her. Where was it? Daytona? Bahrain? She was on the yacht, he knew that.

"Can I help you?" asked Gemma as she hung up the phone. "Oh, it's you. I'm so sorry, my love. I've been so busy. What's up."

"I can't do this anymore," said Chad. "I need to go home. I'm going to go home and watch some TV."

"Chad, please," Gemma started, but she could see the look in Chad's eyes. He was drained. Even she had to admit that he shouldn't even be back to work so soon after a hit like that. "Before you go, do you think you could separate all these papers for me? Yellow folders go with yellow folders. Red goes with red. I'm sure you get it."

"Sure," said Chad as he started looking through the files. He held up the folder he thumbed through when he came in. "What's this?"

"That is what I'm dealing with now," she answered. "Nobody tells you that when you die unmarried, everyone that can claim to be your spouse comes out of the woodwork."

"And this girl in here?"

"Elena Mourinho, one of the women he used to have at his afterparties. She said he went to sleep with her, and she had a kid. One of many who's already come forward with that claim. It's all bull. Nigel may have slept with them, but he was always careful, even when he was drunk. I have at least six or seven DNA tests scheduled."

"What about her?" asked Chad as he gestured at another folder.

"Antoinette Lafleur," Gemma replied. "Same rubbish, different day."

"Seems like everybody wants a piece of the action," Chad commented as he stacked the folders, peeking inside from time to time. "But to be honest, he could've done better. Then again, that's incest."

"Chad, that was rude!" scolded Gemma.

"I'm sorry, love," Chad apologized. "But seriously, it seems like with all these people, they just want what he could have given him. No way any of these people actually loved him."

"People are so selfish," said Gemma. "I just wish I could just tell everyone to go away and leave the man alone."

"Is that all?" asked Chad.

"No, there's more. People who say he promised them favors. 'Nigel said he'd pay me rent.' 'Nigel said he would pay my alimony.' 'Nigel said he'd pay me back for a trip to Vegas.' I wouldn't be surprised if the bloody king called and asked for a bit of his estate. I already know Uncle Sam is coming for a bit of it."

"Okay," said Chad, "I officially hate people. If there's anything I hate more than the state asking for money because you happen to own property, it's the state asking for money because you happen to have a family member that died."

"D'you know how they say that there's no such thing as a stupid question?"

"All the time."

"Yeah, those people never held a real job."

"Why do you think I hate talking to the press?"

"You know, it's all his fault. I would've thought he'd wait to die until we were old and retired," Gemma joked. "Wait, that was inappropriate of me."

"No," Chad interjected. "Nigel would've laughed at that. That's what we need right now. We need to be able to laugh. We have to find some way to move on. Why do you think I got a little dark a few seconds back. Nigel wouldn't want us moping around, right?"

Gemma smiled tenderly at Chad. Her green eyes brightened as she stared at him. Her natural glow warmed Chad's heart.

"I really think I need to get home," said Chad. "This place is getting suffocating."

"Please think of me while you're at it," said Gemma. "Also, I think my car may need some servicing if you could help me out."

"Of course," said Chad as he blew Gemma a kiss.

Chad did nothing for the rest of the day. His mind was restless. One part wanted to get on the track. The other told him to stay put. He couldn't sleep. He had done enough of that in Sonoma. Gemma was busy. He tried calling Clint. They hadn't spoken since June, and he would already be done with the rally season. There was no answer.

"Probably actually spending time with his wife," he thought.

He went through his voicemails. He was usually very meticulous about keeping his voicemailbox clear. It was full.

"Hey, Chad, praying for you," was one message.

"Hey, Chad, we're glad you alright. Praying for you," was another.

"We are calling to inform you about your car's extended 'warrantee", denied.

"Hey, Chad, it's Clint." This was the message he was looking for. "Sorry I missed you. I know you've probably been busy. Anyway, I just want you to know that everyone back home is thinking of you and praying for you. I know what you're going through, truly. When I lost my dad, I was dead to the world. Do what you need to do, but don't let it absorb you. Love you, friend."

Chad turned on the television. It seemed like whenever he wanted to lose himself in the drone of the TV, he was prevented by the exact thing he wanted to avoid being broadcast on every channel. This time, every live channel was talking about Nigel. The death of the number one driver in the world was big news. It had been nearly twenty-five years since a driver of his caliber was killed on the track. Every angle was covered. For the first time, Chad was able to see everything as it happened. His morbid curiosity got the better of him as he watched clip after clip of his friend being killed. He soon snapped out of it and turned off the TV.

He went to his bookshelf. There was nothing good to read, nothing that interested him. It was all boring slog – stuff he had already finished reading. He grabbed a random book and took a look at the cover.

"*Bridge to Terabithia*," he spoke out loud, "seriously?"

Chad fell to his knees and let out a primal scream. He hadn't had much time to himself since Sunday. He chucked the book at the wall, embedding it in the sheetrock. Alone and with no untoward ears to hear, he let loose a string of expletives and curses aimed at whoever came to his mind. First, it was Gerardo. He thought of all the slurs against the Spaniard, every negative stereotype and description that came to his mind. He cursed the man for a solid ten minutes.

Then, he turned his attention to the organizers of the race. Chad cursed them for going ahead with the race when Nigel, the smartest driver in the paddock, raised some valid concerns. He thought up every anti-European insult imaginable. The rage in his shouts would've made anyone who could hear them cower in fear.

He then turned his thoughts and curses to SportStream. He thought of how they built an insufficiently-safe car and had provided inadequate equipment. He thought of the danger they may have put him in as well, let alone his best friend.

Then, he thought of Nigel.

"Why!" he screamed. "Why did you have to go and die, you lobster-back limey! You knew, and yet you did it anyway! Why couldn't you just listen to your gut and sit it out! You just had to go at it hard! You just couldn't hold back, and look where it got you! Sure, you're probably sitting there up in Heaven laughing at us crying for you right now. It hurts, Nige. It freaking hurts! Screw you, Nigel!"

Chad wilted down to the floor and curled up into the fetal position, bursting into tears. He remained like this for hours until he had dehydrated himself. He retreated to the bathroom where he filled a glass of water. He looked at himself in the mirror. He was a wreck. He splashed his face with the cold water flowing from the sink. He took one more look at himself, disgusted with his behavior, and forcefully shut off the faucet.

Gemma had set a strict 9-to-5 policy for herself. That left her an actual life; well, an actual life of going through Nigel's belongings and planning the funeral. She wept with everything she packed. Most were things that held little to no value for her, but they reminded her of her brother.

Nigel's body was flown back to England on the next day, and Chad and Gemma followed on Thursday to prepare for a Friday burial. The king had offered a burial spot for Nigel at Westminster, but Gemma thanked him and refused. Nigel had always loved the estate near Blackpool whenever he got the chance to go home. It was where they had buried their parents and grandmother. Larry, along with five other members of the SportStream crew acted as Nigel's pallbearers, carrying his casket out of the stone church that had housed it, leaving the publicly-broadcast funeral for the private graveside service. The weather was perfectly rainy for the occasion. Chad held Gemma tight as Chad's pastor officiated the ceremony at the graveside, a gesture of goodwill to the man who had shown so much interest in his church just weeks before.

"I had the privilege of meeting Sir Nigel last month," the pastor began. "He seemed very interested in what I had to say, and we talked for almost two hours after church let out. I guess you could say that instead of being hungry for lunch, he was hungry for the Word. I'm glad to say that I know he trusted Jesus as his Savior. As much hurt as we all feel here, we know Nigel is happier than he has ever been. Why is that? Because to be absent from the body is to be present with the Lord. Nigel knew that fact."

Gemma hid her face in Chad's bosom as they lowered Nigel down to rest. This was it. He was gone.

Chapter Twenty-Six
Therapy

Gemma did not return to work immediately when she returned to Austin. What should have been closure for her only sent her deeper into her own depression. The finality of knowing Nigel was completely gone hit her like an eighteen-wheeler. As much as she tried, she found that stiff upper lip the British are famous for only works for so long.

Chad, for his part, still stayed away from SportStream. He never returned any calls. Just weeks ago, he would have stopped everything he was doing when Mr. Singleton called. Now, the great man's phone calls went straight to voicemail just like anyone else. It was becoming clear that Chad had lost any desire to race.

Without direction, he wandered aimlessly, doing whatever first popped into his mind. Several nights, he would just drive aimlessly. He would be gone for hours, only to find himself in the middle of absolutely nowhere. He didn't care. If he ended up in the wrong place, he almost invited the prospect of danger. One night, he even ended up all the way in Oklahoma City. Without a rest, he turned around and drove back down to Austin.

He did, however, try to spend as much time with Gemma as possible. She was worried sick after his OKC escapade. She, for her part, never trusted anyone outside of herself to manage Nigel's estate. As the dust began to settle with all of the claims against her brother, she distanced herself from SportStream and began spending more time at home. There was so much work to do. Chad often found himself there if he wasn't cruising aimlessly. Nigel's belongings needed to go somewhere. Some would be sold; racing memorabilia, especially from someone like Nigel, fetches a good price.

It was a Wednesday afternoon that Mike and Emily paid Gemma a visit. She was in the living room, packing up Nigel's trophies into boxes. Those were staying with her, but she needed to make room. When the knock came, she rushed to the door and embraced her friend.

"I'm so sorry," said Emily as she hugged Gemma tight. "We brought you a ham and potato casserole."

"Oh, thank you," said Gemma. "You can just set it on t' kitchen table. Please, stay for dinner. I'll put a kettle on to boil and get some toys out for Kevin. Nige left some Hot Wheels and Matchbox in a tote somewhere around here."

"Where's Chad?" asked Mike.

"In t' garage working on my car," said Gemma.

"Mind if I?" he asked, gesturing that way.

"Go ahead," said Gemma. "He needs someone to talk to him. He keeps to himself as of late."

Emily gestured at her husband to go. Mike found the garage door and walked in. Chad was underneath Gemma's Miata. The car was on jackstands, all four wheels off of the car, all four brake assemblies on the ground. He could hear Chad ratcheting on something near the back.

"You're a hard man to reach," he told Chad, hoping it wouldn't startle him.

"That's the idea," said Chad as he continued.

Whatever bolt Chad was ratcheting finally came loose, sending his hand hard into the metal subframe.

"Shhhhhhhhhhhh," he said, holding back the expletive.

"The idea, huh?" continued Mike, ignoring Chad's agony. "You don't want to talk to anybody"?

"Not really," Chad replied as he continued his work. "Nothing to talk about. Nigel's dead. I don't need to go back. Simple as that."

"Well, we've been getting calls asking about you."

"You have now?" asked Chad sarcastically. Before Mike could get another word in, a drain plug dropped. "Finally!" Chad said to himself as he watched the gear oil drain into the oil pan.

"We're all kind of worried about you."

"Is that so?"

"They're asking me if you're going back."

"Back to what?"

"Racing. They told me you haven't been in."

"Nope," Chad replied as he replaced the drain plug and opened the top of the rear differential.

"So, you're just going to abandon them?" asked Mike. "That doesn't sound like you're thinking of your team."

"What's it to you?" asked Chad as he grabbed a bag of gear oil and began to fill the differential. "You don't care about it. All you care about is football, your construction business, and whether you can be the biggest man in the room. So, what, now you actually think my racing career is a good idea?"

"Will you just listen to me?" Mike finally raised his voice. "Put the oil down, get out of there, and listen to me."

Chad slid out from underneath the car and sat up. He was already covered in oil, grease, and road grime. His thick mop of hair looked like it had enough oil in it to crank a small diesel.

"Make it quick, Mike. As you can see, I'm busy."

"My son thinks the world of you. As much as I've hated it, he wants to be you. That little boy worships the ground you walk on. Shoot, he refuses to watch any football with me. He even told me football wasn't a sport. That's not how it works!

"If not for you or the guys at SportStream, do it for Kevin. Do you know what would happen if he knew you quit? It would destroy his world. He wouldn't understand. I wouldn't know how to tell him his Uncle Chad doesn't race anymore."

"Good for him," mumbled Chad sarcastically. "Keep him out of this life. Unless you want him to get killed. You really want to bury him?"

"Look, I know how it is," continued Mike, "to lose a friend in a freak accident. I don't talk about it much, but yeah, I've lost friends too. It wasn't long after I started building when I watched my best friend, Justin, die in front of me. We were working on a four-story apartment complex in Salem. It was raining hard that week, and the scaffolding was slippery. He was carrying a table saw up so we could cut some wood on the top level. He slipped on the scaffolding, and the weight of the saw forced him through the railing and over the edge. He died the second he hit the ground. I watched the whole thing. The impact on the ground snapped his neck, and the weight of the saw crushed his chest. I still remember the scream of terror and the look on his face. I almost quit, but I didn't. I realized that I couldn't go my whole life hiding away and avoiding risk.

"From what I understand, Nigel was killed in a freak accident, much like Justin was. Everything to keep him safe in that car worked like it was supposed to except for one small thing. You've cooped yourself up inside like it'll keep you safe. You're staying away from everybody because you're too chicken to tell them that you're scared to die. You watched Nigel die, and you're scared. I know, because I was too; but I had to come to grips with it, Chad. What's to say you won't step outside tonight and get hit by a bus?"

"What are you saying?" asked Chad somewhat annoyed by this lecture.

"Listen to me," said Mike. "Maybe if it comes from me, you'll listen. I have little to no interest in racing, but my little boy does. I will not sit by as his most favorite person in the whole world sulks and quits what he loves. You will go to Abu Dhabi. You will kick that Spaniard in the butt. You will win that championship. If you don't, you know what I can do."

"Is that a threat?"

"Pretty much."

"So, if I refuse to race, you're going to lay me out?"

"You wanna make that bet? I mean, you die in the car, it'll probably be instant. Not me, though. I'll make sure you suffer. Also, I may or may have not gone behind Emily's back a couple weeks ago and placed a few bets"

Chad considered the proposition. Possible death versus certain death really wasn't anything he would have considered. Chad put out an oily hand.

"Deal," he said.

"Maybe wash up first."

That night, Chad and Gemma enjoyed dinner with his cousin. He was happy to see Gemma had a friend there for her. He also found a new respect for Mike. This man who seemed like he wanted to distance himself from anything Chad did was now pushing him to race.

The Stewarts ended up staying late that night. After dinner, Chad ordered desert delivered to the house. As soon as Kevin fell asleep, Mike and Emily decided to go home. As the couples walked out to the car, Chad extended a hand to Mike. Mike grasped it and then pulled Chad in for a bro hug. The warming of a once-frosty relationship brought bittersweet feelings to Chad, reminding him of the friendship that blossomed between he and Nigel earlier that year.

Chad stayed to help Gemma clean up after dinner. He could tell she was exhausted. Hosting guests for dinner wasn't in the plans for today, and she was behind on getting Nigel's belongings catalogued and packed. As soon as the cleaning was done, he headed to the foyer to grab his jacket.

"Where are you going?" asked Gemma. "I thought you were going to stay a bit tonight."

"Change of plans," said Chad. "It's already very late, I need to pack."

"You need to pack? For what? You're not cruising again tonight, are you? You know I get worried sick."

"Abu Dhabi", Chad replied.

"You're not going?"

"Mike talked me into it."

"You're not going."

'Why not?"

"You'll die."

"Maybe."

"I can't let you."

"Any why not? Are you afraid you're going to lose me too?"

"Yes!"

"Gemma, I can't sit around here wasting my time."

"Please, don't," Gemma pleaded. "There's plenty of things you can do. I got a call the other day. Rick March is selling his assets and charter. You could buy the team and run it. You don't have to drive. You could go back to NASCAR as an owner. Even then, you're independently wealthy. Retire. Go home to Oregon. You'll never have to work another day in your life. You can live comfortably."

"Perhaps," said Chad, "but not right now."

"Why are you doing this?" she cried out as she burst into tears.

Chad took her hand and stared into her eyes.

"Because I need to finish what I started," Chad said with determination. "Gerardo Lopez is now tied with me. If I don't go to Abu Dhabi and at least try, he's got the championship."

"What does it matter though. It's just a stupid trophy."

"Do you think the world revolves around just us? There's a bunch of guys in that paddock who've busted their butts all year to get where we are. If not for them, I need to do it for me. I have to at least try and get back behind the wheel. I can't be a quitter. What will I say on my deathbed as I die unceremoniously crapping my diaper? 'I used to race, but I lost my nerve.' Do you think Nigel would tell me not to go? Heck no! Come on, you know if he could, he would've been there for the whole thing. If not for me, or the team, or little Kevin, I'm doing it for Nigel."

"Please, stay for me," Gemma bawled. "I can't lose you like I lost Nigel."

"You won't," said Chad. "I'll come back."

"You can't guarantee that," Gemma argued.

"Gemma, I promise," said Chad, "I will go to Abu Dhabi, I'll win that race, and I'll come back home safe and sound."

"I can't do this," Gemma said in reply. "I'd rather just go off and be all alone than lose someone else I love." She slipped her engagement ring off and handed it to Chad. "I can't do this to myself. I'm sorry. I just can't."

Chapter Twenty-Seven
Finish What You Started

The sun was beginning to set over Yas Island off the coast of Abu Dhabi. The day had been perfect with a high of 77°. With the disappearing sun, it had cooled to 68°, still not too chilly. It was perfect conditions to go racing tonight.

Chad sat alone in a corner of the SportStream paddock. He fiddled with Gemma's engagement ring in his hands. Since he left her house Wednesday night, he continually questioned his decision to return to the track. He had purchased a thin chain before flying out and threaded it through the ring. It would be his good luck charm, though he wasn't sure what good it would do. The girl of his dreams had called off the engagement. She was on his mind, though, the whole time.

His meditation was interrupted by some shuffling from behind him. He turned around to see his new teammate. The kid was barely nineteen. A German-Italian European mongrel who grew up in

Monaco, Klaus Cirnigliaro shared a similar story to Nigel and Chad. Dominating in karts from a young age, he worked his way through the grand prix ladder. The poor kid looked scared to Chad. He couldn't tell if he was embarrassed from interrupting him, or if he was scared to race.

"Hey, Klaus," he addressed the new guy.

"I'm sorry, Chad," he apologized. "I didn't mean to interrupt you."

"It's alright. Hey, congrats on that front-row qualifying. You'll fit in well here."

"It's certainly no Formula Two," Klaus replied.

"It's sure not. Hey, you'll do great today. Just listen to Larry, and you'll be near the front when the checkers fly if not leading."

Chad watched the kid walk away encouraged. He could remember the early days when he first started. Had it really not even been a year? Chad held up the ring to his face again and kissed it.

"I love you, Gemma," he whispered to it, as if it somehow contained her very essence.

He set his eyes to the garage door of the paddock. It was open. The mechanics were busy prepping the cars to go out.

Chad's return was less successful than desired. He was timid the whole time during practice on Saturday. By the time he managed to turn what looked like a hot lap, it was time to qualify. He never made it past the first round. He would be starting P16. He found something poetic about the whole thing. It was exactly where he was last year in Phoenix. It was as if history repeated itself.

The whole team held their breath as Chad lowered himself into the car one final time. It felt to Chad like they were waiting to see if he would actually do it. As he settled himself down inside the car, Mr. Singleton appeared. It was a surprise for Chad. The great man himself was there. It was an encouragement for him to know that this busy man carved out time to support his drivers in this final race. Chad noticed something in his hand as he approached the car: a stick about two feet long with a piece of black cloth wrapped around one half of it. He handed it to Chad.

"Save it for when your victory lap," he told Chad.

Chad pulled the fabric back a little bit. He could make out parts of the outline of a teal number 88.

"Thought it would be fitting for Nigel to take one last ride with you," said Mr. Singleton.

The crowd cheered as Chad pulled his car out of the paddock and onto the track to begin the parade laps. He had gone from a controversial hire to a fan favorite. The American had proven them wrong and shown that the Yanks could be competitive. Amazingly, he heard the response over the roar of the engines.

"It's all for you," said Mr. Singleton into the radio.

"Going green next time around," said Larry. "Pull those belts tight, boys. This is it. This is what we've worked for.

"I'm going to butt in here, Larry," said Lars. "All the gloves are off tonight. As Larry says, checkers or wreckers. Don't let up. Win this race. Make sure Lopez is staring at your brake light at the end."

The Aston Martin safety car ducked into the pits. The twenty grand prix cars came to a stop in their grid spots. Klaus took the outside lane in a renumbered 38 car; SportStream had retired the 88 out of respect for Nigel. Gerardo pulled up next to him on the inside lane. The world all went silent for Chad as he began to pray. While his prayers were directed toward the Almighty, his mind's eye pictured Gemma. He gripped her ring that he had hung around the steering yoke. He imagined that longing look she had whenever he took to the track. He remembered their last meeting. His heart ached. The mental image turned into a vision of Nigel. He remembered the last words he said to him: "Hey, whatever happens, I'm proud of you. Thank you for making this the best year of my life." Chad could have wept over the memory had not red lights gone out that very second.

The race was underway. Twenty cars charged down the frontstretch. Within seconds, the two front row cars slowed down for the first 90° left-hander. Chad held back, allowing his competitors to pass him. He anticipated their move. One or two were always bound to mess up here. He was correct. In the struggle to jockey for position in the turn, two drivers tangled up and wrecked into the runoff zone, collecting two other drivers. Chad reassumed his spot in P16, albeit running last now for all intents and purposes.

The course followed some flat but wide left-handers and right-handers before meeting another, even harder left-hander. The field bunched up here again. This opened to the first DRS zone, though it would not be allowed until the second lap. The field started to spread out here, and Chad was being left in the dust.

"What's he doing?" asked Noodle.

"I don't know," said Larry. "That's not like him."

"Talk to him," Lars ordered.

"Right," replied Larry. "Uh, Chad, is everything okay out there?"

"Yeah, why?

"Because you're lagging behind. Is this some strategy we never talked about?"

"Negative."

"Then pick up the pace. At least get within striking distance if you can."

Larry looked back at Lars and Mr. Singleton. He saw the look of concern in their eyes. There was definitely something wrong. Chad never raced like this.

"He'll be alright," he reassured them. "We haven't even finished the first lap. Fifty-seven to go."

Gerardo led Klaus across the line. The rookie struggled to keep up with the Spaniard. The only ally he had at this point was the top tier equipment from SportStream. This was the same car being prepared for Nigel to race here.

Gerardo was running away with the race. By the second lap, he was already singing victory songs. In his mind, there was no way Chad could make up the time, let alone his stunning near victory at Monaco earlier that year.

Gerardo may have very well been right. Chad was able to make up ground and had P15 in his sights by the start of the second lap, but it was still a long battle to get to the front. His times were off. He just didn't have it in him today, and he knew it. His mind was still on Gemma – still on their last meeting. He missed her. He missed Nigel. It just wasn't the same coming here to Abu Dhabi without them. His drive was just gone.

By the fourth lap, he was able to find an opening. He passed for P15. It wasn't anything spectacular. P15 wavered a bit in turn five, and he sailed past him out of the exit. P14 came to him shortly. He still remembered how to activate his DRS and sailed past the competitor.

"Okay, it looks like he's waking up," said Lars.

"I hope so," said Larry. "Usually, he'd be about P10 by now."

"What's his problem?" asked Lars.

"I don't think he wants to be here," replied Larry.

"Doesn't want to be here?" asked Lars incredulously.

"No, you know what I think? I think he's scared. I think he's had it. He watched his best friend die two weeks ago. He's been like this all week. Did he talk to you, Lars?"

"Not at all. He never said a word. He just showed up with his gear like he always has."

"Did you notice any strange behavior before the race?"

"Well, he kept to himself, but I just thought it was because the McKenzies aren't here. Has he said anything to you? Of all people, he'd talk to you."

"Not a word. He's been all business since the second he got here."

"What have we done?" whispered Lars.

"We're still in this," said Larry. "We just need to stay patient. He'll wake up. Look on the bright side. Klaus is keeping pace with Lopez."

It was true. The kid had talent. He was quickly proving himself worthy of Nigel's car. Even so, he was only playing follow-the-leader to Gerardo Lopez.

Chad was not enjoying himself. He had moved to P13, but again, it was by sheer luck. Someone had retired early. He moved in on P12.

"Chad," came Larry's voice, "why don't you take it out of low power and actually challenge some one?"

"Why can't you leave me alone?"

"Have I said anything all night?"

"No, I just…" his voice trailed off.

"I get it," said Larry. "Just put it in high power. You've saved enough fuel."

Chad sighed and did as Larry said. What Chad lacked in exuberance tonight, the car more than made up for in speed. He easily passed for P12. Coming out of turn nine after the second DRS zone, disaster struck. It was nearing the middle of the race, and one the tires of one of the mid-pack teams had outstayed their welcome. Taking the corner, the right-side tires blew, sending the car spinning out of control. Chad had no time to react. The spinning car clipped his front wing, tearing it in half.

"Dang it!" he shouted, as if it actually mattered to him. "We're done. I'm bringing it in."

"The heck we're done!" shouted Larry. "We're getting a new wing ready. Hards all around. He's going back out there to win."

"No, I'm not," Chad argued. "I'm done. I can't pass. Lopez is running away with the win already."

"And when has that ever stopped you?"

Chad had to take a double take. Larry had all of a sudden become more feminine and British.

"*It can't be,*" he thought.

"Bring it in so they can fix the car, Chad. I'm not going to tell you again."

Chad's heart began to pound out of his chest as he hurried into the pits. He slid to a stop inside his pit stall. With the wing being replaced, he had a few seconds longer to glance inside the paddock. There was Gemma seated next to Larry wearing a headset. She had come back to him.

"Now, get out there and win this bloody race for me!" she shouted at Chad as the jackmen let the car down.

Chad tore out of his pit stall with a new determination.

"Where are we at?" asked Chad.

"You're back to P15," said Larry, "but you were one of the first to pit. You'll make up that ground. Just put the hammer down."

Chad did as he was told. On hard tires and full power, the number 28 SportStream was now unstoppable. He passed for P14 and P13 while he was still on his out lap. P12 was nothing for him as he screamed by the competitor as he crossed the line to start the next lap.

"Larry, I think you should box Klaus next time by," said Lars. "It looks like they're getting Lopez ready."

"Perfect," said Larry. "Chad can make up that ground easily."

The mechanics in the SportStream paddock began preparing for their second pit stop. Larry was unsure what to expect. This was his first race with Klaus. He didn't know how the kid raced. What seemed to work now should work later though.

"Would mediums work, Lars?" he asked his superior.

"Just do it," said Lars. "He's racing for experience, not points. He's holding his own just fine."

"Okay, mediums all around," said Larry. "Okay Klaus," he turned his attention to the rookie, "box this time around."

Klaus brought his car in right behind Gerardo. It was perfect as the majority of the field followed. Chad took advantage of this. He passed P10 and flew around turn sixteen right as Gerardo was heading back on his out lap.

"My gosh, we're gonna win it!" whispered Larry in excitement.

"But he's still so far behind," argued Gemma.

"I'd have thought with him being your fiancé, you would've been paying better attention to him the last few months or so," laughed Larry.

Heading into turn one, Chad picked up three more positions. He was back in the running and back within the pack. Upon exiting turn five, he could use his DRS and overtake.

Klaus followed Gerardo back out onto the track, but he was experiencing trouble. The car didn't feel right. He just didn't have the speed or the grip he wanted. Gerardo was pulling away. Larry could see it on the monitor.

"Everything alright, son?" he asked.

"No, this car is handling like rubbish," the kid replied. "I'm fighting it in the corners."

So, no, mediums were not the answer; but on the other hand, he was lacking speed too. Larry looked to Lars.

"Do what you can, Klaus," said Lars. "Chad's making his way up. Maybe you two can link up. Either way, you've outperformed our expectations this week. Well done."

Chad was flying through the field now. He now had Gerardo in his sights as he picked off P5. He was in the points now, but it wouldn't be enough. He was tied with the Spaniard for first. One of them would have to lose, and Chad knew it wasn't going to be him.

"You're P5, my love," came Gemma's voice over the radio. "Keep it up."

Chad opened up his DRS as he closed in on P4. Clearly this guy did not get the memo that Chad was supposed to win. Of course, it was the other Auburn car of Josue Cardinas. He was putting up a fight, making his car three lanes wide. Someone was going to lose going into turn six. With the speed advantage, he ducked low into the acute turn. Cardinas faltered to avoid contact with Chad and spun into the barrier, ending his night.

"Safety car in sector two," Larry called to his drivers. "That's one down, one to go. Like it ever mattered, right?"

Chad found himself close enough to P3 to activate his DRS again. This time, he was able to take the long way around and pass on the outside of turn nine, keeping his speed and momentum to catch up to the leaders.

By this time, the laps were clicking down faster, or so it seemed. The night had grown dark. It was cold, but not cold inside the car. Chad listened for the voice of his love as she guided him around the track, warning him of hazards and other drivers.

"Ten to go," called Larry as the top three cars crossed the start/finish line together.

"Boss, I'm really fighting this car around the corners," said Klaus. "I don't think I can make it to the end."

"Just hold on," said Larry. "Chad's got your twelve."

"Did you hear him?" asked Gemma.

"Loud and clear," answered Chad as he got in as close to Klaus as safely possible.

The tandem moved to the right of Gerardo Lopez, both activating their DRS as they flew down the back straight. Gerardo was fuming again, much like he did in Sonoma. His crew shut off the live feed as he let off another tirade of Spanish curses. The SportStream tandem proved too successful though. Disaster struck again in turn seven. Klaus was going too fast for his own good. Chad let off the accelerator and applied the brake, as did Klaus, but Klaus' car did not make the turn. Instead, it slid into the barrier, ending his night. Chad now sat P2 behind Gerardo.

"Is he alright?" asked Chad, concern filling his voice. He felt like it was a repeat of Sonoma.

"He's good," said Gemma. "Larry says he's moving around. Safety car in sector two."

Chad was right on Gerardo's tail now. At times, he was mere millimeters away from making contact. He was back to his old tricks again.

"Miss me yet, Tonto?" he said through the radio.

There was another tirade from Gerardo. It couldn't be possible. Chad had come from out of nowhere. With nine to go, he was poised to make a pass for the lead. Gerardo was determined that wouldn't happen. What would it take? It would mean that Gerardo's Auburn would need to be three lanes wide throughout the remaining nine laps. If Chad was going to keep up with him, it also meant a clean race with no time penalties.

"Just keep diggin'," said Larry. "He'll get out of the way soon enough."

Chad kept looking for an opening, but at every opportunity, Gerardo shut him down. Even in the corners, Gerardo somehow knew where Chad would try to go.

"The guy's a freaking clairvoyant," shouted Chad. "It's like he knows every move I'm going to make."

"Oh, but you're doing fine," argued Larry. "Five to go. He'll make a mistake."

Gemma could hear the frustration in Chad's voice.

"Chad," she called him on the radio, "Chad, my love, I need you to calm down and focus. What would Nigel do?"

"He'd cuss me out and wreck me," said Chad.

"After you guys became friends, you silly goose."

"He'd find an opening," replied Chad. "He'd remain calm and patient and wait for me to screw up."

"Then do it," said Gemma.

Chad remained right on Gerardo's heels as they crossed the line for three to go.

"I'm not going anywhere," said Chad.

Chad turned on his DRS again. This time, he had so much speed that his front wing made miniscule contact with Gerardo's rear tire.

"That's for Nigel, estúpido!" he shouted. He hoped Gerardo could hear over the engine noise.

Chad perfectly repeated every move Gerardo made. If Gerardo was going to mirror him, maybe he could throw him off and mirror Gerardo.

"White flag next time by," said Larry as they flew across the start/finish line.

Gerardo was visibly becoming unnerved. Chad would not let up. He still stayed in the fight though. One of them was going to hoist that trophy tonight. Gerardo was determined it would be him. He faltered coming out of turn sixteen onto the frontstretch. It wasn't much, but it was enough for Chad to make a move.

Chad was able to move out from behind Gerardo and advance just far enough to keep him from blocking him. He kept his speed on the outside of turn one. He advanced, literally by centimeters, as the cars made their way into turn five. Chad sent it into the turn. The tires screamed and protested as he nearly drifted the car. He was now halfway down the length of Gerardo's car. He was still gaining ground through six and seven. Chad activated DRS one more time between eight and nine. This boosted his car even further. They were almost neck and neck as they flew around the turn nine carousel. The fierce competitors were still almost neck and neck as they flew along the sector that ran along the Yas Marina.

"Oh, my gosh!" shouted Larry. "It's gonna be close!"

Chad was so close, but his tires were failing. The extra force put on them this lap was causing more wear than they could handle. He barely held on as they rounded turn sixteen. He was still gaining ground as the start/finish line came into sight.

Chad's world went silent again as he pictured a life with Gemma. The whole track disappeared from his mind. He saw it all again: the wedding, their first child, their fiftieth child, his retirement, the five hundred grandkids, his death with her gripping his hand by his bedside. It all happened as if he lived it. Then he saw Nigel. His old friend looked at him with approval. In front of that smile was one thumb up. Just then, a tire blew.

Chad awoke from his daydream and slammed on the brakes. He prayed hard that the safety car would stop any other competitors from ramming him.

"What happened?" he asked Larry.

"We're still waiting," came the reply.

What had happened was this: Chad was still gaining ground on Gerardo Lopez. By the time they had reached the start/finish line, they were neck and neck. Chad's front right tire exploded as they crossed the line, further obscuring who actually won the race.

"Look, even if they can't see on the SportStream cam," said Lars to Larry, "they'll probably give it to him by virtue of starting in the back."

Chad waited in his car. In the meantime, he took off his helmet and his HANS device and replaced them with his SportStream cap. The whole track was silent as they waited for the announcement.

"Attention," came the announcement right as Gerardo was bringing his car cack into the pits. He stepped out, ready to accept the championship trophy. "After careful review of the race-ending footage, we have a new margin of victory."

Gerardo brushed himself off, ready to make his victory speech. There was no way in his mind that a stupid, fat American could win a Formula One championship.

"By a margin of .00001 seconds, Chad Helton is your newest Formula One Champion!"

The crowd burst into applause. Gerardo slammed his helmet on his car, screaming and cursing in Spanish the whole time. The whole SportStream crew jumped the pit wall and stormed Chad's disabled car. Chad pulled out Nigel's flag and waved it.

"Well, I guess we won't have a victory lap," Chad told Mr. Singleton as he hoisted Nigel's flag.

"Who cares?" he cried. "Well done!"

"You son of a gun! I knew you could do it!" said Larry as he embraced the kid he had taken under his wing all those years ago.

Noodle ran up behind Chad and gave him a noogie. "I knew you could do it!" he said, big tears pouring down his cheeks.

The crowd of mechanics and team members parted in front of Chad. There, they made way for Gemma. She had the biggest smile on her face. He bright green eyes sparkled in the moonlight. He rushed to her, and he embraced her. He swept her off her feet. The racing crowd all let out a collective "aww" at the couple.

"I knew you could do it," she told him. "I'm so sorry. I was scared. I didn't want to lose you."

"It's alright," Chad consoled her. "I'm here. I'm safe."

Gemma was now crying. Chad couldn't tell if they were tears of sorrow or tears of joy.

He pulled out the ring from his pocket and took the chain off. He fiddled with it in his palm for a minute while Gemma dried her tears.

"So," he began, "are we still on for February?"

Gemma looked around. It was a big crowd, thousands of times bigger than the first time. Everyone waited on the edge of their seats to hear what she would say, even if they never heard the original question in the first place.

"Yes!" she cried. "Yes, yes! And a thousand times yes!"

The crowd burst into another applause as Chad replaced the engagement right back on Gemma's finger. He took her in his arms and embraced her again. He took in her eyes, her lips, he turned-up nose, and the raven corkscrews that tumbled down her back and shoulders. She was now his, and nothing could ever come between them.

Epilogue
Final Four Revisited

And the rocket's red glare

The bombs bursting in air

Gave proof through the night

That our flag was still there

O say, does that star-spangled banner yet wave

O'er the land of the free

And the home of the brave?

The crowd cheered as the ten-gallon-hat-wearing bearded pop country star finished his heavily stylized acapella rendition of *The Star-Spangled Banner.* Three F-22s from Luke Air Force Base nearly drowned her out as he neared the end of his song. The crowd settled into their seats as forty drivers settled into their cars.

Chad Helton swung his right leg over the door of his Ford Mustang Darkhorse. Well, it wasn't exactly a door, but it was where the door would've been had it been an actual road car. Swinging his left leg over into the window opening, he slid into the driver's seat. With some assistance from his crew chief, he buckled the six-point harness that would keep him glued to his seat for the next three to five hours.

"This is it," the crew chief told him. "Just get out there and get at it."

"That's it then?" Chad chuckled. "Come on, Larry, you can do better than that."

Chad was in the final race of his second year, and it was one for the books. Well, it was his second official year in the Cup Series. After missing nearly the entire season the previous year, he had gone out and won himself a Formula One championship.

Upon returning back to Austin, he received a call from Rick March offering his charter and assets. The price was too good to pass up. What was more, he now had full financial backing from Colin Singleton and SportStream. He left the world of Formula One behind without looking back, bringing most of his crew members with him.

Upon his return to NASCAR, he also bought some additional equipment to run a second team. Before Daytona, Colin Singleton bought into the team and purchased a second charter. They hired a rookie who Chad took under his wing.

Being an owner-driver never slowed Chad down though. He powered through the season, winning every crown jewel event possible. With ten wins on the books by the end of the regular season, he was already a favorite to win the Cup title. Throughout the Playoffs, he lived up to his very name: Mr. Eliminator. He never forgot his friend and brother, Nigel, though. He kept his Formula One victory flag with the teal 88 in his car, so that whenever he took the checkered flag in first, he would turn around the opposite way and salute his fans in honor of his fallen friend.

Chad strapped in one final time. Larry moved out of the way for another visitor. Gemma bent down to see her husband, a two-week-old infant riding in a carrier strapped in front. They had married in February in the interim between the Clash and Daytona. Nigel Chadwick Helton was as fast as his name suggested. He arrived early, just two weeks before Phoenix. Even being a month early, he was already strong. Chad reasoned with Gemma that she should get him to the track as soon as possible. It was never too late to get him started in the sport. The little guy was sure to give Gemma a run for her money trying to keep up with him.

"Be safe out there, my love," said Gemma. "Go out there and make history. Come back to us."

Chad said nothing, but he flashed a smile at her. He put on his HANS and helmet, encasing his head inside for up to five hours. The playoff beard wasn't so patchy this year. He still wanted it gone though. No matter how long he kept it, it still itched like crazy.

Even with a tiny pair of noise-cancelling earmuffs, Gemma covered baby Nigel's ears as the command from the grand marshal was given.

"Drivers, start your engines!"

Forty cars roared to life as the pace car took its place.

"Sixteenth!" he complained into the radio. "Every year, I'm in sixteenth."

"And look what you always seem to do with that," laughed Larry on the other end. "Now, get out there and show me what you're made of."

Gemma climbed into the pit box and sat next to Larry. She watched as her husband joined the throng of stock cars as they made their way out onto the track. This was it. The teal and black number 28 SportStream Ford Mustang gleamed under the hot desert sun. All forty cars swerved back and forth to warm up their tires for added grip. The pace car ducked down off the track. The official perched above the start/finish line waved the green flag, and they were off.

Chapter Four Redux
Dumb Redneck

Nigel McKenzie looked down at his itinerary again as the SportStream jet touched down at the Daytona Beach International Airport. He was hoping this would just be a quick formality. No, he knew it would be a quick formality. These people, these new competitors, were all a bunch of dumb, fat American rubes.

The new cars, modern as they were, were a massive step down from the precision instruments he drove. Sure, they would be a slog for the Englishman to drive, but their build served a purpose. It's not like he'd be weaving around hairpins and hills for five hundred miles. How hard would making wide left turns with a wide-open throttle at 190 for three hours be?

"Why don't you stop worrying and enjoy yourself for once, Nige?" a young smartly dressed woman across from him asked.

"Little sis, if you only knew," he muttered as he dropped the itinerary down onto his lap.

"Well, it's not like you have that much to prove," Nigel's sister went on. "Everyone knows who you are. You've won it all – Formula One, Indy, Le Mans – and you're now afraid of this? You're overthinking it."

"Look, it's nothing about talent or intelligence with these people," Nigel replied. "It's their tenacity, Gemma. You've seen what they do. It's not precision and clean racing. I watched the first flag-to-flag race broadcast here from 1979. It ended with the top two competitors running into each other and taking each other out before the finish line. Then, they got into an all-out donnybrook. No, Gemma, it's not how good they are that scares me. It's how dirty they can get."

"Well, I'm sure they're a lot more civilized forty-five years or so on from then," Gemma chuckled as she unbuckled her seatbelt.

"They had better be," said Nigel. "As much as Mister Singleton is spending on this team, I'd rather not destroy his equipment."

The airport butted up right against the backstretch of the two-and-a-half-mile oval. That was about all that was good about this situation. Nigel felt like he was stepping out into a sauna as he walked down the steps to the tarmac. Immediately, he pulled off his sweater, fearing the knit would stick to his skin like bloodied gauze. Gemma, for her part, seemed unbothered by the whole affair. It didn't matter what, rain or shine, dry desert or muggy swamp, she always wore the same get-up she treated as her unofficial sports agent's uniform: a white button-down blouse, brown cardigan, and matching skirt – something that seemed like she had just stepped from the Wartime world of C.S. Lewis and into the modern day. Upsetting her out-of-time appearance was a Bluetooth earpiece she always kept planted in her right ear.

"Your yacht is docked in the marina ready for your use, Mister McKenzie," an assistant informed Nigel as he strode across the tarmac.

Good, that was a place to stay, but it meant leaving the facility. The thing that sucks about being famous is nobody leaves you alone. It would be straight from the pit box to his Aston that was also waiting for him and then a sprint from that into his yacht. He hoped that maybe there would be someone guarding the marina.

A golf cart met the party, Nigel and Gemma, at the edge of the tarmac. This would take them directly to the garage. He could already smell it: high-octane gasoline, burnt rubber, and motor oil. It didn't matter the vehicle or discipline, this smelled like home to Nigel.

Nigel had just signed on with SportStream, a streaming service that focused on sports broadcasting. The owner, Colin Singleton, had his hands in many different ventures related to the streaming service – mainly sponsoring sports teams. This year, he made his most ambitious move by buying out a failing Formula One team, bringing in his money and his people. This meant hiring a rising Formula One champion in Nigel McKenzie to be his lead driver. This also meant possible NASCAR sponsorship, in addition to the World Rally Championships, IndyCar, and NHRA teams that already wore SportStream teal and carbon black. Uncertain about the success of the team he intended to sponsor, he flew his F1 driver to Daytona to pilot a one-off unchartered entry for the Great American Race. This worked to McKenzie's benefit as it was his goal to win at least one race in every major discipline. As Gemma had mention, he was already a Formula One champion, as well as an Indy 500 winner. He'd won rally races, Formula Drift competitions, as well as a class win a Le Mans with Porsche. NASCAR seemed like the next step.

"Nigel, you made it!" Colin Singleton warmly greeted his driver as he entered the garage.

"Glad to be here, gaffer," Nigel replied.

He took a look at the car. It was meant to resemble a Mustang Dark Horse, though only the nose and tail were even remotely shared with the road-going version, as well as a few body lines. In the place of doors, it had an open window, secured by a net. It was wrapped in SportStream's corporate racing paint scheme: teal in front before fading to black carbon fiber in the back. SportStream's motorsports logo, the silhouette of an open-wheel car against a giant tachometer, along with the name "SportStream", was emblazoned in carbon fiber over the hood, as well as the company's name emblazoned in white on the rear quarter panels. On the front of the doors and the roof was a white number 88.

Nigel swung a leg over the door, and then another, before sliding down into the driver's seat. His crew chief handed him the detachable steering wheel.

"Russ Martin," he introduced himself. "You ever driven anything like this before?"

"Can't be much different from a GT car," Nigel replied. "Five-speed sequential gearbox, not much in the way of messing about in here. How often do you expect me to be shifting out there? This is the big oval race, right?"

"Yeah, you'll be in fifth, basically, the whole race except during restarts and pitting."

"I've done the simulator," Nigel explained. "Any real-world situations I should know about here?"

"I assume you were online," Russ replied. "Well, you won't be dealing with amateurs, that's for certain. However, if you get in the pack, you run the risk of losing it all. You've seen these races, right?"

"One bloke loses it, we all lose it," said Nigel.

"Exactly," Russ went on. "You'll have a spotter. If he's not talking your ear off come Thursday, he's not doing his job."

"Well, I guess I should gear up," said Nigel.

That was Tuesday. On Wednesday, Nigel found himself behind the wheel of his Mustang for the first time. Qualifying would be two laps around the tri-oval. He would have two laps to show that he could conquer any car and any track. The two fastest qualifiers would set the front row. Everybody else would have to try again for their spot on Thursday in the Duels – odd numbers fighting for an inside-lane position and even numbers duking it out for an outside spot.

Nigel's time came. He drove from the garage seeded thirty-fourth and out onto the racing surface. It was just like the simulation; no, better. Down the backstretch, he picked up speed. He knew the lines he would need. He'd watched the previous thirty-three drivers had taken.

Picking up speed coming to the start/finish line, a slight left-hander on the frontstretch, making Daytona a tri-oval, his qualifying laps started. His first time piloting a stock car at speed, Nigel felt some trepidation. It was almost as if the car wanted to go faster but couldn't. Going into turn one, he was amazed at how it stuck. He wanted to fight the car, but he couldn't. There was almost no challenge, and yet that somehow made driving a challenge.

Coming out of turn two, he glided to the right, running up tight against the backstretch wall. Mere millimeters separated his car from the SAFER barrier, cutting off wind resistance as he quickly approached turn three. He swung the car back down as close to the double yellow line to his left as possible. Coming out of turn four, he once again began to drift toward the wall, then back down close to the line as he crossed the start/finish line.

"How'd he do?" Colin Singleton asked Russ.

"49.975," Russ replied. "On par with the mid-pack guys."

"He can do better, I know he can," said Colin.

"Hey, Nigel, that was great," Russ spoke into the radio. "Now, really open her up and show us what you can do this time by."

To the naked eye, it would look like Nigel repeated an identical lap. But inside the car, miniscule changes were made. Millimeters were shaved off of his distance around the track. He'd get closer to the line in the turns. He'd cut off the wall a millisecond sooner or hang on sometime longer. Either way, by the time he crossed the start/finish line again, the results were clear.

"49.838," Russ announced. "That's a top ten. He'll have to fight for a spot tomorrow, but I think he has what it takes to win come Sunday."

Nigel pulled the car into the garage area. There were a few more cars to run their qualifying laps, but he was safely in the top ten. In fact, he was now seeded tenth.

Nigel lazily stirred the pile of corn kernels on his plate as he sat on the deck of his yacht overlooking the marina. He was displeased with himself. He had left the qualifying session as quietly and solemnly as possible. Any answer to any question was just one word – whatever could get the idea across in the quickest and most efficient way.

"Come on, Nige, it wasn't all that bad," Gemma tried to comfort him as she dabbed her mouth. "Nige, it's not going to get any better by you just letting your supper get cold."

"It was a pole-position car," Nigel grimaced. "I could feel it."

"Okay, so the best you can start on Sunday is fourth," Gemma argued. "You'll still have five hundred miles to figure it all out."

"Right, that's if I even make it through the Duel without some muppet taking me out," Nigel went on. "Not to mention, I'll be starting on the outside at a disadvantage."

"And when has a bad situation ever stopped you?" Gemma smiled.

"It's all so simple for you, isn't it?" Nigel chuckled ruefully.

"It's what I'm paid to do."

"So, you're not trying to hype me up because you're my little sister and would support me no matter what?"

"I mean, I would, but a quarter million quid a year for representing you does make it much easier to do so."

"I see," Nigel chuckled. "So, anyone I should be watching tomorrow? Anyone to look out for?"

"There's that bloke in the 5 car that's really good in different disciplines," Gemma explained as she pulled out her notes. "A couple Toyota drivers. Ah, Chad Helton. Heard of him?"

"I may have seen an article or two. Tell me about him."

"He's in the first Duel tomorrow," said Gemma. "I'd encourage you to watch a race or two of his from last year if you have the time. Anyway, he won Rookie of the Year and was runner-up to the whole Championship last season by only a couple meters."

"Wait a minute," Nigel muttered. "That Chad Helton!"

"What?"

"Remember what Singleton told us? He's running our car with full sponsorship as a works team, but he's giving MorrisSport partial sponsorship unless he wins today."

"Either way, you both can make Mister Singleton a very happy man," Gemma added.

"Anyway, tell me more," said Nigel.

"Honestly, if anybody, this is the bloke you should worry about," Gemma went on. "Know how they have a win-and-you're-in points system? Well, absent the playoffs, he would've clinched the Championship ten races before the season ever finished, including all of the Crown Jewels. Look at these stats," she held up her phone. "Thirteen race wins, nine of them before the Playoffs, thirty-two top-10s, twenty-seven top-5s, twelve poles, and six thousand three hundred thirty-seven laps led. You're looking at the most dominant driver in the Cup Series today, and he's only in his fourth year of NASCAR national competition."

"And he's hungry for another 500 win," Nigel concluded.

"I'd say he's bitter and wants to prove himself," said Gemma.

"Well, I'd like to see this Chad Helton in action tomorrow," said Nigel as he tore off a hunk of his ribeye, "try and find a weakness."

The day of his Duel came. He would be starting fifth, an advantage since he would be taking the inside line. Nigel sat cooly by his car, sipping some hot tea and thinking about the competition. That's what encouraged him – the thrill of finding someone to beat.

"Oi, Nige, I'm going to go have a walk," Gemma called as she stepped out of the garage.

"In this heat?" Nigel thought to himself. *"That girl is mad!"*

Moments later, Gemma returned practically beaming. Nigel had never seen her eyes shine as green as they were. She skipped into the garage like a giddy little school girl and plopped herself down on the hood of the car.

"You'll never guess who I just met while I was out there," she proudly announced to her brother.

"Um, Tommy Cooper?" Nigel guessed jokingly.

"Guess again," Gemma giggled.

"Bob Hope."

"Wrong."

"Steamboat Willie?"

"Ugh," Gemma groaned, "it was Chad Helton."

"Our Chad Helton?"

"Yeah, we bumped into each other in the pit lane."

"Anything new I need to know about him?"

"I'm not entirely sure," said Gemma. "Thing is, he's just a kid like me."

"You're twenty," Nigel added. "That's hardly a kid."

"Only when it's convenient for you," Gemma giggled. "But he didn't seem all that remarkable."

"What do you mean?"

"He seemed scared," Gemma answered. "I really don't know if it's nerves, but he just babbled on about some nonsense."

"Hmm, maybe he's thinking about failing," said Nigel. "I get it. You get that sophomore slump, and you look like a total amateur out there."

"Well, he did have a better qualifying position than you," Gemma jabbed.

"Thanks for reminding me, sis."

"What are little sisters here for?"

"To get paid a quarter million pounds to be the best support a big brother could ask for."

Nigel stepped over to the monitor as the field took the green flag for the first Duel. If this Chad Helton character was as good as everybody said he was, perhaps he could learn a thing or two.

The field had shifted quickly. By the time they had reached the backstretch, the front row was three-wide with the number 28 Ford of Chad Helton splitting the middle. On lap twelve, the backmarkers bunched up flying down the backstretch. A lone car driven by a rookie making only his third start fell out of line. The driver, used to taking risks in the lower divisions, swerved back up into traffic, only to cut off another car, sending that one into another and causing a massive pileup. The rookie's car was rear-ended by another backmarker who was even further back, sending the car up onto its nose, its rear end visible sticking straight up in the smoke and debris.

Helton was unscathed. Nigel watched as his rival entered the pits. The 28 car took four tires and topped off on fuel.

"How long can we run on a full tank?" Nigel asked Russ.

"Around forty laps," his crew chief answered.

"So, barring any cautions, he can stay out until the end?" Nigel pressed.

"Who?"

"Helton."

"Let's see, four tires and topped off, yeah."

The green flag waved again, and Nigel watched the 28 Mustang begin to weave in and out of traffic as if all other competitors were standing still. Ten laps later, those who stayed out during the caution lost their gamble and surrendered the lead to pit.

The white flag waved but twenty-four laps later. In the top four were two Fords and two Toyotas, each in a tandem draft with his stablemate. In third on the inside lane was Chad Helton pushing his fellow Ford driver. The two pairs remained neck and neck as they barreled down the backstretch. This was going to be close.

Nigel bolted out of the garage to watch the drama unfold live. The cars came out of turn four. Helton had the momentum as he cut low out of the draft, faster than his stablemate. He had all of the advantage. The number 28 Mustang easily passed both Toyota and Ford, making it to the checkered flag first. Helton would be starting in third on Sunday.

"Can you even follow up that finish?" Russ applauded as he stepped out.

"Is that even a question?" Nigel growled.

It was the first time for Nigel to be in a pack of stock cars. He didn't trust anybody, and he wanted out as soon as possible. With the drop of the green flag, Nigel punched the throttle, his spotter shouting in his earpiece.

Things were getting too close for comfort. Any more bunching up, and Nigel was sure he'd be crushed. Along the backstretch, there was no hugging the wall for Nigel in his position.

"*Forget this*," he thought to himself as he slowly drifted left.

Out of the draft, Nigel lost all momentum, and he started fading.

"Nigel, what am I here for?" his spotter questioned into the radio.

"McKenzie, are you alright?" Russ asked. "What're you doing?"

"It's too dangerous," Nigel replied. "I'm practically asking to be taken out. I'd rather keep this car in one piece for Sunday."

"I get it," Russ admitted. "Better to let the other screw up and keep her in one piece for the big show than to risk it all. Start in the back Sunday if you have to."

"I don't intend on that either," Nigel chuckled.

Sure enough, Nigel had drifted back from fifth all the way to twenty-sixth – dead last in the field of fifty-two entries. Twelve drivers would be going back to Charlotte this week. Nigel was determined not to be one of them, yet fifty-second was not the position to be in to prevent that.

'What the devil is he doing?" Gemma asked Russ.

"Strategy, I think," he replied. "You know him better."

Twenty-four laps in, Russ was sure he knew what Nigel was thinking. The veteran wasn't entirely sure he liked this strategy, but this was the way of the world this week. The field was still green, but fuel was running low for all.

"Oi, Russ," Nigel came in on the radio, still riding dead last, "what was Helton's pit strategy?"

Russ tried to search his memory.

"Four scuffs and fuel," one of the tire carriers recalled.

"Did you get that? Scuffs and a full tank of fuel," said Russ. Bring her in next time by. You'll lose track position, but you'll be out running while everyone else is pitting if we stay green. Gotta take the gamble."

"You know, I always wanted to go to Vegas," Nigel chuckled as he drifted off of the racing surface and onto the apron to slow his approach to pit road.

"Keep her at sixty," Russ instructed as Nigel brought the car down. "Okay, he's almost here. Get ready. Three, two, one."

Nigel's car slid into the pit box. Four men, two carrying air impacts and two carrying tires – one of the tire carriers carrying a floor jack, rushed to the passenger side of the car. With one pump of the jack, the car was sufficiently off the ground to quickly remove the tires. One big lug on each tire came off. The tires came off and were rolled back toward the wall, caught by other crew members. The new tires went on and were secured with one big lug each. The passenger side was let down, and the crew members scrambled back to the driver's side of the car, one of the tire carriers ripping off a layer of transparent plastic from the windshield, effectively cleaning it. The crew members on the other side of the pit wall rolled new tires to the tire changers. The same process repeated itself on the driver's side. Meanwhile, the fuel man plugged a fuel can into the fuel hole and began dumping gasoline into the fuel cell. With one can empty, a crew member handed him another. Two cans were sufficient to top off. Within nine seconds, all four tires were changed, the windshield was cleaned, and the fuel cell was full. Barring any incidents, Nigel's car was good to go until the checkered flag.

Nigel spent the next thirty laps cruising around the track. Sure, he had fresh tires, but it was as if he wasn't trying. With five to go, the field was all bunched back up, Nigel still bringing up the rear, but still on the lead lap.

"Nige, come on, it's go time," Russ panicked.

"Five to go, let's move!" said his spotter. "You've got one on your twelve. Take him!"

"Hey, Russ, you wanna see a trick?" Nigel chuckled into the radio.

Nigel hooked onto the rear bumper of a Camaro and pushed the lucky winner through the pack. Two cars are faster than one, and they found their line. If the driver in the Camaro thought he was receiving a gift, he was dead wrong. Over four laps, the pair pushed their way through traffic, the driver of the Camaro unaware he was the unwitting accomplice of his ill-fated win attempt. As the white flag waved over them one and two, Nigel began to make his move. Coming off of turn two, Nigel kept his Mustang low, as close to the double yellow boundary line without touching it. The Camaro had the advantage as far as momentum, but Nigel was choosing the short way around. They were neck and neck going into three, still neck and neck out of four. It would be close, but Nigel had the inside lane advantage.

Into the tri-oval, it was too close to the naked eye to see. Three one thousandths of a second was all that separated fourth and sixth on Sunday.

"Did we win?" asked a tense Gemma.

"I don't believe it," Russ gasped. "Look at the telemetry!"

Gemma looked up at the monitor.

"I don't believe it," Gemma whispered. "He did it! Won it by a thread!"

"Nige, you won it all, son!" Russ yell into the radio. "Go ahead and enjoy that celebration!"

Nigel had watched Chad's victory lap, and he copied it. He drove around the track the wrong way, saluting the fans. Back on the frontstretch, he then dropped the car into first gear and mashed the throttle, causing the rear tires to spin. The car did several donuts before disappearing in a cloud of smoke. Now, it was time for the victory lane celebration. Nigel brought the car to the infield. He climbed out of the car before being dogpiled by his crew members.

With a victory lane celebration comes victory lane interviews. The raucous atmosphere was perfect for the occasion.

"Nigel McKenzie," began the pit reporter as he made his way into victory lane, "Formula One World Champion and now a winner in the NASCAR Cup Series. What do you have to say about that."

"Well, first of all," Nigel began, "I'd like to thank my sponsors. This SportStream Ford Mustang Darkhorse was tremendous out there. Also, my owner, Colin Singleton, for giving me this opportunity. And finally, I need to thank me agent, Gemma McKenzie, who's also me sister."

He grabbed his little sister and gave her a side hug. The girl looked up to her brother like he was her whole world, as if he were the greatest superhero ever committed to comic book pulp.

"How do you think this bodes for you on Sunday?" the reporter pressed.

"Well, I'm hoping we can turn a fourth-place start into a first-place finish," Nigel replied. "Either way, I'd just like to celebrate this. You know, they really put together a spectacular car. I told them they had a first-place car before the race, and we've proved it today."

"Well, we're looking forward to Sunday to see if you can convert this qualifying result into a win," the reporter said excitedly.

Nigel retired to his yacht that night, satisfied he could hack it. After a glass of porter, he had calmed his nerves sufficiently to lie down for the evening. The Duel was just the first step. Sunday would be the big show. He would make sure that nothing would get in his way. The Daytona 500 was his to win, and no dumb redneck would get in his way.

About the Author

Sam Sitler graduated from Heartland Baptist Bible College in 2015 with a degree in music. He currently serves at his local church as minister of music and 5th and 6th grade Sunday School teacher in Albany, OR alongside his wife, Stephanie.

Other Titles by Sam Sitler

Fiction

Rumble Road

Sleeper

Back to Rumble Road

Racing Through Time

Blameless

Non-fiction

On the Record: What the Bible Really Says About Music